T0193702

The Marsh

Also by Bill Noel

Folly

The Pier

Washout

The Edge

The Marsh

A Folly Beach Mystery

Bill Noel

iUniverse, Inc.
Bloomington

The Marsh
A Folly Beach Mystery

iUniverse Star
an iUniverse, Inc. imprint

iUniverse books may be ordered through booksellers or by contacting:

iUniverse
1663 Liberty Drive
Bloomington, IN 47403
www.iuniverse.com
1-800-Authors (1-800-288-4677)

Cover photo by the author
Author photo by Susan Noel

ISBN: 978-1-936236-87-9 (sc)
ISBN: 978-1-936236-88-6 (e)

Library of Congress Control Number: 2011916988

Printed in the United States of America

iUniverse rev. date: 9/16/2011

Chapter 1

"Found a gnawed-up, rottin' body out there, I hear," said Harley. He nodded toward the marsh fewer than a hundred feet from where we stood.

His whispered tone, slightly louder than a foghorn, turned eight heads toward the short, chunky gentleman standing to my left. It wouldn't have been nearly as distracting if we hadn't been absorbed in a silent prayer at the time.

I was standing in a semicircle with friends and acquaintances in a beautiful, grass-covered meadow surrounded by regal live oaks. I looked in the direction of Harley's nod toward the gently swaying, early-summer salt marsh cordgrass. A bright-blue South Carolina sky, dotted with low, white, puffy clouds, merged with the light green of the awakening grasses and blended with the new leaves on the trees and the lawn of the meadow.

The weather and scenery were perfect; only Mother Nature could provide such a grand vista. I would have savored the view more if I hadn't been staring at a newly dug grave—a grave that would be the final resting place for Mrs. Margaret Klein.

Reverend Vandergriff pointed a devilish stare at Harley—as devilish as permitted, since the good reverend was at work—and said, "Amen." The chords of "Just As I Am" left the well-traveled guitar of Calvin Ballew. The musician, known to most as Country Cal, had rested his right foot on a grave marker to the right of Mrs. Klein's coffin as he began his final tribute to the lady he had known for five years. Cal was six-foot-three, slim, and when decked out in his rhinestone stage coat

1

and Stetson, was a live-ringer for Hank Williams Senior—or what ol' Hank would have looked like if he had managed to stay alive until retirement age.

Cal sang, "O Lamb of God, I come, I come." I leaned toward Harley and whispered, "Tell me later."

When I moved to the small South Carolina island of Folly Beach some four years ago, I would have told you how ludicrous it would be for me to be standing in a beautiful, peaceful corner of the world in a cemetery dotted with polished-stone grave markers and a dozen graves marked with crosses made from white, plastic plumbing pipe. I would have sworn I'd never be there listening to a person who was named Harley after his father's motorcycle, while listening to a washed-up country music singer named Country Cal, while attending the funeral of an eighty-six-year-old woman I had helped rescue from a hurricane and a calculating murderer. Then again, I had learned that something had to travel a long way from normal to be ludicrous on Folly Beach.

Cal strummed the last notes of the poignant hymn. The good reverend shared how Mrs. Klein had "moved on to a better place," how we should "celebrate her ascension to meet her maker," and some other never-to-be-understood-or-proven verbiage ministers preach at funerals. I had attended more of these events since arriving at Folly Beach than I could remember in the balance of my sixty-one years. My mind wandered. What did Harley mean about a body?

There was one thing I was certain of. My friend Charles, who was standing on the other side of me when Harley bellowed his "whisper," would corner Harley and not let him mount his motorcycle before extracting a full explanation—an explanation with photos and video if possible.

Reverend Vandergriff uttered the final "Amen," and the mourners silently reflected upon their memories of the deceased. Two nearby seagulls cackled over a piece of fish. Louise Carson, Mrs. Klein's oldest friend, slowly stood. She had been seated in a rickety, white wooden folding chair, the only seat provided by the funeral home.

A hand gripped my left elbow before I could offer condolences to Louise. "Chris, could I see you, Charles, and Harley a moment before we leave the cemetery?" asked Sean Aker, a partner in one of the two small law firms on Folly Beach.

Charles had already corralled Harley, no doubt asking about the body. "Give us a minute," I said.

I sidled up to Charles and Harley and gently nudged them toward Louise. Tears ran down her cheeks, but she managed a slight smile when I gently touched her arm. Her eighty-plus years showed. Louise worked at Island Realty and was the aunt of Bob Howard, a Realtor friend of mine. Her office tasks were vague at best, but her passion for being the island's busybody was known by all. She regularly monitored the police radios and wasn't shy about expressing her opinions about law enforcement on Folly Beach. She thanked us for coming and said that she'd miss her friend. I knew not to mention "body" within her hard-of-hearing range.

"Let me show you something," I said as I herded Charles and Harley away from Louise and toward the edge of the marsh. It was high tide, and the salt water was only a foot or so below the edge of the cemetery. Our approach startled a heron from its peaceful rest, and I watched it gracefully take to the sky. Sean was still beside the grave.

"Okay," said Charles. He pointed his ever-present, handmade cane at Harley. "What body?"

"Put that weapon down," said Harley. His chubby right hand grabbed the tip of the cane and pushed it away. With his left hand, he took a pack of Camel cigarettes from the back pocket of his best dress jeans. Both Charles and I took a step back; experience had shown us that a cloud of white, nicotine-infused smoke would momentarily surround Harley.

The threat of Charles's cane had diminished, so Harley lit a cigarette and took a long draw. "Damn, I needed that," he said after he exhaled. Charles waited patiently—a skill that had come late in his life, maybe started today, truth be told. "Heard a body was found yesterday out in the marsh, nibbled all to hell by swamp critters." Harley pointed his cigarette toward the center of the marsh. "Surprised you two—being detectives and all—didn't hear about it."

"We're not detectives," I quickly said before Charles claimed otherwise. "We've just helped the police a time or two."

"More like four," said Charles, a stickler for details. "Back to the body, Harley."

"Don't know much," roared Harley. "Heard something at Bert's before heading here." He took another long draw and blew smoke in our faces. Charles had said it was Harley's way of bonding. I'd said it was rude but never shared that observation when Harley was close enough to hear.

"Who was it?" asked Charles, the "detective."

"No idea. Don't think the cops do either," replied Harley. "That's all I know."

Harley flung his cigarette to the ground and stomped on it with his work boot. I translated it as "end of conversation," and I mentioned that Sean was waiting for us at the grave.

I met Sean just after I had moved to Folly Beach. He performed the legal work when I opened a small photo gallery, and we had had several social and business contacts since then. He was always friendly and helpful. Charles had known him much longer. They had been in a skydiving club. Even my expanded, Folly Beach imagination couldn't see Charles jumping out of an airplane, and he hadn't demonstrated that idiotic feat since I had known him. Sean had confirmed that it was true, and after all, he's a lawyer, so it must be true.

Sean looked back toward the drive at a navy-blue Ford Crown Victoria parked behind his look-at-me red Porsche Boxster. Sun reflected off the windows of the Crown Vic, and I couldn't see inside.

"Guys," said Sean, "could you meet me in the office tomorrow?"

Charles and I were retired—me for the last three years; Charles for the last quarter of a century, even though he's three years younger than I. We could be there. Harley, a plumber with a spotty work record, hemmed and hawed and then reluctantly mumbled that he'd make it.

We agreed on a time and slowly headed toward our cars—and one Harley-Davidson.

"Mr. Aker, could I have a word with you?" said a middle-aged man wearing a wrinkled, cheap, gray suit and an equally wrinkled look on his face. He had stepped out of the Crown Vic and was hovering beside Sean's convertible.

I knew the intruder as Detective Brad Burton, Charleston County sheriff's office. There was nothing good that could come from his appearance at the cemetery.

Chapter 2

Detective Burton and I had become acquainted four years ago on my fifth day on Folly. I remembered because it was not easy to forget finding a still-warm body on the beach with a bullet hole through its left eye. Burton and his partner, Karen Lawson, the daughter of Folly Beach's director of public safety, were investigating the horrific event I had stumbled upon. Burton usually addressed me with a disdainful snarl, but as Detective Lawson had shared later, Burton didn't discriminate— "To him, everyone's guilty of something."

Detective Burton invited Sean to the front seat of his Crown Vic, and I had to shove Charles away from the unmarked car. If I hadn't stopped him, he would have squished in the seat between Burton and the lawyer. "Extraordinarily curious" would have been an extraordinarily kind way to describe my friend—*nosy* was the word often bandied around.

The low rumble of Harley's cycle drowned out any chance of hearing what the detective was saying, so Charles reluctantly took his seat riding shotgun in my aging Lexus. The road to the cemetery was off Folly Road and only a couple of miles from the bridge to Folly Beach. The small barrier island was fewer than two handfuls of miles from beautiful Charleston, South Carolina, but was as different from the historic, stately city as environmentalists were from Republicans. The half-mile-wide, six-mile-long island had more character and characters per capita than any city in the United States, unquestionably more than any in Canada. The island had played a critical role in the Civil War and gained popularity after World War II, when wealthy business owners and industrialists from Charleston discovered the cool ocean breezes and relaxed atmosphere. Many of them built small cabins to serve as dressing rooms and places to hang out during a day at the beach. The cabins were eventually outfitted with furnaces and became year-round residences for the more bohemian friends and relatives of the wealthy. Less well-to-do Charlestonians lived in cramped, wooden houses and unsuccessfully fought the humidity of the summer before discovering the get-away beach at Folly.

Folly Beach was well past its heyday, when an amusement park, bowling alley, and large pavilion had provided entertainment for the locals and visitors from afar. Over the last forty years, a series of hurricanes, large and small, had changed the landscape of the island, but many of the small, and patently sturdy, cabins were still around. Many had additions larger than the original structures. And, like everywhere along the coast, McMansions were sprouting up and causing consternation among the residents who wanted Folly Beach to remain unchanged and battled those who wanted the right to spend their millions on as large a house as imaginable.

In a chain-everything world, there were only two establishments on Folly that can be found outside South Carolina: a small Kangaroo gas station/food mart and a micro-sized Subway. Both shared a small building along the main drag.

Charles, without mincing words, reminded me that it was past his lunch hour—"far, far, near starvation" past. I ignored his greatly exaggerated, self-proclaimed deteriorating condition and headed to the best breakfast and lunch spot on the island, the Lost Dog Café. The local landmark would feed my stomach, Charles's starvation, and his nosiness appetite. Rumors, facts, opinions, and bovine manure bounced around the dining room nearly as much as hot coffee and breakfast burritos. There was one additional, and very special, reason I frequented the colorful restaurant: Amber Lewis, five-foot-five, long brunette hair, trim in all the right places, attractive, funny, insightful, and in Charles's words, "Old Chris's main squeeze."

The Dog in an earlier life had been a Laundromat, but with the owner's creativity and love for canines, the restaurant had expanded, with two outdoor seating areas making it canine-friendly. Considering all the anti-discrimination laws in the country, I assumed that cats were welcome but had never seen one inside the dog-bone-shaped railings closing in the front porch. A concrete, life-size dog statue sporting a summer straw hat and a Hawaiian grass skirt greeted us at the front door; Amber provided a much more charming and attractive greeting inside. Most of the lunch crowd had headed back to the nearby beach or to their homes and condos for an afternoon siesta.

"Over here, boys," boomed Harley. He sat in a booth near the kitchen wall and waved as if we wouldn't have heard his voice over the handful of customers. Harley wasn't a regular at the Dog, so I felt obligated to share the booth with him. "So, what's *that* lawyer want with me?" he asked before Charles and I had reached the table.

"No clue," said Charles. "Any idea?" He set his canvas Tilley hat on the edge of table and leaned his cane against the wall.

"Not a one, pard. I've never even met the *little* guy."

Sean was much taller then Harley, so he was referring to the attorney's width, significantly narrower than our biker friend.

Harley slowly looked around the room and lowered his voice—lower for Harley. "I'm not a fan of lawyers. One almost sent me up the river a while back. Guy had a knife. Had to defend myself, didn't I?"

I was clueless; but since Harley looked like he could wrestle alligators for amusement, I wasn't going to press for an explanation. Besides, that's why Charles was along. He didn't disappoint.

"What happened?" asked Charles, on cue. "When?"

Harley fidgeted with a clear plastic Bic lighter. "Few years back. Before I moved to Follyland, I was minding my own business in a dive in North Chicago, lining up the beer bottles on the bar. I'd emptied them all." Harley patted his stomach with his right hand to show where he'd emptied the bottles, and then tapped the lighter on the table. He paused and then looked at the ceiling.

"And?" asked Charles, who thought silence was the work of the devil.

Before Harley could expound, Amber arrived with a large chicken quesadilla and gracefully slid it under Harley's elbow that he had rested on the table. She handed Charles a plate with a large hot dog smothered with cheese. She gave me an endearing grin and a filet of broiled whitefish and some weedy-looking garnish on the side. Amber had paid much more attention to my weight than I had over the last two years. I didn't think one hundred eighty pounds was bad for my five-foot-ten altitude, but the misguided charts in the magazines said differently. I was in a constant battle with the anorexic chart-writers. I wanted to hear more of Harley's story, so I chose not to draw a line in the sand about my lunch un-selection.

Harley already had a huge chunk of quesadilla in his mouth but muttered, "And I had the ten bottles arranged on the bar just like those things in a bowling alley—"

"Pins?" interrupted Charles.

"That's it, pins," said Harley. "Where was I? Oh yeah, the bottles were sitting there all nice and pretty. And this big ol' tall-drink-of-water, Nazi-looking loser walked up and took his hairy arm and swept the bottles off the bar. Said I was in his space." Harley stuffed another bite in his mouth and grabbed the Bic and started to get up. He was on his way outside for a smoke.

Charles wasn't going to have that. "Whoa, big H! What happened?"

Harley glared at Charles but lowered his ample rear back into the booth and took a deep breath. "I politely told Adolf where he could put my ten beer bottles, offered to help him since he'd have a hard time reaching the spot, and then grinned." Harley demonstrated the grin. "Now, how much more hospitable could I have been?"

"And?" I said. Charles was a bit slow.

"And a big ol' switchblade appeared in the bugger's left hand. I didn't think he was going to use it to shell the tin bucket of peanuts parked beside his beer. I removed the blade from his hand, sent his left elbow in a direction it hadn't been before, and helped his nose get better acquainted with the top of the bar." Harley grinned. "Peanuts flew everywhere. Was one of my finer moments, if I say so myself." He paused as his grin morphed into a frown. "And then the police had the nerve to arrest me. Seems that Nazi boy's brother owned the bar. Nobody saw nothing except me attacking the poor, God-fearing Nazi boy."

"Eventually," said Charles, "this is going to get back to why you don't like lawyers. Right?"

"Your mind rolls along on one track, don't it?" said Harley, more perceptive than he will ever know. "Yeah. The PD they gave me— snotty-nosed kid, just out of law school, mail order, I'd bet—said I was guiltier than sin and I'd be lucky if he could save me from the gas chamber. Then the lawyer-baby wanted me to take a plea and go up the river for three years." Harley picked up the salt shaker and pounded it on the table. His face was red, and he looked like he was ready to blow a gasket. "Three years! Can you believe that? Three years for defending my bowling alley."

"Well?" said Charles.

"A friend told me I could demand another lawyer, and I damn well did. New guy actually spent more than five minutes on my case and learned that the bar had more red dots than any other drinking establishment within ten miles. Got the—"

"Red dots?" blurted Charles.

Harley stared at him. "I thought you were a detective."

"Don't know everything, yet," said Charles, the un-detective.

"Red dots were put on a map at the cop-crib to show where crimes happened. Seems that Mr. Bar Owner and his Nazi, bowling-alley-wrecking brother are a two-man crime wave. There were no witnesses to my discussion with the Nazi except for his biased brother, so the judge gave me a fine—no death sentence this time." Harley paused and then nodded. "Is this Aker lawyer guy like my first PD?"

"I've known Sean for a dozen years or so," said Charles. "He's a good guy."

"He doesn't practice criminal law," I added. "He wouldn't be like a public defender."

"So what's he want with me?"

Good question, I thought.

There was only one other table of diners, and they were on the other side of the room. Amber caught a break in our conversation and returned to the table.

"Learned a few things about the body they found. Interested?" Her sly grin showed that she knew the answer. She didn't wait for a reply. "Seems it had been in the marsh for a few days; animals had already begun to feast on it." Her grin turned to a grimace. "Cops think it was a guy but couldn't tell much of anything from the body."

"Who found him?" asked Charles.

"Young couple from New Jersey and their five-year-old daughter were taking one of those marsh tours with Captain Anton. Out to celebrate Memorial Day."

"It'll be a Memorial Day to remember for those northerners," said Harley.

"Better story to tell their friends than about getting sunburned at the beach," added Charles.

Amber swore that that was all she had learned, and when Harley asked her his question of the day, she said that she didn't know what Sean wanted with him. We let her get back to waitressing.

Attending a friend's funeral, learning about a body in the marsh adjacent to my island, watching another friend in deep conversation with the police, and being summoned to a lawyer's office—what a way to begin June.

Chapter 3

The Lowcountry had been mauled by Hurricane Greta eight months earlier. It was the worst natural disaster to hit the area since the infamous Hurricane Hugo ravaged the Eastern Seaboard in 1989. Damage estimates from Greta, already in the hundreds of millions of dollars, were still escalating. But thankfully, adequate warning and Greta coming ashore slightly weaker than predicted had limited human loss. The death toll had peaked at seven in South Carolina: four as a direct result of the hurricane winds and three from subsequent tornados that spun off inland. Regardless of what the official statistics showed, I knew the death count was eight. The lady buried yesterday had been the latest victim.

Seventeen houses had been leveled on Folly Beach, including the oceanfront boardinghouse owned by Mrs. Klein. Fifty or so other structures, including a massive nine-story hotel, received significant damage; the other older houses had survived Hugo, and most built since Hugo's day had been constructed to withstand stronger blows than Greta and only suffered cosmetic damage.

Mrs. Klein's boardinghouse, the Edge, wasn't one of the luckier pre-Hugo buildings. Charles, Harley, and I knew firsthand how it had been ripped apart by rain, wind, and the storm surge. We were in it at the time—in it saving its owner from the wrath of the hurricane and a killer who had been bumping off her residents with a most unlikely and terrifying weapon, a crossbow. She had survived the crossbow killer, Hurricane Greta, her beloved house collapsing around her, and being carried by Harley through raging, waist-deep waters, only to fall victim to pneumonia, depression over losing everything, eighty-six years of life, and excessive quantities of Maker's Mark. Pure stubbornness had kept her alive these last eight months.

"Hey, Mr. Photo Man. We going to sell a herd of photos today?" Charles entered Landrum Gallery and cheerfully spouted off these words, words similar to those he began each day with. It was an endearing but increasingly irritating habit.

Charles was my unofficial—and unpaid—sales manager, helper with everything that needed to be done, and eternal optimist. After I had taken early retirement from a multi-national health care company in my hometown in Kentucky, I bought a small cottage a few blocks from the beach and rented a dilapidated former souvenir and T-shirt shop on Center Street, the figurative and literal center of commerce on Folly Beach. My lifelong passion had been photography, and my plan was to open a gallery of my work. I had made a couple of lucky real estate investments and received a substantial buyout from work, so I could retire while still in my late fifties. I didn't have to make a profit at the gallery named after myself in a burst of egotistical non-creativity, but the last two years had been financial disasters. I thought photographs should be up there with bread, milk, toilet paper, and cell phones as human necessities, but the buying public had disagreed. I couldn't continue to stay open. I had lightly broached on the subject with Charles, but he was a master of deflection, a trait we both shared. I needed to change my tack.

"See anybody lined up outside?" I said. I wasn't ready to have the conversation with him.

"Not yet," he said.

"When was there ever a line?" I asked.

Charles rolled his eyes toward the ceiling. "Well, as President Buchanan once said, 'There is nothing stable but Heaven and the Constitution.'"

In addition to Charles's grating optimism, he had an uncanny habit of quoting US presidents. I hadn't had the energy or interest to verify the quotations, but the couple of times I called him on one, he had cited the source—chapter, page, and verse.

"Whatever," I replied—shy of articulate, but I had no interest in what the obscure president might have said.

"So what does Sean want to see us about?" said Charles.

I knew he had wanted to discuss it when we were at the Dog, but Harley had seemed antsy enough without more lawyer talk being thrown around. His previous encounters with the legal and law enforcement community appeared to lean toward the *bad news* side.

We moved to the office/break/storage/goof-off room behind the gallery and took our traditional seats around the rickety kitchen table that was used for everything from matting photos to holding invoices that usually exceeded available cash to holding pizza boxes, beer cans, and wine glasses during impromptu parties.

"I have no more idea than I did yesterday," I said. "We'll find out soon enough."

"Then what do you know about the marsh body?"

"About as much as I know about what Sean wants," I replied.

"I could have learned that from from old Mr. Schmidt's schnauzer tied up in front of the Dog."

"Yeah, but it wouldn't get you coffee," I said as I pulled two semi-clean ceramic mugs from the sink and filled them from the Mr. Coffee machine on the counter.

I smiled as I returned to the table, but my stomach churned. There would never be a good time to tell Charles that I was closing the gallery. I needed to get it over with.

"When I—we—opened the gallery, all I wanted was to not lose money," I said. "I came close that first year."

Charles leaned back in his wooden chair, the mug in his left hand. "Because of your fantastic sales manager, of course," he said. He set the mug on the table and nervously picked some lint off the sleeve of his University of Hawaii long-sleeved T-shirt.

"Since then, I've been losing a boatload of money." I tried to make eye contact but couldn't manage it.

"I guess a raise is out of the question," he said.

He was kidding, but he had on anything but a happy face. He knew what was coming. I hated it; he hated it.

"I'm going to have to close," I said. My head was down; I still couldn't bring myself to look him in the eye.

He balled his right hand into a fist, shoved away from the table, inhaled, and pushed the chair back. "No," he whispered. He walked to the door that led to the showroom, hesitated, and then returned to his chair but didn't sit. He stood behind the chair and gripped the backrest. His knuckles were chalk-white.

I hadn't moved. "I'm sorry, but ..."

"Do what you have to," he said. He grabbed his cane from the corner of the table, pivoted, and stomped through the door to the gallery. A moment later, I heard the front door slam.

Truth be known, I should have closed two years ago. I wasn't wealthy but could survive a no-frills retirement if the gallery had not been such a drain. Charles hadn't held a tax-paying job since he moved to the island twenty-five years ago at the ripe old age of thirty-four. His only source of income was a few off-the-books jobs for construction companies, a handful of days a month helping local restaurants clean, and an occasional on-island delivery for the surf shop. The deliveries were in a limited radius because his mode of transportation was an immaculately maintained 1961 Schwinn bicycle. He owned a 1988 Saab convertible that hadn't moved from outside his small apartment in the last two years.

Money wasn't an issue with Charles. He always found enough to squeak by. Landrum Gallery had given him a sense of pride. He had told me last year that it made him feel important, something he had never experienced before we met.

Charles would do anything for me—in fact, he had come close to sacrificing his life on a couple of occasions to save my hide. I had never paid him a penny for his work at the gallery, and now I was slamming the door on his self-respect. I felt terrible.

I stared at the hardwood floor and walked to the front window overlooking Center Street. I thought about the first time Bob Howard had showed me the "beach-aged, quality retail space," his words to describe the worn-out storefront location. The floors still had the paths furrowed by thousands of feet, sandals, flip-flops, and clogs that had traipsed around display racks that cluttered the souvenir shop that had occupied the space before Landrum Gallery was born.

The bell over the front door jarred me out of my pity party. A middle-aged couple entered and gave me a vacationer's grin. I put on my best retailer's face and asked if I could help them.

"Saw the sign and thought we'd come in," said the man dressed in a baggy bathing suit and a Nike golf shirt. His bright-red flip-flops appeared new. "See anything you like, hon?" he said as he looked at his partner.

"Nice stuff," she said, her grin matching his. "Maybe."

There's nothing like my fine-art photography being called "stuff," but if they were going to buy any, they could call it anything they liked.

I glanced out the window to see if Charles was anywhere around. The customers slowly looked at the larger framed pieces on the wall and then through the black, cloth bin in the corner holding matted images.

I was thinking how ironic it would be if they made a large purchase when the doorbell chimed again. Charles bounded in with a smile on his face. He handed me his Tilley, asked if I could put it in the back room, and turned his attention to the potential buyers. I heard him tell them that he was sorry he hadn't been there when they first came in; he said something about having to go on an errand for the owner.

I stayed in back and let Charles play sales manager. Besides, I couldn't find it in myself to put on a happy front. I knew I had hurt Charles, and hurt him deeply. He was one of the first people I'd met when I arrived on Folly Beach. He and I were about as opposite as two people can be. He was a voracious reader; his apartment was nearly filled floor to ceiling with books—fiction, nonfiction, biography, history, and a selection of cookbooks that the Food Channel would envy. He claimed to have read all of them, with the exception of the cookbooks. I, on the other hand, avoid reading anything. I took the more traditional route in life and actually had worked for a living; Charles gave up that pursuit decades ago. I had spent many years paying back loans to banks and mortgage companies; Charles didn't have a bank account, a cell phone, or an operable gas-powered vehicle. He's outgoing—nosy—and talks to everyone; I semi-avoid people. In one of the perplexities of life, we had become close, and I couldn't imagine my world without him in it.

Would my decision to close drive him away?

I heard the doorbell ring, and seconds later, Charles peeked around the corner. His grin was wider than when he had returned. He waved three crisp one-hundred-dollar bills over his head and in one breath, told me how he had convinced the couple to buy one of the more expensive prints, how they had said it was great that there was a gallery on the island, and how they would return each year—he repeated, *each year*—and *buy* more.

"Think we'll be able to stay open?" he asked. It was clearly a question but sounded close to the border of begging.

I shook my head and reminded him that several large sales wouldn't come close to covering a month's rent. "I don't see a way. Sorry."

"Come on, Chris, please—I'll do more to help sell the photos." He paused and looked at the tin ceiling. "Please?"

I shook my head. "You've been great. There's nothing more you could possibly do. I don't want to close either. There's no choice."

Charles looked in my direction, but I didn't think he saw me. He was angry and hurt; and it was my fault. He started to say something but closed his mouth and opened the back door and looked out on the gravel lot. I didn't know what to do, so I sat and waited. The veins in his neck throbbed, and his hand wobbled on the cane. After what seemed like an eternity, he turned back toward the room. Tears rolled down his cheeks, and he slowly walked to the table, placed both forearms on the top, and rested his head on his arms.

I didn't say anything and walked back up front into the sales gallery. For the first time in three years, I prayed that no customers would come in.

How could things get worse?

Chapter 4

I listened to the sounds of truck engines and children laughing along Center Street in front of the gallery and to the overworked, aging air conditioner roaring in a losing battle to keep the building comfortable. The outside temperature had already topped eighty-five, above average for this early in June. Sadly, I was used to standing by myself and watching the world pass by the large front window.

"Time to head to Sean's, isn't it?" yelled Charles from the back room. He had rinsed his face and dampened and combed his mostly gray, thinning hair. His eyes were red, but no one would guess why.

Sean's law office was on the second floor of a two-story wooden building less than a block, and across the street, from the gallery. The first floor held Sweet Sue's, the island's only candy store. "Aker and Long, Lawyers" was stenciled in black on a florescent orange surfboard hanging horizontally above the first-floor entry to the stairs. I had thought the surfboard was strange during my first visit a few years ago. I didn't give it a second thought now that I had been inoculated by the quirkiness of the island.

Harley puffed on a cigarette as he leaned against the front of Sweet Sue's. I knew he was as uncomfortable as he appeared. "What if we're in trouble?" he said by way of a greeting.

Charles reminded him that Sean didn't practice criminal law and that he was one of the good guys. Harley dropped his cigarette on the sidewalk and twisted his boot on it. He fell into step behind Charles and me as we headed up the stairs.

The second-floor door reflected the more traditional image of a law office. Three chairs were arranged around the perimeter of the small waiting area. We were greeted by Marlene Ryle, the receptionist and administrative assistant. I had met Marlene on my first visit to the office and had seen her occasionally walking around town with her shih tzu. Marlene was in her thirties, wasn't especially attractive or unattractive, and always greeted me with a smile. She was swallowed up by the oversized secretary's desk.

"Marlene," I said. "Do you know Charles and Harley?" I turned and nodded toward Charles and had to step aside so she could see Harley. He stood directly behind me and reminded me of a sad-eyed bulldog that had been rescued from an abusive owner.

"Sure, I know Charles." She grinned in Charles's direction. "He and Sean used to jump out of perfectly good airplanes."

Charles turned toward me. "I've worked a couple of jobs a while back for Aaron, Marlene's husband," interrupted Charles. "He has a construction company." Charles smiled at Marlene and tipped his Tilley.

She grinned and then leaned to her left to see Harley who was still directly behind me. "Don't believe I've had the pleasure of meeting Harley."

There was a small conference room behind Marlene with two walls full of the obligatory, leather-spined law books. To the right of her desk was a door with a brass plate inscribed *Tony Long, Attorney at Law.* Tony was Sean's law partner; I had only met him a couple of times at social events. He had given me the impression that his attendance was required but no one could make him enjoy the gatherings.

I didn't have the feeling that a lengthy conversation was brewing between the two, so I got down to business. I nodded to the door to the left of her desk, the one with a wood cutout of a pie-sized parachute with *Sean* printed in bright red, green, and blue paint on the canopy. "Is he in? We have an appointment."

She looked at a stapler on the desk like she hadn't seen it before. "Umm, he was here earlier." Her hands wrestled with a silver paperclip. The small piece of twisted metal was winning.

"Be back soon?" asked Charles.

Harley backpedaled toward the stairs.

Marlene made a strong effort but managed a weak smile. "I don't know," she said. "I really don't know."

After an awkward pause, I asked if she knew about the appointment. Silence followed.

"Where'd he go, Marlene?" asked Charles. He moved closer to her massive desk.

She looked up from her mangled paperclip. "I shouldn't tell you this," she said, barely audible. "Since he stood you up, you should know." She paused and looked at each of us as if she was waiting for permission. "He got a call on his cell about a half-hour ago. I don't know who it was for certain, but from what I heard, I'd guess it was the police. He hung up and rushed out of his office; barely looked my way. Said when you got here to apologize and tell you he'd have to reschedule."

"Anything else?" asked Charles.

Harley already had his foot on the top step and was ready to bolt.

"Not really," she said. "Sorry. I'll call when I hear when he's available."

Not knowing what else to do, we took the safe route and headed to the stairs. Harley was already halfway to the sidewalk.

"It's not like Sean to miss an appointment," said Marlene to the back of our heads.

"No it's not," mumbled Charles to no one in particular.

Chapter 5

I assured Harley that I'd let him know when I heard from Marlene. Charles and I watched him walk the short distance down Center Street to his motorcycle parked in front of the Sand Dollar Social Club. Instead of mounting his Harley, he entered the bright-green-painted private club, most likely to drown his traumatic visit to a lawyer's office in Budweiser—proudly advertised by the Sand Dollar as the Home of the One-Dollar Bud Can. The abuse he had shared at the hands of law enforcement and members of the bar (lawyers, not the Sand Dollar), had a palpable impact on him. What he shared would have been traumatic, but his reaction to Sean was over the top. Could there be more to it?

Charles and I decided that the last thing we needed was the dark, cigarette-smoke-filled pool hall ambiance of the Sand Dollar, so we ventured across the street to Rita's, one of Folly's newer, and more popular, restaurants. Rita's stood on the spot that years earlier had been a bowling alley, and since I moved to Folly, the restaurant had operated under three names. The new owner had completely renovated the building to the point of demolishing one section and adding outdoor seating. We entered the main door, which was surrounded by rusty corrugated steel panels, and were greeted by John, the owner. Charles nodded his Tilley at the cheerful proprietor—a habit that Charles had picked up from one of the etiquette books. I had asked him if the book had been published in the last fifty years, since hat-tipping was an art that had come and gone—thankfully. He didn't answer but said that the photo illustrations were in black and white.

Charles stopped at two tables, tipped his hat to the three couples peacefully having a late lunch, commiserated on how hot it was, and continued to the patio, where we were fortunate to get seats at a small, bar-height table shaded by a hurricane-proof wood and steel roof. I resisted the urge to shove him along.

A waitress arrived as soon as we were seated. Before she had time to take our order, Charles said, "Heard anything about the marsh body?"

"Excuse me?" she said.

I didn't recognize the blond, college-age waitress and didn't know if she knew Charles. Her startled reaction answered the question for me.

"The body found in the marsh Monday," he said in a tone like he was accusing her of killing the poor soul.

She looked at him as if he were speaking Swahili, and said, "Can I get you something to drink?"

"Never mind," said Charles. He shook his head.

I ordered drinks for both of us before the perplexed waitress got more confused.

"Whatever happened to people being helpful?" asked Charles. He slammed his hat on the table and kicked the table leg.

"Maybe she didn't know anything," I said. "Or didn't know what you were talking about?"

He didn't reply, so I continued, "What's wrong? You're—"

"Nothing," he blurted.

"I know you better than that," I said. "What's going on?"

The waitress was back with a beer for Charles and a glass of white wine for me. She avoided Charles and asked if I wanted water. I declined for both of us.

He took a sip and stared at the attractive, blue Tides logo on the façade of the nine-story hotel across the street. "It's just got to me," he said, and continued to stare at the hotel. I waited. "Standing at the grave yesterday got to me. You and I helped save her last year; she was a courageous old bird … and looking out at the marsh during the funeral, I thought how pretty everything was, and she would never see it again … never see it again."

"She led a long—"

"Don't interrupt," he said. He grabbed the handle of his cane and rammed it on the concrete patio. "And Harley tells us there was a body rotting out in the same marsh the day before. And then we get stood up by a lawyer—a lawyer, for God's sake! You know how many times in my entire life I've been to see a lawyer?" He still faced the hotel's sign but held his left hand in front of my face. "Don't guess. Today was number two, and he stood me up."

I didn't know what was so fascinating about the blue hotel sign, but his gaze never left it. I swore to myself I wasn't going to interrupt if we sat here until July. It felt nearly that long before he spoke. My curiosity about his first visit to a lawyer tempted me to ask, but he finally continued.

"Now you fire me, take away the best job I ever had."

He chose this moment to turn his attention from the neon sign to me. Hurt seeped from every pore in his body. I felt three layers below scum.

"Guess that's what's bothering me," he said and faked a smile.

My cell phone rang and drew me from of the depths of hurting. I was on the border of tearing up.

"Oh, hi, Marlene," I said. I was surprised that I recognized her voice. "Sure, yeah, Charles is with me ... I'll let Harley know ... No, I haven't heard anything ... You're kidding ... Is that where Sean went? ... Wow! Are you sure ... Okay."

I punched *end call*, set the phone on the table, and looked at Charles. He stared at me and had his arms extended, palms up. His body language screamed, "What?"

"The body in the marsh," I said. "It was Tony Long—Sean's law partner."

Chapter 6

The school year for Amber's son, Jason, had ended yesterday, so I had promised to take him and his mom to supper to celebrate. There was never doubt about his dining spot of choice. His favorite restaurant was Planet Follywood, a block from their tiny, second-story apartment.

Amber and I spent three hours listening to the recently-turned-thirteen-year-old's perspective on teachers, the school curriculum, what he needed to do and read to get a head start on next school year, and why his mother should let him start surfing or learning to fly an airplane. His mother's tan became a little less red with Jason's last two ideas. The best thing about the night was that there was absolutely no mention of Mrs. Klein's funeral, the mysterious discovery of Tony Long's body, or the firing of Charles Fowler, sales manager, Landrum Gallery.

I arrived at the stairs leading to Aker and Long five minutes before the designated time. Charles and Harley were in front of the building waiting for me. Charles was decked out in a long-sleeved UCLA T-shirt, threadbare cargo shorts, and his ever-present canvas hat. He held his cane over his shoulder like a soldier preparing to march into battle. Harley puffed on a cigarette, his right foot nervously tapping to a silent beat on the sidewalk. He wore a grease-stained, short-sleeved work shirt, dark-blue work pants, and boots I wouldn't want to be kicked by.

"Hurry up," said Harley. He flipped the half-smoked Camel in the street. "I've already missed two hours of work."

He was a plumber but only worked part-time for a couple of plumbing contractors off-island.

We traipsed up the steps in the same order as the day before. Marlene's smile was more sincere when we entered the reception area. Sean was in. I swallowed hard when I looked at the closed door to Tony Long's office.

Sean stepped out of his office and walked over to greet us before Marlene could properly announce our arrival. He was a couple of inches taller than me but weighed approximately fifty pounds less. Sean was well-toned and as athletic as all get out. No one would confuse the two of us. To make me feel more inadequate, he had a full head of short, curly black hair, no gray showing, and was at least two decades younger. Instead of stomping on his toe to level the playing field, I moved so he could see Harley. Sean shook Harley's hand and told him that he was sorry about the loss of his friend, Mrs. Klein. He nodded to Charles—his skydiving buddy. Sean looked at Charles and widened his grin. "Remember the time ..." He paused and looked toward his late partner's door. "Never mind. Come in the office."

There were two leather chairs in front of Sean's desk, so he pulled one of the chairs from the waiting room so we could all sit. He offered coffee or water, but we declined. Harley looked at his watch, saying bye to his hourly rate, I suspected.

"I'm sorry I couldn't meet yesterday," he began. "I hope it wasn't too inconvenient to have to reschedule."

Charles and I said it wasn't; Harley groaned.

Sean picked up a manila folder from a stack of several on the corner of his desk and opened it. "The reason—"

"Whoa," said Charles. He raised his cane and held it over Sean's hand so he couldn't open the folder. "What happened to your partner?"

Sean moved the cane away and alternated his gaze from Charles, to Harley, to me, and shook his head. "I don't know," he replied. "The detectives talked to me yesterday but said they weren't certain." He looked toward the ceiling. "That's what they said, anyway."

"Okay," said Harley. He leaned forward and looked ready to bolt. "He don't know nothing about the dead guy. Why are we here?"

Charles turned to Harley and started to say something, but Sean held up his hand. "Let me answer that, please," he said.

If he had his way, Charles wouldn't let Sean stop until he had told him every word the police had uttered, what they were wearing, and the kind of aftershave they had on. He was equally curious about the contents of the file, so he let Sean continue.

"Gentlemen," said Sean—a stretch, but we let it pass, "this is the last will and testament of Mrs. Margaret Lanier Klein."

I heard Marlene's phone ring for about the fifth time since we entered the office.

Harley scooted to the front of his chair; Sean had his attention.

"I've done legal work for her for the last nine or ten years," continued Sean. "She was widowed in 1984 with the passing of her husband. I helped her change her will seven years ago. She didn't have any living relatives and wanted to leave everything in an account to maintain her boardinghouse until the money ran out."

Joseph, her husband, had built the house on the beach and made her promise that when he was gone, she would divide the large structure into small apartments. He told her he hated that only the rich could enjoy living on the beach and wanted to provide low-cost apartments for the not-so-wealthy.

"Last September's hurricane royally screwed up her plan," said Sean.

After Hurricane Greta, all that was left of her husband's grand gesture, the Edge, were the foundation and two of the four concrete block walls.

"So what?" said Harley. His voice, always loud, had reached new heights. He wanted to be anywhere but in a lawyer's office and didn't hide it.

"So," said Sean, "Mrs. Klein called me on Valentine's Day and asked if I could 'come a callin'.' Her health was deteriorating; she really never recovered from the hurricane. I met her at her apartment. I had planned to take my wife to Charleston for a fancy dinner at Slightly North of Broad. She didn't rightly appreciate me standing her up for another woman on Valentine's Day—even if the other woman was in her eighties. That turned out to be a very cold February night when I got home ... never mind." Sean looked down at the double-spaced document in front of him. "Mrs. Klein wanted to change her will." Sean paused and made eye contact with each of us. "Guys, she left her entire estate to you."

"Shit fire," blurted Harley. Sean now had his undivided attention.

"Huh?" said Charles.

I waited for Charles and Harley's eloquent comments to subside and added, "Why?"

"If it weren't for you, she wouldn't have survived Hurricane Greta and as she told me, 'that deity-damned, crazy-assed crossbow killer.' You saved her life; that's why."

Harley focused on Sean; his need to get to work instantly fell off his priority ladder. "How much?' he asked.

"Don't get excited," said Sean. "I tried to get a handle on her net worth but couldn't get a straight answer. She told me she still owed a 'shitpot load' of money on the house but didn't know how much; she thought her husband had some insurance on the property, but she didn't know how much; she told me her dear husband had put a 'bunch' of money away in 'some' banks, savings and loans, had some gold, and some investment accounts, but didn't know how much." Sean paused and looked at the ceiling.

"How could she have gone all these years without knowing any of that?" I asked during the lull.

Sean shook his head. "She said she kept getting checks each month from several places and the rent her boarders paid took care of the rest. She stuck the monthly statements in a big freighter chest and never opened the envelopes. I was afraid to ask her about taxes."

"Let me guess," said Charles, "Hurricane Greta washed the chest away."

"You got it," said Sean. He closed the folder and tapped the pen on the desk. The phone in the outer office rang again—Marlene was earning her pay.

"Then what's it all mean?" asked Charles.

Sean looked back down at the closed folder. "Could mean that you are rich or that you still owe a lot of money on her—your—oceanfront property." He smiled.

"How can we be in debt over something we didn't even know about?" asked Charles.

"Yeah," said Harley, as he glared at Sean.

An excellent question, I thought.

Sean looked at Charles and smiled. "Really, you can't; you'd have to sell the lot and whatever she had and pay what you could from the proceeds. If that's the case, all you've inherited is a hassle."

"How do we find out about all the other stuff?" I asked. "The accounts, gold, and the other things she mentioned."

Sean looked down at the desk and then up at me. "We executed the new will, and I asked her to start collecting the statements she's received since Greta. They were all coming to her post office box, so nothing went to the street address of the Edge. I haven't been to her apartment to see what she's accumulated. With any luck, there should be a decent trail to her wealth—or poverty. Her oceanfront land, especially with its proximity to the center of town, should be worth a lot; but I don't know what she owed."

Harley wiggled in his chair. "When will I know what I get?" he bellowed.

"There should be at least three months of statements at her place ... if she did what I asked. That'll give me a good idea of where we stand. She paid the mortgage quarterly, so I'll have to find who she owed it to and contact them. Unfortunately, her checkbook went the way of all her other possessions during the storm, so I don't know who the mortgage holder is." Sean giggled. "She said she sent the mortgage check to some old bank in Kennedyland. I assumed she meant Massachusetts."

"Sean, I'm confused," I said. "Mrs. Klein and her husband built that house many years ago; He died more than twenty-five years ago. Why would there still be a mortgage? Wouldn't it be paid off?"

Sean nodded. "That's a good question," he said. "But I don't have a good answer. I asked her the same thing when she said she still owed on it. She said something about her husband 'forgetting' to pay taxes when he sold his chain of movie theaters. This was back in the sixties or seventies, not sure when. Anyway, he had to take a second mortgage on the property to pay the IRS. I don't know how much, but Mrs. Klein said the interest and penalty were more than the amount Joseph owed. It was none of my business then, so I didn't push it."

"Yeah, yeah," said Harley. "Can I smoke in here?" He swiveled in the chair and looked around the room. "When will I get my money?"

"No," said Sean in a tone that left no doubt that *no* meant *no*. "Harley, I have a couple of things on my plate right now. It'll be a couple of days or so before I can get a handle on this. I'll let you know."

With that, Sean moved the folder back to the side of his desk and asked if there were any other questions. I had about a zillion but knew this wasn't the time to ask. Charles shook his head. And Harley was already out of his chair and had a pack of Camels in his hand. He headed to the door.

"Oh, I forgot," said Charles. We were in the waiting area saying bye to Marlene. "Sean, there is one other legal question I wanted to ask. Do you have another minute?"

Charles asking a legal question was as rare as the American Heart Association endorsing Dunkin' Donuts.

"Uh, sure," said Sean.

Harley had heard enough legal mumbo-jumbo. "I'm out of here," he growled and headed down the stairs.

Charles was already walking to Sean's office. "Chris, you can join us."

"Gee, thanks, Charles," I mumbled under my breath.

The three of us took our familiar seats in Sean's office. Charles had closed the door once he had us herded together.

Sean smiled. "Charles, a legal question?"

Charles pointed his cane at Sean and glared. "Spill it. What's going on?"

Chapter 7

Sean returned Charles's glare, looked around the room, fiddled with a surfboard-shaped, orange paperweight, and moved some papers from one side of the desk to the other. I wondered how much longer he could stall before giving in to Charles's cane-pointed question.

"I don't know Harley," began Sean. "I didn't want to say more while he was here." He paused. "Hell, I don't know much more than I said anyway."

Charles lowered his cane. "Sean," he said, "The police didn't call yesterday, get you all irritated, have you go wherever, meet with you, to tell you they didn't know anything about your partner's death."

"Routine questions, that's all," said Sean. He shuffled the paperweight from hand to hand. "They asked when I saw Tony last. If he seemed worried. If he had enemies. Did I know if he went out in the marsh often. If he and I had any disputes. If—"

"Stomp on the brakes!" said Charles. His cane came up from his lap. "You're a lawyer and you thought that last one was a routine question? Where did you go to law school—Sesame Street U?" Charles shook his head. "Did you and Tony have disputes?"

Sean tapped his fingers on the desk. "They're just reaching," he said. "They don't know what happened ... I would have asked the same thing."

For someone who had repeatedly jumped out of planes, surfed, and scuba dived with sharks, Sean seemed mighty nervous.

"Sean," I said, "what'd you say to their questions?"

"The truth, of course. I hadn't seen Tony for two weeks before Memorial Day."

"Was that unusual?" asked Charles. "That's a long time."

Good question, Charles, I thought. For law partners, two weeks did seem like a long period not to see each other.

"Not really. We have a small office in North Charleston, and he works there most of the time. Tony had his own clients and took most of his meetings at their offices."

"Was he worried about anything?" asked Charles. "How about enemies?"

Sean giggled and looked down at the paperweight. "He should have been worried ... never mind. Enemies? He's a lawyer—what do you think?"

Marlene knocked on the door and stuck her head in before Sean said anything. "Sorry to interrupt. Want to take a call from Abe Fox?"

Sean looked at Charles and then me, and back at Marlene and asked her to get a number and see if he could call him back in a few minutes.

She closed the door, and Charles said, "Why should Tony have been worried?"

I knew Sean's "never mind" wouldn't fly past the master inquisitor.

Sean stood and walked to the wall behind Charles's and my chairs. We turned and watched as he looked at a photo of a significantly younger Sean Aker free-floating in the air before his parachute deployed. Whoever took the photo had been no more than fifteen feet from Sean and captured a wide grin on his face. *Fearless,* I thought; *until a few minutes ago.*

"I was here on Sunday evening about a month ago; a rare event, I admit. Tony's light was on and on his desk the brown accordion file we keep our bank statements in." He looked toward Tony's office. "We have several accounts—each of us has an individual account; there's a partnership one; and several escrow accounts. Marlene handles most of the checks, and I seldom get involved. Tony's the detail person and finance guy, and he works with her on reconciling the statements every so often. I hate it." He paused—too long for Charles's comfort.

"Was something wrong?" asked Charles.

"Yeah," said Sean. He had returned to his desk and had both elbows plopped squarely on the surface. "I'll spare you the details; let's just say the partnership account was nearly seventy-five grand light."

"As in seventy-five thousand dollars?" said Charles. "Vamoosed?"

Sean raised the paperweight and sidearmed it against the wall to our right. Charles was closest to the point of impact. He ducked and nearly slid out of his chair. The paperweight missed a framed photo of Sean scuba diving but sounded like a gunshot when it hit the wall. It hit the floor with a *clink*.

"That mean yes?" said Charles after he had regained his balance on the chair.

Sean simply stared at my friend.

"Did you tell all this to the police?" I asked.

"Yep."

"What'd they say?" asked Charles.

"They'd be talking to me again."

I'd put money on that, I thought.

Chapter 8

Sean shed little additional light on the missing money and said he had to make a call—a polite dismissal. Vacation season had begun, and we had to weave among the visitors to make the short trek from the law office to the gallery. The number of vacationers thinned considerably as we reached the door to Landrum Gallery; unfortunately, not that unusual an occurrence. It was still before noon, but the temperature pushed the upper eighties; the air conditioned gallery would feel great.

"Do you know who Abe Fox is?" asked Charles as I unlocked the door.

"One of the top criminal attorneys in the state, if his press clippings are accurate," I said. I got a dollop of satisfaction knowing the answer to Charles's question; he gets way too much enjoyment telling me things I don't know.

Charles grabbed two Diet Pepsis from the refrigerator in the back room, underhanded one to me, and frowned; he had missed his teaching moment. "And do you think it was just a coincidence that one of the top *criminal* attorneys called Sean?"

"Could have been." I pulled the tab on the drink and sat in one of the rickety chairs at the multi-purpose table. "He may want to buy property here and wants Sean to handle the paperwork; they may have a client in common; he could be calling to get Sean to buy tickets to a big charity event the legal association is sponsoring; he—"

"He could be Sean's long-lost father wanting to tell him his son that his mother was from the planet Uranus!" interrupted Charles. "Stop being so dense. Sean's hiring Fox to defend him. Defend him against a charge of murdering his partner."

I had known where Charles was headed when he asked if I knew Fox. I wanted to slow down his conclusion-train. "How long have you known Sean?"

"A dozen years or so," he said. "I met him just after he opened his practice. Why?"

I ignored his question. "So, how well do you think you know him?"

"Fairly well, I guess. We were in the skydiving club together for a couple of years—you get to know someone pretty well when you're sitting in that little plane getting ready to step out into nothing. He and his wife live over at Mariner's Cay; we don't do any socializing together, if that's what you mean."

Mariner's Cay was a large condo development across the Folly River from the island.

"Have you ever seen anything that would make you think he could be a killer?" I asked.

Charles leaned back in his chair and rubbed his chin. "Not really," he said. "But I've never seen him deal with someone who ripped him off for seventy-five thousand bucks." Charles paused and then nodded his head. "When that paperweight whizzed by, it entered my mind that he might have a temper."

"Jumped right on that, didn't you?" I smiled. "We really don't know, do we?"

"No, but I don't want to think Sean's a killer. Besides, we don't know that Tony was murdered. He could've drowned, had a heart attack, or been grabbed by a sea monster, or, or ..."

"Now you're being dense. What are the odds that he wasn't murdered?"

"Give or take, zero."

The bell over the front door interrupted our mathematical probability discussion, and Charles jumped up to greet a potential customer. I jumped up at a much slower speed and got another Pepsi from the fridge. I didn't know Sean as well as Charles did but still couldn't picture him as a killer. He had handled some of the legal work for the gallery, had even helped me get information to help find a murderer a couple of years back. And last year, during one of my lowest moments in memory, Sean had sprung Charles and me from jail. On a non-professional level, we had had several conversations at social events and even shared a conversation over an alcoholic beverage at The Crab Shack, one of a handful of Folly's outdoor restaurants. I also realized that none of this would preclude him from killing his partner.

"I've got it. Brilliant!" said Charles as he bounded back into the room. "Wait till you hear this," he said.

I ignored his enthusiasm and asked if he had sold anything.

He nodded his head in the direction of the gallery. "Idiots," he responded. "Wouldn't know a great photo if it bit them on the big toe."

It didn't make a *bit* of sense, but I figured it meant they had left without buying anything.

"Forget them," he continued. "Wait until you hear this." He headed to the fridge and grabbed a Bud Light.

Oh, oh, I thought.

"Okay, here goes." Charles had returned to the table. "Now that I'm unemployed, I can devote my work hours to another pursuit. Now that I'm heir to a fortune, I can devote my resources to my new business. And because I'm such a generous, helpful individual, I can offer you a job in my new business." He paused and squinted his eyes in my direction. "I can do that even after you fired me."

"First," I said and made a fist of my right hand and extended my thumb, "you were never employed, so your status is unchanged. Second," I raised my index finger, "you have no idea what you inherited; remember, Sean said you may owe more than you get." I extended my middle finger. "And third, when the gallery closes, I will go back to being retired, full-time—never to go to work again—retired."

"You haven't even asked what the business is," he said.

"I'm pretty sure I don't want to know, but tell me anyway ... like I could stop you."

"FDA—the Fowler Detective Agency."

Since I moved to Folly Beach and had the "honor" of meeting Charles Fowler, he and I had developed the knack of being in the wrong place at the wrong time. I had stumbled on a murder of a prominent developer; another friend of mine had convinced us that an apparent suicide was actually a murder; someone had killed innocent people to serve as an overture for murdering our friend Larry; and a crazed crossbow killer had bumped off some of our friends and acquaintances.

Through some minor detecting, stumbling into places where we had no business, and pure luck, we had helped the police find the killers. Each time, we found ourselves in places where the police should have been, and Charles had created an imaginary detective agency. He called it the C & C Detective Agency. Depending upon his mood, the first C was for Charles or for Chris. I called it absurd, impossible, dangerous, and totally a figment of his imagination.

Now it seemed he wanted to move it to the possible category, and in a glimmer of poetic justice, according to its new moniker, it would appear that I had been fired.

"I think FDA is taken," I said. "Unless you are going to be investigating norovirus illnesses linked to oysters, you better not steal the US Food and Drug Administration's initials."

"Good point," he said without any hesitation. "They would see me as a threat. Wouldn't want them to have to change their name. How about CDA, Charles's Detective Agency?"

"Do you know what it takes to start a detective agency?" I asked. "I would hope not anyone can hang out a shingle and claim to be a private detective."

"Why not? Anyone can open a restaurant. Look at those places that serve seriously sucky food; they're not restaurants, but their signs say they are."

Arguing with Charles was like trying to teach a turtle how to ride a bike; it'll look at you, bob its head, and then nothing.

Charles looked at me and then nodded. *A bit turtle-like,* I thought. "I've already got my first case," he said.

"Finding Tony's killer?"

"Yep."

Chapter 9

Brian Newman was Folly Beach's director of public safety, shortened to "police chief" by most everyone. He and I had slowly become friends. I, along with a few quirky friends, had stumbled in his way a few times; we had provided him with invaluable leads on a couple of cases and given him more than one headache; and once, he had had to save my life.

The chief had suffered a serious heart attack in September—so serious that the doctors had thought he was a goner. But Brian was a fighter. He was in his mid-sixties but was in excellent health at the time of the attack. His overall health saved him, according to his doctors.

Brian was a week away from returning to full-time duty the first of the year, when he suffered another attack. It wasn't as serious as the first, but the doctors "highly encouraged" him to retire from the force and cite pressure, stress, and fighting battles for funding from the city council—all things he didn't need more of. The doctors didn't know Brian. He had served thirty years in the military, in Special Services and as an MP; he had been Folly's chief for nearly fifteen years. He wasn't near ready to quit.

After much wrangling and a direct order from the mayor, Brian agreed to "rest" until the fall, when he would resume his duties part-time until he could con his doctor into releasing him for full duty. He was as happy about "resting" as I would be about an outbreak of shingles on my back.

A low front pushed into the area overnight and helped lower the near-record high, late-spring temperatures. A steady rain replaced the sweltering heat, and I decided it would be the perfect day to visit the "resting" chief. I told Charles my plan, and he asked if he could tag along. He would normally chide me for leaving the gallery during the busy season and then give me his martyr's grin and say to go ahead, he would mind the store. Not today—he was up to something.

Brian lived in a three-story condo complex across Folly Road from the Piggly Wiggly. The rain had intensified as we pulled into the development. The large, relatively new, attractive complex was nicer than most condos in the area and was convenient to both the island and downtown Charleston.

Visitor's parking was across the drive from the building. Brian lived on the second floor, and we were drenched by the time we ran from the car up the stairs. My Tilley protected my receding hairline, but my golf shirt and shorts weren't so lucky; they were soaked. Charles had had me stop by his apartment on the way so he could change into a NYPD long-sleeved T-shirt in honor of our visit to Folly's highest ranking law enforcement official. The wet, black T-shirt stuck to his thin frame.

Brian greeted his waterlogged visitors with a smile and waved us in. Despite the precautions dictated by his doctor, he looked fine. His six-foot-two frame stood erect. He was still slightly under his fighting weight, but his face was tanned; he had lost the pasty-white pallor I had become accustomed to seeing since his first attack. He was dressed in bright, glow-in-the-dark-blue shorts, a short-sleeved Folly Beach T-shirt, and chocolate-brown Crocs; however reluctant, he had clearly become acclimated to the life of leisure. I didn't want to drip on the floor, but Brian said not to worry. The combination living room and kitchen had a tan, ceramic tile floor, so the drips wouldn't hurt it. He offered us coffee and headed to the high-tech-looking, Bunn coffeemaker before we could decline.

I had been to the condo several times since his heart attack, but this was Charles's first visit. He looked around the room and appeared surprised by the décor. The living area and dining room were furnished in high-end, light oak Scandinavian furniture. The furnishings were sparse but high-quality—a reflection of Brian's many years in the military, when he was unable to put down roots. A fifty-five-inch Sony Bravia was on a five-foot-wide, natural wood, low stand along the far wall. Clear glass doors on the stand revealed a Sony Blu-ray disc player and sound system. I didn't know about the television but suspected that the stand cost more than all the furniture in my living room, including my thirty-two-inch television.

Charles walked around the room like a dog deciding where to spin and light for a nap, or worse. Brian returned with a mug in each hand and pushed one on each of us. Charles looked at the recliner situated in the center of the room, about fifteen feet directly in front of the television. The chair was white leather and would have been more at home in the Starship Enterprise than in a Lowcountry condo. The chair was centered on a five-by-eight-foot area rug covered in overlapping circles of varying sizes and bright colors.

"Can that thing fly?" asked Charles as he stared at the chair's round, steel base.

"Never tried; don't know," deadpanned Brian as he walked back to the kitchen to get his drink.

There were only two other chairs in the room, so Charles and I didn't have a difficult time deciding where to sit.

"It's a Kiri," said Brian. He slowly sat in the contemporary recliner and swiveled toward Charles.

"That anything like a Goodwill?" responded Charles.

Brian laughed but didn't answer, the best response to Charles most of the time.

There was a small, glass-topped table beside each of the bleached-wood chairs Charles and I occupied. The chairs were contemporary, stylish, and as comfortable as sitting on a flagpole. The only other piece of furniture in the room was a three-shelf bookcase by the entry. Charles had lost interest in the Kiri—whatever that meant—and stared at the books on the shelves.

"Got some of those myself," he said as he continued to read and lovingly touch the spines. "Military history, war strategy, history of the US navy—fun reading."

Truth be known, I would have been shocked if Charles didn't have some of the books, since his apartment resembles a used book store on steroids.

Brian looked at Charles with new admiration. "I didn't know you had an interest in the military and military history."

Charles blew on the coffee and then took a sip and looked from the bookcase to Brian. "Oh, I don't. Bought them for a dime each; couldn't pass up the deal."

I had even less interest than that, so I interrupted the "fascinating" conversation and asked how Brian felt. He said "fine" and didn't elaborate, so I asked when he would be back on the job.

In a fit of governmental wisdom—a contradiction, I realized—Mayor Amato had hired an acting director of public safety last September. The acting chief, Clarence King, had been a long-term member of the Charleston County sheriff's office and was nearing retirement. He had a "distinguished" career that included numerous citizen complaints, an unexplained shooting, and at least three sexual harassment charges. To make up for these shortcomings, he added anger management issues to the list. To put it mildly, Mayor Amato didn't have to twist the sheriff's arm too hard to let him borrow the services of Clarence King.

Before I had the pleasure of meeting the acting chief, word was being bandied around that he was a hard-ass. That proved to be a gross understatement.

The city limits of Folly Beach were now under the control of acting chief Clarence King, and the best chief the city had ever had was lounging in a Kiri, wearing glow-in-the-dark-blue shorts, and watching daytime soap operas on a television the size of a ping-pong table.

Brian glanced at Charles and turned to me. "When will I return to my job?" he said. "Good question. There's no reason I couldn't have been back last month. I've heard from a little bird at city hall that the mayor is trying to make my medical leave permanent."

"Is the mayor still upset about traffic problems?" I asked.

"Yeah," said Brian, "like I can do something about all the people coming over here in the summer." He abruptly stood and headed back to the Bunn machine. "Now he's forced us to cut staff and park one of our patrol cars. Budget cuts—bunk." He returned to his chair, but instead of sitting, Brian continued to the window and stared out. "The real problem is the wealthy newcomers. They come from wherever, buy a teardown house, and spend millions building a monument to their wealth. They move into their damned McMansions and complain about noise, traffic, trash, and the laid-back lifestyles of people who have lived here that way for decades." He finally returned to his chair and plopped down. "They think Folly Beach should be another Kiawah, or Isle of Palms. Hell, some wing nuts have proposed we put a gate at the bridge and charge folks to visit the island."

He took a swig of coffee, and I took the opportunity to interrupt his rant. "You still have the council's support, don't you?" The mayor has the upper hand in hiring and firing the director of public safety but must have the backing of the six-member council or could face the embarrassing situation of having his decision overturned.

"Barely," said Brian. "Before the last election, they supported me five to one on most issues. Now it's four to two; wouldn't take much to go the other way, and with the mayor's strong pro-growth ideas, I'm standing in his way."

"So what's up with the murder of Tony Long?" asked Charles, who had been sitting quietly—a condition almost worthy of a YouTube video. He had heard all he wanted to about city politics.

Brian smiled. "I wondered when you would get there," he said as he looked at Charles. "First, they don't even know it was murder. We're at the beach; we have a river behind the island; there's the marsh back there; people drown—accidents, drunks fall off boats, fools zipping around on jet skis, idiots kill themselves on purpose—"

"Yeah, yeah, yeah," interrupted Charles. "But I'll bet ya my Saab against your condo that this was a murder."

Brian laughed; finally. The only thing Charles's car and Brian's condo had in common was that neither had moved in years. "No bet. The odds are that it was foul play; but I don't know anything more about it than you do. Actually, with your rumor network, you might know more."

"How would you investigate it if it was your case?" said Charles.

Now Charles's interest in coming with me had begun to make sense—CDA was on the job.

Chapter 10

Brian sat erect in his chair and gave Charles a fifty-watt version of his police stare. "Well, the first—the very first—thing I would do *if I were you* would be to say to myself, 'Am I a duly sworn law enforcement officer?'" He intensified his stare. "And then I would answer, 'Whoops, no! Time to butt out and leave it to the cops.'"

"So, if you weren't me and investigating the case, what next?"

Charles was on a mission and wasn't about to be rebuked by a mere chief of police.

Brian shook his head in mild surrender. "Charles, there's nothing mysterious about an investigation. Nothing that the world doesn't see every week on *CSI*, *NCIS*, and a dozen other television shows."

"But they're all fiction," said Charles.

Exactly like your detective agency, I thought. I leaned back in the extraordinarily uncomfortable, but stylish, chair to watch the show.

"Okay, I give up," said Brian. He took another sip of coffee and leaned back in the recliner. "The first thing I would do is secure the crime scene; not just where the body was, but expand to anywhere the perp may have entered or exited the area. The first responder on the scene gets a good overview of what happened, can usually tell if it was the kill site or just the dump site. Crime scene techs from Charleston would do their thing. While the techs collected evidence, I would talk to witnesses and anyone around the area. The quicker a motive can be established, the easier the case. Some are obvious, like a store robbery gone bad; others nearly impossible—"

"Like a body in the marsh?" blurted Charles.

Brian gave Charles a sideways glance and then continued, "Then the hard work begins—talking to family and friends, co-workers, neighbors, anyone who had a connection to the victim. Motive, means, and likely suspects become part of a giant puzzle. In the real world, murders are not solved in sixty minutes, like they are on TV." Brian giggled. "And that's with giving the viewers the chance to learn about the latest prescription drugs for depression, allergies, and erectile dysfunction."

"Do you know much about Tony Long?" I asked.

"Not really," said Brian "He's not over here that often; think he mainly works out of an office off-island, maybe in North Charleston. A few years back, a buddy of mine on the force up there told me Long was on the *periphery* of a mob-related investigation."

"Good or bad periphery?" asked Charles.

"Bad. He was representing some shady characters in a money-laundering scheme. His clients had business ties—close business ties—to the bad guys."

"That doesn't sound like something Sean would be part of," said Charles.

"Not the Sean I know," said Brian. "But you never know. For what it's worth, I've heard that Tony had a weakness for the fairer sex; that's only a rumor, though."

For Charles, a rumor-collector extraordinaire, that was all it took. He had moved to the front of his chair and was on the verge of falling off. "He was married, wasn't he?"

Brian grinned. "Yep. Connie's her name; met her once at the Christmas buffet at Planet Follywood. Heard she has money—inherited from her grandparents, or some relative."

Brian's front door opened and nearly startled me off my chair.

"Oh, sorry, Dad. I didn't know you had company," said the attractive, trim, almost regal Detective Karen Lawson.

Charles and I stood. Karen's long, chestnut-brown hair was tied in back, and she was dressed in a navy pantsuit. Her look oozed professional and on-duty. She set her purse on the floor beside the door and moved quickly to Charles and gave him a brief hug and then turned to me and did likewise. She walked to Brian, who was still seated, and gave him a peck on the top of his head.

"Going or coming?" asked Brian as he looked up at his daughter. He remained seated.

"Working," she said. "On my way to talk to a witness about a mile from here. We got an anonymous tip in a three-year-old case. Amazing what a ten-thousand-dollar reward will bring out of the woodwork. Thought I'd see how you're doing."

"Was doing fine until these pests arrived," said Brian as he waved in Charles's and my direction. He smiled as he said it.

I had met Detective Lawson my first week on Folly Beach, the same time I met Detective Burton. I had gotten to know her much better last year when Brian had his near-fatal heart attack. It was a terrible way to get to know someone, but I thoroughly enjoyed it despite the circumstances. She and I had shared a few meals together, a few drinks, several hours of conversation, and a mutual admiration and concern for her father.

Friends tried to convince me that Karen wanted to share much more with me, and truth be told, if I hadn't felt the way I did about Amber, I would have pursued the opportunity.

"Is Long yours?" asked Charles. He wasn't going to pass up this golden opportunity to gather information.

Karen looked at Charles and then walked over to the Bunn coffeepot. I doubted that it had received so much attention since Brian bought it. "No," she said after taking a sip from her mug. "I tried, but the sheriff is still pushing me away from cases on or near Dad's kingdom. Stupid, but not my call."

Karen wouldn't say it, but I suspected it was because of the harassment complaint she had filed against the acting chief four years ago when they were colleagues in the sheriff's office. Before acting chief King was appointed, Karen had been assigned to every murder on Folly Beach since she had been promoted to detective. She had an excellent relationship with the law enforcement officials on Folly; she respected their insights and abilities and was extremely effective. That all changed nine months ago with King's new job.

"Heard about it?" asked Charles. He was still standing and leaning against his cane.

"They still don't know COD," she said. "The body was pretty cut up, bounced around on the razor-sharp oyster shells. Eyeballs gone—probably crab food."

"Yuck," said the always articulate Charles. "Look like murder?"

"Again, they're not sure. The coroner is backed up and hasn't done the autopsy. One of the detectives on the case told me he was no expert, but he'd put money on it."

"Enough of this cheery topic," said Brian.

"I have to go anyway," said Karen. "Bad guys won't wait." She returned her mug to the kitchen counter and gave her dad another kiss on his head. She turned and smiled at Charles and slowly walked to me and gave me a hug before turning to the door.

"Be sure and say hi to Joe for me," I said.

She turned and gave me a radiant smile before opening the door.

Charles's head was turned to the closing door, but his eyes were turned toward me. He knew Karen was single, and I suspected he had no idea who Joe was. It would have been easy for me to tell him that Joe was Karen's eight-year-old cat, a cat named after Joe Friday from the old television show *Dragnet*. It would have been easy to tell him, but not nearly as much fun.

We stayed at Brian's condo for another hour, letting him regale us with stories from his military days and Charles talking about his first few years on Folly Beach and how strange, iconoclastic, and in the view of some, corrupt some of the members of the local government were back in those days. Brian said that it might not be corrupt now, but "strange and iconoclastic" would still apply. He didn't get an argument from us.

The last thing Brian said to us on our way out the door was, "Thanks for stopping by. Stay out of trouble, and don't meddle."

Charles only heard *thanks*.

Chapter 11

The Folly Beach Arts and Crafts Guild sponsored an arts and crafts show in the Folly River Park the first Saturday of the month during the summer. I would need an outlet to sell my photos once I closed the gallery; the monthly show—dubbed First Saturday on the Edge—fit the bill. When I lived in Kentucky, I participated in a handful of juried shows throughout the region and loved the outdoor atmosphere—loved it when it wasn't pouring rain or when the temperature didn't shoot past ninety.

The show didn't officially open until eleven a.m., so I had plenty of time to set up the tent and displays. The small park, on the corner of Center Street and the Folly River, was only two minutes from my house and no more than five minutes by foot from the entire commercial district of the island and the Atlantic Ocean. My gallery staff, Charles, waited for me as I backed into a parking area to unload the tent and display racks. He stared at the spot on his wrist where most mortals wore a watch. He waved his cane in my direction and informed me that it was about time I arrived. He pointed his cane toward the metal-roofed open pavilion and said our space was to the right of the crisp, beige-and-white structure and the pier over the marsh. As my luck normally goes at these shows, the space was as far as possible from where the car was parked. Newcomers to the event can't be choosy.

I had hoped that I wouldn't have to erect my ten-by-ten-foot Lightdome tent, but the warm front that had come through the area yesterday lingered, and there was a fifty-fifty chance of afternoon showers. The tent setup was a tedious process, and I had often envied the artists who worked in steel, who seldom worried about the weather and could be ready in fifteen minutes. Matted and framed photographs were not as forgiving as steel lawn birds.

The sun, coming from the direction of the ocean, peeked out over the clouds. A couple of artists had already completed their setup and stopped by to share bits of gossip and conversation about the weather. The event was not large by art and craft show standards. Fewer than fifty booths were permitted, but the quality of the art was outstanding and the venue pleasant and easy to get to. The city had completed a major overhaul of the park a few years ago and added the covered makeshift stage and new restrooms—the improvements cost a bundle but were worth it.

Despite the countless notices plastered around town listing the start time, the sidewalks that meandered through the park overflowed with visitors and potential buyers an hour earlier. Most artists were ready to take the vacationers' money. Traffic arriving from Charleston was already backed up on the bridge to the island, and two of Folly's finest were stationed in front of the park to keep vehicles moving. As usual, once vacation season arrived, they failed.

I sold a couple of hundred dollars of prints before the official opening, which was kicked off by a welcome from the president of the Arts and Crafts Guild, a prayer from the minister of an African-American church located just off-island, and an enthusiastic rendition of the national anthem sung by a high school senior at Charleston County School of the Arts.

I was selling a matted photo of the Folly Pier to a couple from the Sullivan's Island when I heard Charles yell, "How's Joe?"

I turned and was surprised to see Karen Lawson headed toward the booth. She was either off-duty or undercover. She had on a sleeveless, pink blouse and tan shorts. Her hair flowed freely and shimmered in the light breeze. Her pale, well-toned legs revealed that she had spent too much time working and not enjoying the spring sunshine.

She frowned when she got about five feet from Charles. With a straight face, she said, "He was out cattin' around last night." She shook her head in disgust.

I hadn't told Charles about Joe's pedigree and could tell he didn't know what to say. I stood behind him, smiled, and gave Karen a thumbs-up. She shook her head like she was near the end of the line with Joe's shenanigans. If I didn't sell another thing today, this moment was worth all the trouble.

The couple from Sullivan's Island had left a hundred bucks lighter and with two photos. Karen, Charles, and I were alone in the booth. Apparently she felt guilty about teasing Charles—unnecessary, since he had made a crusade out of insulting and teasing friends and foe alike— and told him about her feline. The booth filled before she completed her story about Joe and how he got his name. I had learned over the years that customers arrived in waves. Without any danger of rip currents, I welcomed all visitors to the booth, regardless of how they arrived.

Karen started twice to tell us something but was interrupted by questions from customers. A rock-and-roll band from James Island began a sound check at the bandstand. In seconds, we wouldn't be able to hear anything. Charles said he would take care of the booth if Karen and I wanted to walk and talk. She said, "Thanks" before I weighed in on the offer.

A recently updated, narrow pier started at the park, spanned part of the marsh, and ended overhanging the Folly River. I guided Karen toward the pier and slowly walked with her to the end of the seven-hundred-foot-long, wood structure. She had something on her mind, so I didn't compound the situation with words. Several walkers were on the pier, but by the time we arrived at the covered end that overlooked the river, we were alone.

Karen leaned against the rail, made a couple of benign comments about the weather and the large number of boats on the river. And then, her reason for coming. "One of our detectives called last night," she said. "Long was murdered."

I wasn't surprised, but it still turned my stomach sour. "How?"

"Gunshot," she said. "No slug in the body, but no doubt about the cause."

"Leads?"

"Zilch," she said. "Doubt they'll ..."

Her next words were drowned out by the roar of a speedboat as it zipped down the river—too fast and too close to shore. Insanity season at the beach had begun.

I asked her to repeat the last part.

"I doubt they'll find anything useful. The body was near the narrow channel out by Secessionville. The doc said he wouldn't be able to pin time of death closer than a two-day window. The body was found on Memorial Day and had been there at least three days and up to five; high tide had come and gone at least six times, could be as many as ten. Our guys couldn't even tell if the body was killed or dumped where it was found or washed there from somewhere else." She paused and followed the path of a sailboat that was gracefully passing. "To be honest, I'm sort of glad someone else has this one." She tapped me on the arm. "You didn't hear that from me."

"Hear what?" I said.

"Thanks," she said and tapped my arm again. "I need to head out. I promised to take Dad to lunch in Charleston."

The rock band was going full tilt when we got back to the tent. I didn't recognize any of the music, but that wasn't the case for the group of early-teens who stood in front of the screeching musicians and mouthed the words. I didn't want to immediately be tagged as an old geezer, so I didn't put my hands over my ears.

Karen waved bye to Charles and leaned over to me. "I'm not going to tell you not to get involved; I know it won't do any good. Just be careful." She gave me another arm tap and walked away.

Excellent advice, I thought. *And what's with the arm taps?*

Chapter 12

I returned to the tent to find Charles deep in conversation with Marlene Ryle, the receptionist at Aker and Long. Their heads were inches apart so they could hear each other. Her white linen slacks and a light-blue top contrasted with her professional garb she had worn each time I was in the law office. Her shih tzu was cradled in her arms. She and Charles were laughing, but I couldn't hear what they were saying because the lead singer was screaming something about either Danny Glover or a fanny lover.

Two huge speakers with "Cosmo Rentals" stenciled on each side suddenly turned silent, proof that there was a god and that he did work in strange and mysterious ways. The Goth-attired lead vocalist and the geeky-looking teenager working the sound board looked at each other, and then at the cables snaked between the board and the amps, and then toward the sky, and then back at each other. My guess was that neither of them was an electrical engineer.

The unexpected, and welcomed, silence gave me a chance to interject myself into Charles and Marlene's conversation. I made the obligatory comment about her "adorable" canine and then listened as Charles filled me in on what I'd missed. Marlene had told him that even though she was one of the signers on the firm's checkbook, neither Sean nor Tony needed the second signature. She seldom had access to the checkbook; Tony hoarded it and was the numbers person. This was consistent with what Sean had told us.

"Anything bothering Tony?" asked Charles.

Marlene set her dog, whose name I'd already forgotten, on the ground and wiped a couple of hairs off her blue top.

"Well, fellows," she began, "I don't like to speak unkindly about the dead, but ..." She hesitated.

Charles wasn't about to let her stop. He picked up the dog, gave it a hug, and told her how precious it was, and said, "It's okay. We won't tell anyone."

"These are just rumors and feelings, you understand," she said as she looked around to see if anyone was near.

A few words of profanity came from the bandstand—a good sign, I thought. The peaceful silence would continue. The Goth-attired lead singer leaned on the metal sculpture of a frog playing a guitar that guarded the shelter. I realized that I was feeling my age when I thought the frog statue looked more human than the young vocalist.

Marlene continued, "I think Tony may have had a wee bit of a drug problem."

"What makes you think that?" I asked.

"I have a young cousin who's been in and out of rehab for years, lives out near the plantations. We used to be close ... until—until he got so paranoid he didn't trust anyone. He'd steal and pawn anything that wasn't screwed down." She stopped and wiped a tear from her left eye. "He was all nervous-like. Tony's behavior the last year reminded me of him. I said there wasn't anything specific; a gut reaction."

Charles set the dog down. "Anything else?" he asked.

"God, I feel terrible telling this," she said. "I think his wife was going to leave him."

"Why?" I asked.

"I'm not certain she was," said Marlene. "The last couple of weeks she called the office three times I know about. He usually talked to her with his door open, but the last few times he closed it before having me put the call through. The walls in our offices are not the best construction. Normal conversation is okay, but if someone talks loud, you can hear it in the reception area. Tony was cussing and pounding his desk as soon as the conversation started with Connie—that's his wife, you know."

"Are you sure it was about her leaving him?" I asked.

Marlene grinned. "Pretty sure it wasn't over getting bananas at the Pig on his way home."

She pulled her shoulders back; she was beginning to like the attention. Charles's way with dogs worked wonders.

She continued, "Seriously, I heard him say something about money, her attorney, 'you'll regret it,' and 'just try!'" She shook her head. "No, I didn't hear him say she was leaving, but that was the impression I got, you know. After two of the calls, he slammed down the phone, yanked the door open, and ran down the stairs without saying anything to me."

"Did Sean hear any of this?" asked Charles.

"No," she quickly said and then looked toward the top of the tent. "No—I'm pretty sure he didn't. He was out a lot. I don't even think he saw Tony."

Two elderly couples had walked into the tent. They appeared to be together and started asking about the location of several of the photos, oblivious to our conversation with Marlene. She wasn't about to continue with the growing crowd and said she'd talk to us later. We had no choice but to let her leave. Charles would have followed her out and continued the interrogation, but the chance of taking money from customers held him at bay.

Around one o'clock p.m., the clearing sky and sun began to win the tug-of-war against clouds and rain. The crowd wasn't as heavy as it had been earlier, but there was still a steady flow of visitors to the booth. Charles was much more comfortable talking to prospective buyers than I was, so I walked around and looked at the other booths. I had met one of the two other photographers at the exhibit, and we spent a few minutes talking about the plethora of photo opportunities around Charleston and the Lowcountry. We both bemoaned how difficult it was to sell enough photography to make a living. He said he was planning to publish a photo book of Folly Beach. I wished him well and continued my walk.

"You just missed William Hansel," said Charles when I returned to the booth. I waved my Tilley in front of my face to get some air movement. Perspiration covered my body.

William was my neighbor when I rented a house during my first extended stay on Folly Beach four years ago. He was a tenured professor of hospitality and tourism at the College of Charleston. On the surface, nothing sounded unusual about that, but in the spirit of Folly, he broke the mold at that point. William was African American, was a strong Republican, had never worked in his field of expertise, and would rather live on an island with an extremely small minority population than in Charleston. He would still be my neighbor if a killer hadn't decided that I was a threat and burned my house down—with me inside. Fortunately, that was ancient history, although I would occasionally awake in the night imagining the smell of burning wood from that horrific night.

I handed Charles a hot dog and Diet Pepsi that I had picked up during my tour of the show. "Is he going to come back?" I said.

Charles took a bite about the size of half the hot dog and then mumbled, "No. Said he had to get somewhere; I didn't catch where." A sip of the Pepsi was next. I waited patiently. "He did say you were overdue for a visit."

He was right. I hadn't talked to William since Christmas.

Chapter 13

Storm clouds gathered in the west; thunderheads rolled closer by the minute. The rock band had given up on restoring electricity to its thunderous performance. All there under age sixteen were disappointed; all with eardrums over forty, relieved. The temperature must have been ninety, and the humidity soared. Most visitors had abandoned their cover-ups by mid-afternoon and pranced around in bikinis, swim trunks hanging below the knee, and worst of all, men in Speedos. I would rather have watched a chorus line of alligators amble by. Summer had arrived early on Folly Beach.

Power to the bandstand still hadn't been restored, but it didn't stop Country Cal from beginning his half-hour set of country classics. With nearly fifty years of singing for a living, he had seen it all—from the stratospheric heights of the Grand Ole Opry to standing on hay bales crooning for crowds numbering in single digits. Thirty minutes without a live mike would be a snap.

The first chords of "I Never Go Around Mirrors" were coming from his beat-up guitar when Marlene edged back into the tent, shih tzu in hand.

Charles immediately took the dog and kissed it on the nose; Marlene beamed. "Tony have problems with any clients?" asked the budding detective and canine-kisser.

"Come on, Charles," she said as she looked around the tent. "You know I shouldn't tell you this."

I saw that as a good sign, since she had started that way earlier and then talked and talked.

"It's okay," said Charles—whatever that meant.

Marlene continued to look around and saw that no one else could hear. "You have to understand," she said, "we don't do criminal law; mostly boring stuff like wills, estate planning, real estate closings, business incorporations, occasionally a divorce. Every once in a while, Tony got involved with clients he never brought to the office. I think it's, as they say, 'family' business …"

"Like Mafia?" interrupted Charles.

Marlene's eyes darted around the tent once again. "You didn't hear that from me," she said. "Anyway, he keeps—kept—whatever it was separate from anything in the office. To be honest, I have no idea if anyone was mad at him about that work."

"Was Sean involved?" I asked.

Marlene waved her right hand in front of her head, palm facing me. "No way," she said. "He wouldn't touch that if he were flat broke. In fact—oh God, I shouldn't be telling you this—I know he and Tony had more than one, let's say, heated discussion about some of Tony's clients. They've been at each other more and more lately; not out-and-out arguments but sharp words, nasty looks, slammed doors." She hesitated and looked down. "Please don't tell Sean I said anything. I've been with him, well, with both of them, but mainly Sean, five years. I love the job."

"He won't hear it from us," said Charles. A promise I wasn't sure he would be able to keep.

"One other thing, and then I need to go," she said. "When you asked about problem clients, it made me think of Mr. Elder, Conroy Elder." She looked at Charles and then me, and said nothing.

"What about him?" asked Charles, who was uncomfortable with Marlene's pause.

"It may be nothing," she said and continued to move her gaze from Charles to me and back. "A couple of weeks, or maybe it was three, before the holiday, Mr. Elder stormed into the office and demanded to see Tony, demanded to see him *right now!* Fortunately for Mr. Elder—not for Tony—it was one of the rare times when Tony was there. He was meeting with a client about a will. Tony heard Mr. Elder yelling and cut his meeting short and hurried the client out the door. Confused the heck out of the client, I think." Marlene shook her head. "Thought we were going to have a scene right then and there."

"What happened?" I asked.

"Well, Mr. Elder stormed into Tony's office and waited for Tony to follow … I thought Tony should have hightailed it down the stairs and out of Dodge, but he followed Elder and closed his door."

I thought I knew the answer after having heard Marlene's comment about the walls but still asked. "Did you hear what it was about?"

"Aside from a lot of profanity, all I could gather was that Mr. Elder accused Tony of screwing him out of a huge payoff. Something about Tony brokered the deal where Elder sold half of a business to his partner. Mr. Elder thought that Tony had gone behind his back and negotiated with the partner to where Mr. Elder sold his half for less than he should have. I didn't get all the details, but I thought Mr. Elder said he got ripped off for several million dollars."

"What business?" asked Charles.

She shook her head. "Don't know. He has a bunch. Mr. Elder lives most of the year in Baltimore, and several of his businesses are there. They have something to do with the Internet; cloud technology—whatever the hell that is—and software. He yelled about something else, but I couldn't catch what it was."

"Does Mr. Elder have a home here?" I asked.

"Oh yeah," said Marlene. "One of those humongous houses on the ocean out past the Washout. It's got a large enough lot he could build another house on it if he wanted to."

"Not hurting for money, then?" said Charles.

"You never know," said Marlene. "I have to go. Please, nothing to Sean about this, please?"

A clap of thunder accented the second *please*. The expanding large, and increasingly darker, thunderheads were almost overhead, and the last verse of Cal's 1962 hit, "End of Your Story," was winding down while most visitors and artists were looking skyward at the clouds.

You never know. How true, I thought.

Chapter 14

The show was scheduled to run until seven p.m., but by four-thirty, the looming threat of rain, the painfully high temperature, and the palpable, stifling humidity had thinned the crowd to near- nonexistent.

Charles and I cowered in the back of the tent to avoid the direct sunshine that competed with the rolling, ominous-looking clouds.

Charles fanned his sweat-dripping face with his Tilley. "You know, Chris," he said, "if you keep the gallery open, we wouldn't have to be sitting here *enjoying* this wonderful weather."

"We've sold more today than we did last month in the gallery," I said.

"Got more sunstroke, dehydration, and insect bites too," said Charles. With a dramatic swoop, he smacked his hat against his leg. A symbolic insect killing?

"True," I said, "but it cost less—no rent, utilities, insurance, and—"

Charles interrupted, "Yeah, yeah, yeah. I got it." He paused and pulled his shirt away from his sweaty chest. "What do you think about this? We could take one wall of the gallery and make a used book store. I could bring my books and sell them. Wouldn't that help?" He didn't make direct eye contact but looked in my direction.

Charles collected books like some people collect friends, or money, or stamps. I knew the offer to sell his valued collection was the ultimate sacrifice he could make. I felt like a heel. I also didn't want to give him false encouragement; I didn't see a way in the world that selling a few books would significantly stop the bleeding.

"I'm losing hundreds of dollars a week now," I said. "Do you really think selling your prized possessions would help much?"

He looked down at the ground. "Maybe … could … oh crap, not really." He looked up and finally made eye contact. "Just thought it might help. You're right."

"You'll never know how much I appreciate the offer." I turned away and hoped that he thought the water running down my cheek was perspiration. "I don't have a choice."

Charles smiled, "Maybe we'll inherit a zillion dollars from good ol' Mrs. Klein, and then we can open a chain of Landrum-Fowler Galleries across the United States, Canada, and Alabama. And … drum roll, please … the Charles's Detective Agency could have a branch office in each gallery."

"And then you can wake up from your dream and help me take down the tent, pack up these photos, lug it all to the car and gallery, and let me buy you supper."

"Inside, with air conditioning?" he asked.

I nodded.

"So who killed Mr. Long, Esquire?" asked Charles in one of his typical atypical segues.

"The police'll figure it out," I said. "From what little we know, it doesn't look good for Sean. You know him much better than I do, but he seems to have a good motive."

"He couldn't have done it," said Charles with the confidence only he can muster—more confidence than he expressed the other day. "We're not close, but I've known him for years; we've skydived together; we've shared a few adult beverages together. He's as honest as June 21." He glanced out the tent and up at the sky. "Sean didn't kill Tony Long—period!"

"He also said Tony stole seventy-five thousand dollars," I said. "And according to Marlene, he and Tony had been fighting. If the police don't already know that, they will. Sean will be at the top of their list."

"They'll also know that Tony had one very wealthy enemy," said Charles. "They'll also know Tony worked for the Mafia—not quite a Sunday-school-teaching, pope, preacher, prophet group of guys. And …" Charles stopped; he looked over my shoulder toward the sidewalk, and his mouth broke out in a wide grin.

It had to be something important to stop him in the middle of lecturing me. It was.

Since I've known Charles, his total number of love interests has peaked at one. Amber once told me that with the exception of a couple of dates he had with her, she was unaware of anyone he had dated in the last decade. In fact, the widespread rumor was that he was gay. He embarrassingly confided in me the first year I knew him that this wasn't true; he simply couldn't afford to "court the ladies."

That changed nine months ago, when he met Heather Lee, the lady headed to our tent. She was smiling from crystal earring to crystal earring.

Heather and Folly Beach were perfect companions—both were quirky, bohemian, conflicted about an identity, easy to love, and charming beyond belief. During the day, Heather plied her trade as a massage therapist at several local spas and occasionally went divining along the beach for whatever people divined for. By night, she was an amateur psychic and country music singer. I had no way to determine how good she was at divining, or as a psychic, but I did know in no uncertain terms that her singing sucked. That was not my opinion alone. Everyone, with the exception of Charles, who had heard her sing was in total agreement. Before she and Charles started dating, he had agreed with the rest of the universe, but lately he leaned to a more generous analysis of the quality of her crooning. His reevaluated position is that she might just have some untapped potential. A lump of coal also has untapped potential to become a diamond—a transformation that will occur long before Heather taps her potential. But music is in the ear of the behearer. If Charles is happy, I'm happy.

"Just got off work from Milli's," she said. She was in her daytime work clothes, an off-white outfit that looked like a cross between medical scrubs and a karate *keilogi*. Milli's was a local spa and salon that met most of the beauty needs of the locals and many visitors. "There's only so many massages I can give to old, sunburnt vacationers and wrinkled local biddies. Thought I'd give a couple of old locals a hand with this tent and stuff." She laughed and pointed to Charles and me.

Charles thought being called old was hilarious. I wasn't nearly as enamored but was pleased it got us some help with the tent and him off the topics of murder and keeping the gallery open. Her "aw-shucks" smile and tilt of the head brought a smile to my face. She gave Charles such a powerful bear hug that it knocked her wide-brimmed straw hat off when the brim met his forehead. She wore the distinct hat most everywhere.

Normally, it would have taken Charles and me more than an hour to huff and puff and take the tent down and load the photos in boxes and haul it all to the car. Heather was nearly twenty years younger than either of us, radiated enough enthusiasm for five people, and had powerful hands and upper body strength conditioned by kneading, probing, and punching "old, sunburnt vacationers and wrinkled local biddies." We managed to complete the task in a record thirty minutes. And best of all, Heather only broke into song twice.

Chapter 15

Restaurants had come and gone as often as some vacationers during my four years on Folly Beach. Lazo's was the fourth iteration of restaurant in an attractive, large building on the main drag. The building was originally a grocery before it began playing musical restaurants.

There was a waiting line of hungry patrons on the sidewalk in front by the time Charles, Heather, and I arrived. Being a Saturday in-season, we knew it would be the same at every restaurant on the island. Charles had worked on the remodel for the manager and walked around to the back entrance to see if he could move us up on the waiting list. Five minutes later, he peeked around the corner and motioned for us to follow. There was one booth being cleared, and the manager waved for us to have a seat.

"Charles the connected," cooed Heather. She squeezed his arm.

"What'd that cost you?" I asked Charles as we both removed our Tilleys and set them on the empty space beside me. Heather topped both hats with her wide-brimmed straw one.

"You don't want to know," he said. "But dessert's on you."

"Charles tells me you two are going to find poor Mr. Long's killer," said Heather after she had wolfed down her organic shrimp salad.

I gave Charles my best dirty look and turned back to Heather. "I'm sure *he* misunderstood," I said and smiled. "That's for the police."

Heather returned my smile, watt for watt. "Nope—I don't think so. I know how good you two are at solving murders—you saved Mrs. Klein and Harley last year. No, Charles was pretty certain you would solve this one too." She continued to smile but wrapped her arms around Charles's left arm and squeezed.

Heather, along with Country Cal, Harley, Cindy Ash, and four less fortunate souls who didn't survive the crossbow killer escapade had lived in Mrs. Klein's boardinghouse. After Hurricane Greta flattened the building, my friend and Realtor, Bob Howard, commandeered low-rent housing for the survivors at Mariner's Breeze Bed and Breakfast, an over-the-hill business on the marsh side of the island. The B&B was teetering on bankruptcy and saw little chance of recovery after Water's Edge Inn, a new, upscale competitor, opened three years ago less than a half mile away.

I looked at the two lovebirds and smiled.

Heather shrugged and apparently channeled Charles's talent for un-smooth transitions. "Saw Cal when I was on the way to work," she said. "Said he got to sing at the art show."

"Yeah," said Charles, "sounded better than that rock band that blew out the power."

Heather took the last bite of her roasted vegetable Napoleon and looked down at her empty plate. "Suppose they would have asked me to sing if I didn't have to work," she said.

"No doubt," said Charles; a love-biased truth, or a whopper of a lie.

I didn't think *when the Folly River freezes over* would have been the best thing to say after Heather had helped take down the tent. I continued to smile.

"Oh yeah," said Heather as she snapped her fingers. "Greg said he might let me sing two songs Tuesday at open mike night. You need to be there."

Greg Brile owned GB's Bar, formerly called Greg's: Home of Rowdy Rock, until the bankers and tax collectors were on his doorstep. He had realized that if he wanted to stay in business, a change to country music was his only hope. Charles and I had become semi-regulars at GB's and hadn't seen a single banker or IRS agent grace the premises; the transition must have worked.

GB's open mike night rules were simple. If you had ever released a record—or CD, or download—you were allowed three songs. If Greg thought you had a glimmer of hope, you were awarded two opportunities; and if you were a nobody and talent-wise, destined to stay that way, one song was your maximum. Greg figured his patrons could hold their ears for one tune. Over the last couple of years, during which she had appeared almost every Tuesday, Heather had worked her way up to one song.

"You can count on us being there," said Charles.

He had the irritating habit of speaking for me.

Heather shook her head. "Don't put too much money on me getting two songs. He probably isn't good at his word."

"Why not?" I asked.

"Don't know," she said, her voice turning serious. "He's got an aura of unpleasantness. Demonic sparks fly around him sometimes."

Or, I thought, *he has two good ears and knows how Heather sounds behind a guitar.*

"Hmm," said Charles. That said it all.

Good to his word, Charles ordered the last two slices of key lime pie and an oversized bowl of ice cream for Heather and made sure the waitress put it on my tab. I was exhausted and looked forward to bed rather than dessert. I think I stayed awake while they savored their sweets, but wasn't certain.

What a day, I thought as my head hit the pillow. Marlene had shared more than she should have, Karen had shared that Long was murdered, Charles had shared with anyone who would listen that *we* were going to solve the murder, and possibly worst of all, Heather had shared that she might get to massacre two songs on Tuesday.

Chapter 16

I hadn't paid enough attention in school to know how many muscles there were in my body, but I could unequivocally say that every one of them hurt as I slowly and carefully rolled out of bed. A "quick shower" took a half-hour, and bending to put on my slacks took on the appearance of an aerobic exercise. I reconsidered having a booth at the park, even if it was only one day a month.

I was running late to meet Charles at the Dog, a condition totally unacceptable to Charles, who considered himself late if he arrived five minutes early. He would have to adjust. Despite being late, I knew that walking would be the best thing I could do. I was not a fan of exercise, but it would loosen my aching joints; and besides, there wouldn't be a parking space near the Dog on Sunday morning.

Charles's Schwinn leaned precariously against a tree beside the restaurant. Dude Sloan's light-green, rusting, classic 1970 Chevrolet El Camino was parked in one of the few spaces directly in front of the patio. He was either lucky or had been there since the Dog opened.

According to local lore, the first surfboard arrived on Folly Beach in 1966. The war began within days between the evil, iconoclastic surfers and the saintly, law-abiding fishermen and swimmers. Four and a half decades and several restrictive laws later, the battle has subsided into minor skirmishes, but it hasn't gone away. Jim "Dude" Sloan arrived twenty-two years after the first surfboard and bought the surf shop—proof that things beyond most people's imagination could happen. In an age of business plans, profit-and-loss statements, and committees in faraway cities making lending decisions, Dude's explanation of how he purchased the shop would be a textbook example of how not to get a loan. He once told me that he "Needed job; liked the area. Couldn't cook; didn't have any skills. Saw ad in the paper; went to bank. They made dumb decision and lent me the money. Rest be history." I still have not learned why he didn't capitalize the first letters in the name of his store—surf shop. Dude epitomized the folly in Folly Beach.

I was surprised to see the surf shop owner in my regular seat opposite Charles. Charles saw me enter, looked at his watchless left wrist, and stared at me until I was at the table.

"Well, look who finally decided to roll out of bed," he said with nary a smile. He turned to Dude. "Beauty sleep didn't help him, did it?"

"Beauty be in retina of beviewer," said Dude.

Dude was leaned back in the booth. He wore a faded, multiple shades of green, tie-dyed T-shirt with a florescent orange peace symbol on the front. If you were looking to cast a character in a movie about an aging, long-curly-haired hippy who looked like Arlo Guthrie, the search would end at Dude. If you wanted the actor to speak in long, flowing, comprehensible sentences, the search would need to continue.

I ignored Charles's rebuke and Dude's philosophic analysis of beauty and slid into the booth beside the surf shop owner. Amber nearly beat me to the table and had a mug of hot coffee in front of me as I moved Dude's latest issue of *Astronomy* magazine out of the way. Charles had often speculated that Dude was from another planet and his interest in astronomy was so he could learn more about his homeland. I occasionally agreed with Charles but most of the time thought that Freud would conclude that Dude's interest in astronomy was simply an interest in astronomy.

"The Chuckster say you two be finding aggro idiot who kilt Long," said Dude.

I thought I understood but looked at Charles for help.

"Aggro means pissed off," translated Charles. He still hadn't cracked a smile. Tardiness made Charles aggro.

I didn't waste time with a denial. "Did you know Long?" I asked.

Dude held his thumb and forefinger an inch apart. *"Un poco.* Know the Seanster better—he be good guy; Long be ungood." Dude stopped and took a sip of hot tea.

Most people who met Dude for the first time thought he had
smoked too many illegal substances or had way too many encounters
between his head and a surfboard. I was no different, but after spending
several nonsensical and sentence-challenged hours with him, I had come
to realize that he was extremely bright—by earth standards—and had
a good feel for the goings-on on Folly Beach.

"Why *ungood*?" asked Charles.

"Never helped wobbly chicks across street; never bought from surf
shop; hung with shady, pinstripe-suit goons from Chi-town; drove
Mercedes; cheated on wife—ungood. Clear as day. But hey, you two
be the detectives."

The first two reasons would apply to me, but I got his drift.

"Dude," said Charles, "know anyone who could take us to where
they found the body?"

Oh no, I thought.

"Know latitude and longitude?" asked Dude.

"What's that got to do with finding someone?" asked Charles.

"Nada," said Dude. "Just like saying it—cool words."

Charles pointed his fork at Dude. "The man was found in the marsh,"
said Charles. "Don't know where, but we can find out if we can find
someone to take us there—latitude and longitude to be determined."

"Piglet waves in marsh," said Dude. "No fun surfing. But this be
your lucky day." He stopped and took a bite of his cheese grits and
then looked around the full restaurant. The comforting smell of bacon
wafted up from his plate.

Marc Salmon approached the table. He was one of two city council
members who spent a couple of hours most mornings at local eateries
consuming food and rumors, and sharing "wisdom." He reminded
me of a bee flitting from bloom to bloom, leaving bits of what it had
picked up from the previous plant. "Did you hear that Tony Long was
murdered?" he asked.

He leaned into our space like he was confiding in us with the
salacious information; he would proceed to share this with everyone else
he encountered the rest of the day. He was a talker and never passed up
an opportunity to spread rumors like melted butter on toast. He even
shared facts if they were juicy enough.

"Old news," responded Charles.

"Oh," said Marc, clearly disappointed that he wasn't the first to break the news. "Hear his wife's going to take the body back to Chicago for burial."

"Uh-huh," said Charles.

I suspected that was news, but Charles didn't want Marc to know he had told us something new.

"Okay, gotta go," said Marc. He wheeled and walked toward the door and stopped at the last table before the exit and began telling the occupants about the murder.

Dude watched him go. "Connie be sticking Long's bod in ground far from here ... good plan."

"Real good plan," said Charles. "A funeral we can miss. I'm funeraled out."

"Amen to that," I said.

"I'll try again, Dude," said Charles. "Know anybody who could take us to where they found Tony?"

"Sure," said Dude.

Charles sighed. "And you couldn't tell us that twenty minutes ago?" he said.

"Could—didn't," clarified Dude. "Chuckster, you be fun to twiddle with."

I liked Dude more each day.

Charles grabbed his cane from the floor and pointed it at Dude. "Who?"

Dude had been on the pointed end of Charles's cane before and slowly reached out, wrapped his hand around the tip, and pushed it toward the wall. "Good bud of mine. Mad Mel—Mel Evans."

I tried to hide my shock that Dude actually had a bud, much less a *good bud*, and asked, "Who's he?"

"Well duh," said Dude. "Everyone knows about Mad Mel's Magical Marsh Machine—Tours, Etc."

Two of the three of us at the table didn't, and one of us, Charles, prided himself on knowing everything about almost everyone on Folly Beach. Dude went on to explain, the best I could translate, that Mad Mel operated a marsh tour business based out of the Folly View Marina, just off-island behind the Mariner's Cay condo complex and marina. He specialized in taking college groups on non-traditional marsh tours that often led to moonlight parties on the sandbars that were uncovered at low tide. Dude hinted that large quantities of adult beverages just might be part of these enlightening tours. He'd talk to Mel about taking us to the scene.

Then for some reason Dude began to tell us, in great detail, about tides and how they were influenced by events in some faraway galaxies, and how meteor dust and the moon controlled everything, from the mating habits of sea turtles to lightning bugs to Amway salespeople.

I lost interest once he mentioned galaxies; it returned when he was getting up to leave and I heard Charles say, "No problem; we'll catch the killer."

Chapter 17

"When are you padlocking the door?" asked Charles. "When are you throwing me out on the street?"

I had felt guilty about hogging the booth at the Dog, so Charles and I had moved our conversation to the gallery, less than a block away. Dude said he had to check on the tattoo-toters at the surf shop. I assumed he meant his two surfer-looking, tattoo-covered, rude-most-of-the-time employees. From what I had observed on my infrequent visits to the surf shop, I didn't blame him.

"The end of the month," I said. "The rent's paid until then; I called the landlord before Memorial Day and told him."

Charles rubbed his chin. "Try this idea out," he said. "What if we kept it open until we know what happens with Mrs. Klein? I'll give you my share to help pay expenses."

He gave me a hopeful grin but didn't maintain eye contact. I had considered that option, but hadn't said anything to Charles. I didn't want to lift his hopes and have to dash them again. I was clueless as to what I had done to have such a loyal friend. I turned and walked to the refrigerator so he wouldn't see tears. I was surprised he didn't ask why it took me so long to find two Diet Pepsis. It wasn't as if the shelves were cluttered with stuff like food.

I regained my composure, and the two of us settled around the table in the back room. "We don't know if we'll have anything after the dust settles with Mrs. Klein's estate," I said. "Besides, what about your detective agency? That'll take money."

"I'll do both," said Charles. He tapped his fingers on the table like he was counting. "I figure the North American office of the CDA won't take a coven of cash. I don't have any highfalutin' diplomas, so I won't need a wall to hang them on; I'll have to give in to modern technology and get a cell phone; I can use the computer here for Internet clue-collecting, maybe subscribe to a newspaper to learn about all the latest tomfoolery so I can troll for clients." He paused and looked toward the ceiling. "That should be about all, shouldn't it?"

I smiled. "You may need a good lawyer on retainer to bail you out of jail for the times you'll be arrested for meddling, trespassing, stalking, and—"

"Speaking of a good lawyer," he interrupted. "It seems to me that unless we can do something, the cops will be arresting you-know-who."

"Charles, you think he didn't do it; but he could have. You do know that, don't you?"

"My gut says no. Sean's a big donor to all the local charities; he cares about others; he even calls me a friend; how generous is that?"

I didn't want to argue with Charles but couldn't help thinking that some of the most bizarre and high-profile murders have been committed by society page regulars.

"He has motive," I continued. "Long stole a lot of money from him. They've been fighting over things for a while, and that's before Sean knew about the money. We know Sean has a temper. He would have easy access to a boat that could have taken the body into the marsh."

"But," said Charles, "from what Marlene said, it seems like there's a passel of good suspects: the Mafia; or rich man, Conroy Elder; then there's Long's wife, Connie; heck, maybe the husband of one of the women Long was sneaking around with." Charles held out both arms, palms up. "And that's only what we learned in the last day; there could be others."

There was no stopping Charles from the path he was beginning to head down. "So what do we do?" I asked.

"Now you're talking," he said. "First, remember what Chief Newman said. We have to visit where they found the body. Then I don't know what from there."

"The body's been gone for five days; tide's gone in and out twice a day; the police have already combed the scene; what could we possibly find?"

"Don't know—haven't been there yet."

A flurry of customers interrupted Charles's detective planning. The vacationers were welcomed for their business and also as a distraction from the path I didn't want to go down with my staff. I had been thinking about what William had said to Charles yesterday: I was long overdue for a visit. Charles agreed to sacrifice all his afternoon plans and man the gallery while I visited William. I was absolved of any remorse when he told me his plans included counting the number of dog breeds crossing Center Street on their way to beg for treats at Bert's. The life of the leisurely poor.

William Hansel lived in a small, neat, clapboard house two blocks from the beach on West Cooper Avenue. It was within walking distance of the center of the town, but I drove.

"Ah, my guilt trip worked," bellowed the powerful, bass voice of Dr. William Hansel before I was out of the car.

I smiled.

He was in his side yard, hoe in hand; sweat rolled down his forehead. His twelve-by-thirty-foot garden covered most of the yard and was his summer activity of choice.

He wiped the sweat from his eyes with his forearm. His short-sleeved College of Charleston T-shirt and work denims with a hole in the left knee were his summer gardening uniform of choice. William was in his late fifties, a widower, about my height, and rail-thin, a weight I envied. "Well, my friend, would you like to share some ice tea?" he asked. Regardless of his slovenly attire, his words were always prim, proper, and often professorial.

Sure, I thought, but said, "I would be honored." I didn't want my grade lowered for inappropriate grammar.

William had been battling weeds too long; he quickly leaned the hoe against the house and headed for our drinks. He was back before I had time to sit in one of the two small metal chairs beside a round table that he had strategically placed in the shade of a large bay tree in the back corner of the yard.

He returned with a large, blue, plastic tray with a matching pitcher in the middle and two tall ice tea glasses that also matched the color of the tray.

"The new house appears quite attractive," he said as he set the pitcher on the table and looked at the recently completed, two-story, elevated house next door.

"Not the same character," I said. "Bet it even has a shower in the bathroom."

William laughed. "I'm certain of that."

The new house was built on the lot where an old cottage had stood for many years. In fact, it had withstood all the wrath Hurricane Hugo had brought when it destroyed approximately 80 percent of the homes on Folly Beach in 1989. What the old house couldn't withstand were the flames after being torched by a murderer determined to kill me. The quaint cottage became a pile of charcoal in a matter of minutes, the most frightening minutes of my life—my life up until that time.

The experience was horrific, but William's concern and assistance, along with those of numerous other residents, solidified my belief that Folly Beach was a magical place and where I wanted to spend the rest of my life.

"How is the world of a college professor?" I asked after my first taste of the refreshing brew.

That question opened a floodgate of thoughts, complaints, and humorous stories. I knew it would. He had little interest in the travel and tourism industry and had little actual travel experience himself. He was far from a fan of the academic bureaucracy that stifled most institutions of higher education. What he did love was his students. William was a dinosaur in a world of iPhones, iPads, Blackberries, MP3 players, text messaging, IMs, GPS systems, tweets, twerps, and electronic stuff beyond me even knowing what to call it. He didn't own a cell phone, only carried basic cable on his television, spelled words in their entirety, and spoke in complete sentences—a bit stilted, but complete sentences nevertheless. Regardless, he was able to connect with many students because he listened to them. He, as a minority, could understand when they felt isolated. His wife had died of cancer in 1999, and he understood the students when they talked about loneliness. He had talked about getting out of the "academic torture chamber," but he was still relatively young and needed the income. Besides, he would miss his students too much to walk away.

His rants about deans, department heads, and the over-air-conditioned classrooms were finally winding down. He took a deep breath and poured each of us more tea. "I've a question to ask, if I may," he said.

I nodded that he might. How else could I respond?

"When you moved over there," he said and nodded toward the new house, "I was unable to detect a strong indication that you were a strongly adventurous person. You seemed a bit stuffy, if I might say. No offense taken, I hope."

I laughed and took another sip before responding. "None taken. You summed me up quite well." *Well, but a bit pedantically,* I thought.

"So, what has occurred since then?" he asked. "You, and some of your nonconforming friends, appear to be a crime-solving gathering of citizens without law-enforcement authorization or training." He shook his head. "My level of fear increases when I watch a police show on television. Why do you needlessly risk your life?"

Fantastic question, Professor, I thought. In fact, it is such a good question I've asked it to myself hundreds of times since I moved to this side of the Folly River.

"I wish I knew," I said. "I've thought about it myself."

"And you have concluded?"

"Concluded," I said and then giggled. "Sometimes I conclude that I'm an idiot; sometimes that I have lost touch with reality; sometimes that I have a death wish; sometimes that I must be atoning for all those years of boredom in sales and HR in my former work life; sometimes …"

William raised his forefinger to his lips in the international symbol for silence. "This is where I would stop my student and say, 'Let me clarify.' In other words, I've heard enough."

"Yes. Dr. Hansel," I said and smiled.

"Remember a couple of years back when my good friend Julius was murdered and I was hospitalized for depression?"

How could I have forgotten? Charles and I were almost killed trying to prove that William's friend Julius was the victim of a murder and had not committed suicide like the police had concluded.

"Sure," I said.

"You had become my friend—for reasons I cannot understand—and when I told you that Julius could not have killed himself, you took it upon yourself to seek the truth. And then last year, you and Charles were compelled to seek out that horrific crossbow killer rather than letting the duly sworn police officers do their job." He paused.

"Of course I remember. Almost got killed in the process."

"You got involved—foolishly got involved—because some of your friends were in danger. Is that not correct?"

"Yeah, but …"

"But nothing," said William. "I believe you can stop asking yourself why you get involved. I, of course, am not a professor of psychology. I know very little about that soft science, but it is abundantly clear that you have an extremely strong, possibly latent, gene about friendship. Except for the time you were simply in the wrong place at the wrong time and were almost incinerated"—he once again nodded toward the lot where my former residence stood— "friendships were why you acted—acted foolishly, but still took action."

"I don't know anything about strong or weak genes," I said, "but you're right about friends. I've made more good friends in the last few years than I had accumulated in my life."

He smiled. "Folly Beach does that to people," he said. "Don't ask me why; it just does."

The smile left his face, and he shook his head. "I fear that you're going to be in danger once again. Your friend Charles told me Saturday that the two of you are looking into the untimely death of Mr. Long."

"Not really," I said. "Besides, Long wasn't a friend of mine. Why would I care?"

"Charles is your friend; he said that Sean Aker is a friend of his and is a suspect, perhaps the only suspect. Don't forget, you had never met Julius before he was killed, but you got involved because of me."

"That's different … that's different," I said and changed the subject. "Are you still active in Preserve the Past?"

William let me off the hook and didn't ask how it was different. "I am. We are finally making significant headway on saving the lighthouse. Sean Aker, the attorney everyone is talking about, is a major contributor to the cause. He doesn't make it public, but he's very generous to the group. You should join us sometime."

"I will."

The primary focus of Preserve the Past was to raise funds and awareness to the plight of the historic, but deserted and deteriorating, Morris Island Lighthouse, just off the eastern end of Folly Beach. It was interesting that Sean's generosity had been mentioned twice today.

William bragged about his garden and a couple of his students who had won prestigious scholarships to study in Italy over the summer before I said I needed to be going. He said to stop by any time; I knew he meant it.

Chapter 18

I left William's house and drove off-island to the small cemetery where Mrs. Klein had been buried less than a week ago. I offered a silent prayer at the recently disturbed, dirt-covered resting spot of her empty shell. I didn't spend much time at the grave; my memories of Mrs. Klein were of her in life, not in the concrete vault below my feet.

I walked to the edge of the cemetery, the spot where the well-groomed meadow dropped into the salt marsh. It was a couple of hours past low tide, and the water level was beginning to rise in the low-lying troughs. Three blue herons were majestically perched along the shore, patiently waiting for lunch. A handful of fiddler crabs scampered to safety when they sensed my presence. The distinct marsh smell filled my nostrils. Newcomers often believed the smell, reminiscent of rotting eggs, was sewage; but my walking encyclopedia, Charles, enlightened all who would listen, explaining that it was hydrogen sulfide caused by decaying bacteria. The temperature must have been in the low nineties, but a westerly breeze made it tolerable.

I was certain that I couldn't see the spot where Tony Long's body had been discovered, but the surroundings would have been nearly identical. The marsh between Folly Beach and much of the coastal areas had as much personality as the ocean; I often preferred it to the ocean side. The marsh was ever-changing; the seasons were defined by the color of the active marsh grasses. It had its own beauty and mystery.

William's analysis of my behavior was also shrouded in mystery. Was he right? Sure, I thoroughly enjoyed the friends I had accumulated in the last few years and knew I would do almost anything for them. But would I put my life in danger? Would I risk gracefully fading off into the sunset? If anyone had asked me four years ago, I would have shouted, *No!* Had I changed that much? Could it be that I realized that I didn't have that long left? Other than a few photographs, and memories in the hearts of those who knew me, what had I contributed to the world? If I were honest, I'd conclude I'd not made any meaningful contribution. I had no children to carry their memory of me, or lessons learned; no wife to remember me as no other could.

If my professorial friend was right and friendships were that important to me, perhaps my legacy would be through helping my friends. What better way than helping them stay alive and out of trouble?

My cell phone ringtone interrupted my solving the nature of man and my place in the galaxy. Larry LaMond, former cat burglar and current owner of Folly's only hardware store, Pewter Hardware, called to ask if I could join him, Cindy Ash, his main squeeze in Charles's chatter, Heather, and Charles that night at Rita's Restaurant. He wanted me to see if Amber could join the group. Larry was one of my new friends and had participated in several of our impromptu parties over the years but to my recollection, had never initiated one. Something was up. I said I'd be there and would call Amber.

I overcame a minor twinge of guilt about making calls from a cemetery and punched in Amber's number. She was still at work and couldn't talk long, but said that Jason was spending the night with a school buddy and she would meet us at Rita's.

"Guess the rumors are true," she said and rang off.

"What rumors?" I asked the dead phone.

Chapter 19

Larry and Cindy were already at the restaurant and had commandeered two tables pulled together in the center of the patio. I met Amber at her second-story apartment on Center Street, and we walked hand-in-hand two blocks to the restaurant. I was surprised that Charles wasn't there; after all, I was ten minutes early. Larry speculated that Heather might have corrupted my always-early friend. *Fat chance,* I thought.

The waitress brought two glasses of white wine to the table before Amber and I had a chance to settle in our bar-height chairs.

"It's on us," said Cindy. One empty and two full beer bottles were in front of the smiling couple.

Amber was right; something definitely was up.

Cindy was dressed in an oversized, white T-shirt and pink short-shorts. During her work day, she would be attired in the dark-blue uniform of the Folly Beach Department of Public Safety, where she had served as a police officer for the last two years. She had moved to Folly Beach from East Tennessee and become the first sworn female member of the force, a distinction she still held.

Cindy was in her mid-forties, full-figured and a couple of inches taller than Larry. Even with the additional two inches of altitude, she was still short. Larry under-weighed her by twenty pounds and had been mistaken for a jockey most of his life. He was equinophobic and wouldn't get within a furlong of a horse; but his diminutive size was an asset in his previous career of breaking into houses. He wisely chose to change careers after spending an eight year time-out as a guest of the Georgia State Department of Corrections.

"What's the occasion?" I asked.

"Just hold, you hyena," said Cindy. "Wait for the rest of the party."

How many prisoners has she said that to? I wondered.

Amber leaned on my shoulder and whispered, "Told you the rumor was true."

I felt like I was in the middle of a chick flick but was saved when Charles and Heather walked through the dining room and out to our tables.

"Sorry we're late," said Charles as he looked at his watchless wrist. "My darling date dallied."

"Oh hush, Chucky," she said as she took off her straw hat and waved it at us. "We're still early."

I almost choked on my wine. *Chucky!* Charles would nearly go ballistic if anyone called him Charlie; duck if you heard *Chuck*. Dude gets away with an occasional *Chuckster*, but only because Charles ignores most of what Dude says.

The smell of frying onions was replaced by the fattening aroma of French fries. The waitress delivered two heaping baskets of Rita's Folly Fries. "On us," repeated Cindy for the sake of Charles and Heather.

All the outdoor tables were full, and the dining room wasn't far behind. Small groups of vacationers walked across the street from the Tides. Most would have a long wait for a table at any of the nearby restaurants. The sun was low in the sky and heading for a stunning, late-spring sunset over the marsh.

Charles stuffed a couple of fries into his mouth and then looked at Cindy. "Anything new on the murder?" he mumbled.

"What a pleasant conversation," said Heather.

Cindy had known Charles longer than Heather had; she knew he wouldn't be distracted until he got an answer. "A friend in the sheriff's office said that they were looking at rumors about Sean Aker and Connie, Tony's wife."

"Fling?" asked Charles.

"Yeah," said Cindy. "Rumors."

"I don't believe it," said Charles.

"Well," said Cindy, "like we say back home, where there's smoke, there's barbecue."

Even Charles—alias Chucky—didn't know what to say to that.

Larry jumped in and filled the silence. "Umm, Cindy, don't we have something to tell our friends?" He leaned close and put his arm around her.

"Oh yeah," she said. "The honor is yours." She turned back to Larry and smiled affectionately.

Larry gave her a tender hug and then tapped two empty beer bottles together. Charles gave Larry his attention, even though I knew he wanted clarification of Cindy's barbecue comment.

Larry slid off the bar-height chair and stood erect. He didn't gain much altitude from the move. "Cindy is giving up her apartment," he said and paused.

Cindy shot him an exasperated look. "Larry!"

"And we're getting married."

"I knew it," said Amber.

"Whoopee!" said Heather as she waved her hat in the air. An elderly gentleman sitting at the table behind her came within an inch of having his toupee removed by the flailing, wide brim of Heather's headdress.

John, Rita's owner, magically appeared at the table; he carried a bottle of Moet and Chandon champagne in a bucket of ice and six plastic champagne flutes. With much aplomb, he uncorked the bottle of bubbly.

"Go, hardware store man, go!" yelled a man from two tables away. I didn't recognize him.

Larry turned the shade of five hours in the sun. His face clashed with his bright-orange polo shirt with the Pewter Hardware logo on the breast pocket.

The older I got, the more emotional I had become. I was thrilled for Larry and Cindy and brushed back tears.

Charles smiled at Larry. "Congratulations," he said and paused for a moment to savor the excitement, and then turned to Cindy. "Rumors?"

I elbowed him and said, "Later." Cindy gave him her official, police, you're-drunk-but-I-won't-arrest-you-if-you-just-shut-up look. He did and gulped the champagne like it was Budweiser.

"Blah!" he said.

"When's the hitchin'?" asked Heather.

"Could be July," said Larry. He raised his flute to the sky.

"*Will* be July," countered Cindy before she raised her drink even higher.

Charles leaned over to me and whispered, "President Jimmy Carter once said about his wife, 'I've never won an argument with her; and the only times I thought I had, I found out the argument wasn't over yet.'"

Conversation over the next hour and over burgers could have been an episode on the Wedding Channel—dress options, guest list, location of nuptials, reception or not, kind of flowers, maid of honor, on and on. During each lull, Charles asked Cindy if she were pregnant. Other than tipping over her water glass the first time he broached the subject, she never responded. Occasionally, the conversation was interrupted by others on the patio who garnered the nerve to walk over and congratulate the happy, not-so-young couple. Traffic on Center Street and East Arctic Avenue was heavy and added to the distractions. The patio was fewer than twenty feet from the busy intersection.

"Isn't that Harley?" asked Heather as the pulsating rumble of a Harley engine drowned out Cindy's comment about holding the wedding on the beach.

We turned in the direction of the sound. "Who's with him?" asked Larry.

"Colleen, the waitress from GB's," said Charles. "She looks like she's on the Burundi diet."

"Huh?" said Heather. She spoke for all of us.

"Burundi," said Charles. "One of the poorest countries in the world. Starving people; no food; scrawny. Get it?" He shook his head. "Gee, there's skyrocketing ignorance in my midst."

"Oh," said Heather. "Colleen, the anorexic-looking chick. She's real sweet; always says nice things about my singing."

Cindy stared at Harley's Harley that was parking directly across the street in front of the Sand Dollar Social Club. His bike sparkled under the streetlights. The Sand Dollar was a private club that tripled as a biker bar, an occasional movie set, and the perfect hangout for vampires, blood and beer drinkers who couldn't go out in the sun. It was a Folly Beach landmark. Harley hopped off the bike and wasn't much taller than when he was on board. He was no more than five foot five and was low, wide, and loud—same as his bike. He wore a bright-blue Harley-Davidson jacket and a helmet that looked like one soldiers wore in World War I. Colleen towered over him at six foot one or more but weighed about the same as the handlebars on the hog. A Harley-Davidson jacket wrapped around her body twice.

Larry noticed Cindy staring at Colleen. "What?" he asked.

"That bod isn't from diet," she said and continued to look across the street at Harley's date. "I'd put money on drugs. I've seen too much, way too much, of that look on addicts."

I only knew Colleen from GB's; she was friendly and even laughed at some of Charles's comments—rare for anyone sober. Her pleasant, attentive attitude made even the most mundane item on the menu flavorful.

Heather watched Harley slip his left arm around Colleen and open the door to the Sand Dollar with his right hand. "I hope she's a good influence on him," she said. "He's been a constipated horse's keister the last week or so."

"Bad vibes?" asked Charles.

Heather looked around the table. "Vibes; couldn't hear them. He's louder than his motorcycle, so all of us in the B&B hear everything he says."

Cindy nodded. The rest of us waited for Heather to continue.

"He's been obnoxious—says he's going to be rich; nobody will be able to stop him from splitting this 'backward, backwater burg' ... same stuff over and over, over and over. *O-B*-noxious."

"Any idea what the three of you are going to inherit?" asked Larry.

"No," I said. "Neither does Harley. Could be a pile of debt. Sean has to get more information before he'll know."

"Hope he figures it out soon," said Heather. "I'll be happy to see Harley put his big butt on his hog and rumble off to the gone-land."

The drink choices headed to the slums when beer and pedestrian-quality wine replaced champagne. Two hours later, I was thrilled with the lower priced drinks; Charles told everyone that I would pick up the check for the announcement ceremony. He was generous like that.

I quickly forgot the major expenditure when Amber invited herself to my humble cottage for the night. I momentarily pondered ways to find her son more friends to spend nights with.

No sooner had we entered the front door than my cell rang. I would have been terrified of getting a phone call after midnight in my earlier life; I had learned that Folly Beach was much like Las Vegas—time was meaningless.

"Yo Chrisster," began Dude's distinct voice, "Tour guide here."

"What's up?" I said and shrugged at Amber.

"Be at Folly View Marina; next little hand lands on seven, big hand on six; Mad Max be debarkin'." The phone went dead.

As frightening as it was, I understood what he said and translated for Amber, begged her to give me a minute, and called Charles to see if he wanted to go.

"Does a bear meditate in the woods?" he said and then followed Dude's precedent and hung up.

I had no idea about bears' meditation habits, but knew he meant he'd be there. I love my world!

Then I wondered what I would think of it after a trip to where Long's corpse had been dumped and eaten by marsh creatures. And then I turned to Amber, and my world bloomed with happiness.

Chapter 20

The Folly View Marina was just a hop, skip, and two blocks off-island, a three-minute drive from my house. Charles hadn't mentioned me picking him up, but we both knew I'd be at his door no later than ten minutes before the time we were to arrive at the marina.

Charles paced the gravel and shell lot as I pulled into the small parking area that served both his apartment building and the Sandbar Seafood and Steak Restaurant. He wore a long-sleeved, navy-blue T-shirt with an angry-looking animal with "Fear the Goat" and "Navy" on the front in block letters. The new T-shirt contrasted with his ripped and wrinkled, tan cargo shorts and mud-stained Nike tennis shoes. His ever-present Tilley topped off his outfit. His left shoulder held the camera strap for the Nikon I had given him. He waved my direction with his homemade cane.

"Come on, come on; where've you been? We're almost a little early," he yelled.

I stopped beside him and lowered my window. I ignored his obsession about time and nodded toward his shirt. "Join the navy?"

"Not navy," he said. "Naval academy; goat's their mascot."

"Then let's head to the ship." If he caught my attempt at humor, he ignored it. I would have done the same.

He moved to the passenger side and threw his cane in the rear seat. He looked over at me. "Boring, boring, boring."

Years earlier, I had chosen not to make statements or commercials with words on my shirts, and Charles had never failed to remind me how boring my clothes were. Today's faded-red polo shirt and khaki shorts were no exception. He never commented on my hat, since it was identical to his, just a few years older.

The sun had been up for more than an hour, and the fog lifted as we crossed the two-lane bridge leading off-island. A few early-morning fishermen were already navigating the river on their optimistic quest for food. Immediately past the large Mariner's Cay condo complex and marina, we turned left at a hand-painted wooden sign that read, "Folly View Marina, private property." The marina was in stark contrast to its upscale neighbor. The tire-rutted parking lot was covered with a mixture of crushed shells, gravel, and dirt. Parking spaces were unmarked, and the lot would be challenged to hold more than a dozen cars.

Only two vehicles were in the lot. Dude's El Camino was parked perpendicular to a new, shiny, black, retro-styled Chevrolet Camaro. An equal number of people were standing in the lot beside the Camaro. Dude either had a closet full of tie-dyed, peace-symbol-adorned T-shirts, often washed the one he had on, or stank. With his disheveled, long, white, curly hair and sun-wrinkled face, he looked nearly the same as he had every day I'd seen him except when the temperature dipped below forty degrees. He was in deep, animated conversation with the other man, whom I deduced to be the infamous Mad Mel.

Dude heard my door slam and walked toward Charles and me. His acquaintance followed. Mel was at least a half-foot taller than Dude and had what appeared to be a surgically implanted frown on his face.

"Chuckster, Chrisster," said Dude, "see Mad Mel, a friend." Dude turned and pointed to the man now standing beside him.

Mel stared at Dude. "Friend—shit!" said Mel, his frown still permanently affixed. "Damned, draft-dodging hippy druggy." He then turned to Charles and stared at his T-shirt. "You a damned sailor?"

"Nope," said Charles. "Naval academy shirt."

"You went to Canoe U? Un-damned-believable."

"Nope," said Charles, repeating his word for the day. "Eighty-five percent off at the army surplus store."

"Overpriced," said Mel. "Damned navy."

Charles looked directly at Mel. "Your mom must have been psychic to name you Mad," he said. A sly grin appeared.

What could be construed as a smile in some circles appeared on Mad Mel's face. "You must be smart-assed Charles." He grabbed Charles right hand and gave a vice-like squeeze.

Mel wore a leather bomber jacket with the sleeves cut off at the shoulder; his woodland camo field pants were sheared off at the knee. What appeared to be a bald head was topped by a camouflaged fatigue cap with *Semper Fi* in script on the crown. His camouflaging would have been successful if he hadn't been wearing a pair of bright-white Adidas tennis shoes.

He turned to me. "Then you must be the damned dull one— Chrisster, or something like that."

I saw Charles giggle as he massaged his smushed right hand. "I'd prefer Chris," I said and reluctantly held out my hand. Mel took my hand and squeezed. Apparently, the "dull one" got a more socially acceptable handshake.

"We be going?" said Dude. He was standing behind Charles and was tapping his left foot in the loose gravel.

Mel tilted his head toward Dude. "Shut the commie-pinko trap up," he said. "We're breaking the damned ice ... Oprah bonding." He turned away from Dude and looked at Charles and then to me. "Damned surfing hippy." He shook his head.

"You and Dude been friends long?" asked Charles.

That was the last question I would have asked after Mel's comment.

"Too damned long," said Mel. He turned to Dude and gave a big stage wink.

"Been buds two decades," said Dude. "The last two."

"See?" said Mel. "Too damned long."

"Bonding be done," said Dude. "Vamoose time."

Without another word, Mel turned and walked toward a wooden bridge on the left side of the small parking area. The bridge led to a floating pier that had twenty slips that would hold small to midsized boats. Half of the slips were occupied. The three of us followed like baby ducks paddling along behind their mother. Dude turned to Charles and gave a thumbs-up sign.

I wasn't nearly as much of a detective as Charles thought he was, but I quickly figured out our destination. A low, white boat bobbed in the water in the slip farthest from the bridge we were on. The craft was about twenty-five feet long with *Carolina Skiff, 24DLX* in small letters near the stern and a huge Evinrude engine. The rest of the fiberglass side was covered with "Mad Mel's Magical Marsh Machine" in nine-inch-high, black letters.

"Step aboard," said Mel. "And when on my craft, you call me Major." He held out his right hand to offer leverage. His muscular forearm sported a faded-blue tattoo that said "Dale." The name was in the center of a heart.

"Major Mad Mel?" asked Charles.

"Did I say that, smartass? No, I didn't," he answered his own question. "Just Major."

I looked to the beautiful sunny sky and prayed that Charles wouldn't say, "Aye aye, Just Major."

My prayer was answered when he limited his response to a nod.

"Before we shove off, the damned law says I have to tell you there are lifejackets in the storage area up there," Mel—whoops, Major—pointed to the front of the boat. "For damned wimps," he continued. "And if we start sinking, you have to throw all damned pinko commie draft dodgers off first."

Dude smiled and shook his head. "Law be silent on that." He covered his mouth with his right hand. "Law say Captain Major go down with ship."

"Commie crap," said Mel as he untied his mystery machine and started the one-hundred-fifty-horsepower Evinrude. "Sit!"

We didn't have to be told twice. Dude and I sat on the bench seat along the gunwale near the bow, and Charles scooted toward the stern, close to Med and the instrumentation. We slowly pulled away from the marina, the only slow thing we did for the next fifteen minutes. As soon as we were past the no-wake zone, Mel gunned the powerful engine and we headed east on the Folly River—Folly Beach to our right, the marsh on the left. Despite the warm morning, the sea air was brisk in my face. I felt like I was a gnat sitting on the back of a water bug, scampering on a narrow pond. I had been on Folly Beach for nearly four years but had never seen the marsh from this view. From land, the marsh and river appeared to be one continuous plain; from water, there was a distinct channel we followed.

I couldn't hear everything Charles and Mel were talking about but caught snatches of conversation. Something about the boat having a flat bottom ... low draft of three and a half feet ... eighteen-gallon fuel tank ... eleven-hundred-gallon bilge pump. I watched with admiration as Charles soaked up these arcane facts; his face beamed at the opportunity to expand his trivia collection. He took photos of driftwood floating by as he talked. I had never been a boat fan, knew little or nothing about them, and had no interest in starting now.

I took the opportunity to ask Dude how he had met Mel and if they had really been friends for two decades.

"Saved his Marine Corps ass back in ninety-five," said Dude, who then turned to watch the shore zip by. "One point six decades in truth; rounded to two."

"Saved his life?" I said. I didn't want to confuse Dude with too many words.

"Rip current grabbed him. Be out at Washout. He be on swift trip to dead." Dude pantomimed a swimming motion. "He be surfing; me be surfing. Ditched my board when saw him sinking. Grabbed him and dragged him sideways, away from rip current." Dude laughed. "He be screaming, 'Leave me alone; everything's fine.' Same time he whispered, 'You saved me, little buddy, thanks.'" Dude nodded. "Me saved Mel; Mel saved pride." Dude began humming the Marine Corps hymn. "Surfer dude, Dude, saved the day—and saved big, burly retired United States Marine. 'From the Halls of Montezuma,' la, la, la."

I laughed. Major frowned—again. And Charles smiled.

We were having way too much fun. Then I realized why we were out in the marsh with Dude and Major Mel.

Chapter 21

As quickly as Mel pushed the throttle after we left the marina, he yanked it back. We had reached the east end of Folly. His passengers were still seated, or we would have been hurled into the river.

"Low tide's thirty away," said Mel. "No sense in getting to the A/O before then. I'm going to slip onto that sandbar. Hold on." He pointed his skiff at the low, smooth, light-brown field of sand directly in front of us.

I leaned close to Dude. "Thirty? A/O?"

"Mad talks unnatural."

And that was spoken by Dude!

Dude rolled his eyes and continued, "Thirty be minutes. A/O be area of operations. All be Marine jabber. Mad be et up with it. Me be around enough to figure some out. Don't clutter your noggin. Not worth remembering."

The boat slid about six feet onto the sandbar, and Dude jumped off the bow and pulled it up another three feet. Major cut the engine, and I finally enjoyed a bit of silence. We stood on the spot I'd often photographed from an old coast guard station property on the tip of Folly across Lighthouse Inlet from where we were. The iconic Morris Island lighthouse stood directly behind us and was surrounded by the Atlantic Ocean.

Charles's tennis shoes had no sooner hit the sand when regurgitation of trivia began. "The Morris Island lighthouse was built in 1870 and decommissioned in 1962." He had turned and stared at the wide-striped, faded red-and-white structure. "Thing's 158 feet tall. And get this, when it was built, it was nearly three thousand feet inland from the shore." He pointed away from the ocean, like I wouldn't have known which direction inland was. "In the 1940s, it was on the shoreline, and now it's not even near land." Charles snapped away with his Nikon the entire time he talked. He had never been this close to the lighthouse.

"Sucker sure moves slow," said Dude. "When it be in England?"

Dude stared at Charles. If I didn't know Dude, I would have thought he was serious. Everyone who had been on Folly Beach more than a week knew the history of the lighthouse and how it had fallen victim to the changing sands, the tide's destructive powers, and technology.

"Damned commie pinky draft-dodger," mumbled Mel as he opened the storage compartment beside his seat and removed a red-and-white, plastic flip-top cooler. He still had a frown on his face as he opened the cooler and took out four cans of Miller High Life and handed one to each of us. It wasn't much after eight o'clock a.m., and I wasn't much of a beer drinker, but I saw nothing positive to be gained by arguing with a United States Marine, retired or otherwise, who called himself Mad.

Mel took a swig, gazed at the waves lapping against the base of the aging lighthouse, took off his Semper Fi cap, wiped his totally bald head with the back of his other hand, and explained that it was against the law for him to be drinking if this was a charter, but since we weren't paying "a damn cent," he'd do whatever he wanted. He then turned to Charles. "Now, friend of Dude, why in the hell are we traipsing all over the marsh?"

"Chris and I wanted to visit the spot where they found Tony Long's body," said Charles as he sipped the Miller.

"They be detectives," said Dude.

"Did anybody ask you? Damned commie, pinko hippy." Mel downed the last of his beer and threw the can at Dude.

Dude stepped out of the way of the projectile. "You be cute when you're irritated," he said.

"How long have you had the business?" asked Charles. He apparently didn't want to participate in the beer can fight or explain being a detective.

Mel, Mad, or Major, like most business owners, liked to talk about his pride and joy and looked at Charles with new admiration. "Joined the corps in '73—got a free trip with the Second Marine Division to sand-land in '91." He grinned. "I got the privilege of running that damned Hussein out of Kuwait in Operation Desert Storm; nearly didn't make it back. I put in my twenty and got the hell out."

Charles soaked up the facts, but still didn't have his question answered. "So you started the business when?"

"You damned sure like questions," said Mel. He was close to a smile, but not there yet. "I'm from a pissant town outside Palm Desert, California; didn't grow up around water. I took my military training up at Camp Lejeune in North Carolina and fell in love with the area. When I mustered out, I moved to Charleston and got a job with a septic tank cleaning company and hitchhiked over here on weekends. Got into surfing—"

"Gremmie," interrupted Dude.

"What the hell does that mean?" asked Mel.

Dude folded his arms. "Sucky surfer."

"Damned pinko," said Mel.

Charles looked at Mel. "Got into surfing, and?" said Charles.

Dude interrupted again. "And he be saved by me—hero surfer, Dude."

"Hell if you did," countered Mel. "I was just fine, and ..."

"And you got the business how?" said Mr. Persistence.

Mel ping-ponged his head back to Charles from Dude. "After the commie there screwed up my day at the beach, he felt guilty and told me about an old codger who had a marsh tour business and wanted to sell. The guy was a real dolphin-hugger, all ecology obsessed, knew everything about the fauna and flora of the marsh, what critters lived in here, salt marsh ecosystems, gee-ology, blah, blah, blah." He pointed to the marsh, the lighthouse, the water, and then to his boat. "I didn't know any of that crap—looks like weeds, tall grass, mud, and water to me. But I figured there were a bunch of vacationers who didn't care either and even a bigger bunch of college students who would want to come out here in a boat, get away from the cops, and party hearty on these dunes."

"The rest be history, or sociology," said Dude.

Mel glared at Dude. "Damned dumb commie pinko hippy," said Mel. He then turned his attention back to Charles and me. "What in the hell makes you think you're detectives?"

Charles had started to walk to the boat but then turned back to Mel. "We have a friend who may be in trouble," he said. His voice was barely heard against the slow-rolling waves lapping on the sandbar. "We've got to help him."

Mel nodded and picked up the can he had thrown at Dude; he grabbed the cooler. "Why in the hell didn't you say so? Friends are priceless. Unless they're commie hippies." He nodded toward Dude, who was standing behind Mel and smiling. "Let's shove off," said Mel as he jumped up on the bow of the skiff.

We left Lighthouse Inlet and headed northwest; the marsh got thicker and the waterway narrower. Mel slowed the craft to a more leisurely pace, and I watched a pod of four dolphins, two adults and two pups, swim alongside. The beautiful, playful, mammals didn't appear to fear our intrusion, but several egrets were startled out of their morning rest and gracefully flew away from the noisy boat.

We came to a T in the waterway; Mel yelled that if he had turned right, we would have gone past Cummings Point and on to Fort Sumter, a key battleground of the Civil War. He said the body had been found to the left and we would have to save the Civil War tour for another time. We made the turn, and numerous small creeks branched off the main waterway, like blood vessels as they branched off arteries, going in all directions, creating a maze of options. I was glad it was morning and the sun would be up for many more hours. I'd hate to be here after dark.

"This is the A/O. The body was somewhere around here," said Mel.

I was curious how he knew that, or for that matter, knew where we were, but didn't ask. We were going slow enough for us to stand without fear of being thrown overboard, although I watched his hand on the throttle out of the corner of my eye.

"Now what?" asked Charles.

Dude was closest to him. "You be the detective," he said and waved his arms in the air. "Detect."

"That's Secessionville over there," said Mel. He pointed off to the right.

I saw a tree line and the back of a handful of large houses, but nothing else. Charles photographed everything that looked like a building—his collection of patio furniture photos was expanding rapidly.

"The Confederate Army built a small fort near Secessionville in 1862," said Charles. "It was called Fort Lamar," he continued and stared at the shore. "Yankees tried three times to take it and got whipped—about a hundred dead Yanks; fifty Confederates." He paused, but still looked toward the shore. "What a waste."

The reverence was broken when Mel yelled, "There's what you're looking for."

Our heads swiveled toward Mel, who pointed to the left about fifty feet from where we were. The stream was twenty feet wide, and the marsh grasses were can't-see-through dense on both sides. I finally saw what Mel was pointing at. The yellow crime scene tape was spread in what had once been an orderly rectangle measuring maybe fifteen by twenty-five feet. The multiple tide changes, combined with a brisk breeze over the last few days, had taken their toll on the marked-off area. One end of the tape flapped in the brisk breeze, and the corner closest to the water had pulled loose from the grasses where it had been secured and dipped into the water. The last five feet of the garish tape floated. A shelf of ragged, black oysters covered much of the area. The marsh grasses were beaten down in three spots near the tape. Deep craters dotted the soft mud. I assumed this was from the police, coroner, and crime scene techs who had secured and inspected the scene. You could see where many other craters had been eroded by the high tides.

Mel pulled the boat as close as he safely could to the muddy bank. I heard crabs splash in the salt water and something much heavier land in the current a couple of feet behind the boat.

The marsh cordgrass rose at least five feet above the pluff mud bank and was thicker than any we had seen since we left the marina. The marsh stink competed with a swarm of mosquitoes as major irritants. There was no way I was getting out of the boat.

Mel leaned over the side of the skiff and tried to see into the thick grasses, but the view was blocked by the first wall of tall, green grass. "It's a damn miracle that anyone saw the body."

I agreed. "Whoever did this didn't want Long found."

Charles used his cane to push the grasses aside; it was a futile effort. "Whoever it was knew the body could easily have been undetected forever."

Mel stood on the seat along the side of the boat and looked back toward Secessionville. "Look around," he said. "There could have been a battle of two Civil War Ironsides here, and nobody would have seen anything." He hopped off the seat and walked to the spot closest to the tape. "This was the perfect spot to kill someone."

"Nope, Mad Marine," said Dude. He had seen all he wanted to and sat on the bench with his legs stretched out in front of him. "Not be perfect."

"Why not?" I asked.

Dude stated at the tape. "Bod found. Long be in Charleston; cops all in a fritter; and Chuckster be on the case ... Nope, not be perfect killin'."

Mel took off his hat, wiped his sweat-covered, bald dome, and then put the hat back on. "Charles and Chris," he said. "There is a first for everything." He turned his constant frown to Dude. "He *be* right."

We floated around the crime scene for another thirty in Mel's lingo before unanimously agreeing that there was nothing else to learn. Mel gunned the Evinrude, and we continued west through the marsh past Goat Island and Long Island, where Dude asked, "Manhattan be nearby?" The rest of us ignored him. We crossed under Folly Road and around the next bend, past another of Folly's famous, and unique, landmarks, Bowen's Island Restaurant. Mel traversed a couple of more turns and carefully guided the boat back to the dock where we had begun.

We secured Mad Mel's Magical Marsh Machine and slowly walked to our cars. I asked Mel if he wanted to join us for lunch and a beer. He said he had more important things to do than hang out with a commie pinko hippy and two "no chance in the world of becoming detectives."

We jumped out of the way as Mel's Camaro threw gravel, shells, and dust as it peeled out of the parking lot.

Charles took a photo of a candy wrapper in the lot and then turned to Dude. "Who's Dale?" he asked. I had already forgotten about Mel's tattoo.

Dude looked down at the wrapper and then at Charles. "DADT."

"Surfer word?" asked Charles.

I smiled, knowing that there was something Charles didn't know.

"Be Marine term," said Dude.

"So who is she?" Charles wasn't about to give up.

"Who say Dale be she?" said Dude.

Chapter 22

"Charles, I may not be a detective *like you*, but it looks like all roads, and streams, lead to Sean."

Many of my attempts at sarcasm are lost on Charles, but that hasn't stopped me from trying. We had returned to the gallery after our morning in the marsh. Charles insisted that we give customers a chance to spend money; I argued that it wouldn't make any difference. I got depressed each time I unlocked the gallery door. We sat around the table in the back room with a Diet Pepsi in front of each of us and a rapidly emptying bag of Doritos within arm's reach. Amber had tried for two years to get me on a healthier eating regimen. She might as well have been trying to get me to flap my arms and fly.

Charles didn't respond. I wondered if he had heard me. I spoke louder, "Charles?"

"I heard you. Just thinking it can't be Sean."

"He has more than enough motives—money, betrayal, his *alleged* affair with Tony's wife," I said while Charles stuffed his mouth with Doritos. "He also had means; we know he has a boat that could easily navigate the marsh, and he's lived here long enough to know his way around it. And he's contacted a top criminal attorney."

"I know, I know. It looks bad," said Charles. "But unless something more damning happens, I'm going to stick by my friend." Charles hesitated. "Even if he's guilty, I'll stick by him." He then looked toward the door leading to the gallery. "Will you help me?"

Cute the way he slipped that into the conversation. I didn't think there was anything we could do. I didn't know what Charles had thought we would find in the marsh today, but if I had learned anything that could possibly lead to the killer, I didn't know what. I didn't see what it would harm to keep our ears open, ask questions, possibly look at angles the police might miss.

"I'll try, but if Sean's guilty, we have to accept it."

A huge grin appeared on Charles's face. "President Lincoln once said, 'He has the right to criticize, who has a heart to help.' Criticize Sean all you want, but wait and see—he's innocent."

Once Charles finagled a commitment from me, he said he had to run an errand for Dude and hurried out; most likely, he didn't want to wait for me to change my mind. I wasn't worried about being able to handle all the customers without my sales manager. In fact, that had just been lowered on my list of worries.

Was I serious about meddling in police business? Did Charles and I have a chance at succeeding? Had I gone off the deep end—again?

Mid-afternoon rolled around, and only three potential customers had found their way into Landrum Gallery; one actually bought something. They were followed by an hour-long lull before Charles burst through the door.

He was out of breath and waved his cane around his head. "Just saw Sean," he said. "He wants us to meet him on his boat tonight at seven. We'll be there, right?"

"Why not?" I said. Although if pushed, I could easily come up with a dozen reasons not to wade deeper into the shark pit.

Sean lived in Mariner's Cay, a gated community a short walk off-island, just past the bridge that separated Folly Beach from the rest of the country. Sean had given Charles the code for the punch-in keypad at the entrance. Rather than meeting us at his condo, Sean asked us to meet him on the marina dock. The development was U-shaped, with the condos around the perimeter. A pool, two tennis courts, and a clubhouse were at the center of the complex.

The marina entrance was halfway down the left side of the U. The floating dock was shaped like a fork; the walkway to the dock was the handle, and four docks protruded over the Folly River. I could see Charles's small apartment building and the adjacent Sandbar Seafood and Steak Restaurant directly across the river.

Sean had been waiting for us on the dock. He was leaning against the retractable handle on a large, white cooler and waved as we turned the corner. He smiled, but looked behind us. His body language screamed tense.

There were slips to hold seventy or so boats, and most were occupied. The upscale marina held about a zillion more dollars' worth of watercraft than were in the workingman's Folly View Marina, Mad Mel's base of operation, located only a couple hundred yards away.

I had known Sean had a boat, but had no idea what kind. He waved us to a ten-foot-long, aluminum johnboat that bounced in the wake from a boat that had just sped by. To put it kindly, it was far less than what I had expected.

Charles leaned toward me and whispered, "Told you he had a yacht."

Sean shook my hand and gave Charles a weak man-hug; the entire time, he looked back toward the condos. He held the tiny, bobbing vessel steady while Charles and I carefully climbed aboard. Charles then helped Sean with the cooler.

"Thanks for coming," said Sean as he untied his "yacht" and started the electric trolling motor.

Our trip in the johnboat lasted a couple of minutes at most. We pulled alongside a Chris-Craft that was anchored close to the Folly Beach side of the river within a hundred yards of the bridge and the Folly Beach boat ramp.

"Welcome to my doghouse," said Sean as he tied the johnboat to the side of the much larger craft.

"It's a beaut," said Charles.

Charles must have been looking at another vessel. The Chris-Craft was in dire need of work—much work. The stain on the wood trim was peeling, and the hull paint followed suit. If it had been a house, it would euphemistically have been called a fixer-upper. Once we stepped aboard, I realized that the view from the johnboat was its best. The teak flooring was rough, badly in need of sanding and stain; the glass-paneled door opening to the pilothouse from the rear deck was off its rusted hinges. Two fire extinguishers sat on a ledge at the stern; not a comforting sight.

Sean moved four wooden panels he had been sanding on so we could sit on the only empty horizontal surface. He laughed at Charles's comment. "Beaut—not quite. It's a 1968 forty-five-foot Constellation; an almost-classic. A client paid his bill with it a couple of years ago."

"Does it run?" asked Charles.

"Nah," said Sean. "It'll take thousands to get it moving on its own. It's my therapy. I have a twenty-four-foot runabout when I really want to go somewhere. Best thing about this one is it's a place for me to think and bunk; it's got a full queen-sized bed in the aft cabin." He looked at Charles and giggled. "Lately it's been more bunking than thinking."

"Sara Faye kick you out?" asked Charles. Subtle!

Sean opened the cooler and handed Charles a Bud Light before fishing through the ice and pulling out an airline-sized bottle of white wine and a plastic wine glass and handing them to me. Finally, he pulled out a bottle of Jack Daniel's whiskey and a green plastic cup with "Folly Beach" in script on the side. I was impressed.

"Kicked me out … no," said Sean after he took he took a swig of his Jack Daniel's. "Let's just say that the condo is mighty cold, even with the A/C off. Folly's a small place. Rumors spread like fleas and bite harder." He hesitated for another swig. "Sara Faye is in her store every day and hears everything. The coffee pot—the rumor pot, I call it—is nearly as popular as the romance section."

Sean's wife owned, and was the sole employee of, Readers' Roost, a small used bookstore off Folly Road a couple of miles from the beach. Charles, with his ravenous reading habit, is a regular customer—regular when I take him. The only time I would even think about going in a bookstore would be to drag Charles out and bring him home.

Continuing in his not-so-subtle ways, Charles asked, "Rumors about what?"

"Oh, this and that."

I didn't think "this and that" would get Sean banished to his floating doghouse and knew it was only a matter of time before Charles would home in on it. Sean tried to deflect the coming questions by talking more about his pet renovation project: something about new Italian light fixtures in the cabins, new four-blade props, strut bearings, a new 2500 Trace Inverter, and a 300-hp 6V turbocharger. I tried to look interested, but he lost me with light fixtures.

"This and that what?" said Charles.

Sean didn't have a chance. He looked down into the green cup and swirled it in his left hand. "She heard that I was having an affair with Tony's wife." He continued to stare into the cup.

To Charles's credit, he remained silent.

Sean slammed his cup down on a small wooden box beside him; whiskey sloshed out on the deck. He grabbed the top of the cooler; yanked out another beer, and tossed it to Charles. Then, more cautiously, he took out another mini-wine bottle and handed to me. The weather was gorgeous; the sun was leaning toward the west and would be setting behind the marsh in less than an hour. A couple of large sailboats gracefully floated by, and a nice breeze kept the hot temperatures tolerable. And tumultuous storms raged inside Sean.

He closed the cooler and looked over at a sailboat floating near his fixer-upper. "Guys," he said without taking his eyes off the billowing, white-and-blue-striped sail, "I think I'm in big trouble—and not just over there." Sean sighed and nodded toward the condo complex. "Tony and I met in law school at the University of Alabama. He was from Chicago; never did learn why he really ended up in Alabama—he made it clear that he never wanted to go back there. We were never close; our partnership was more of convenience than anything else. He brought some family money to the table to get us started. We didn't talk about much of anything, much less our cases."

Sean finally looked toward Charles and me and kicked one of the boards that leaned against the side of the boat.

"Crap," he snarled. "Tony's been a skirt-chaser forever; hell, in college he spent more time in the Crimson Motel than in the law library. And I'm being castigated about Connie and me." He slammed down his fist on the table. "He steals seventy-five thousand dollars, and people are looking at me like I'm the criminal. And the drugs—yeah, drugs—that he was getting into were a hell of a lot stronger than this." He held up his green cup and then turned away from us and flung his empty Folly Beach cup against the sidewall. "He takes on all sorts of nefarious clients; I try to stick to boring wills, estates, real estate transactions—business to pay the bills. What the hell does it get me ... what does it get me? What does trying to be good get me?" He paused and took a deep breath.

Charles leaned forward and set his beer bottle on the table next to the bottle of whiskey. "You're alive; Tony's dead," said Charles.

Sean looked at Charles and gave a slight nod. "Good point."

"What do you want us to do?" asked Charles. He pointed his cane at me as he said it.

"First, believe me," he said. "I didn't kill Tony. If I were the police, I would have me as the prime suspect. Shoot, if I didn't know better, I'd think I did it. Keep your ears and eyes open. I know you've helped the police before ... Guys, I didn't do it."

Chapter 23

Morning was my favorite time of the day, especially in the summer. The temperatures were at their moderate best; traffic in front of my cottage was light; the irritations of the day hadn't developed; and most of the vacationers were still snoring in their rentals.

Today was an exception. Yesterday's marsh tour and troubling meeting with Sean weighed heavily on me. I tossed and turned throughout the night and finally gave up on sleep at five a.m. I walked aimlessly around the house for an hour and then decided to venture three blocks to the Tides. The massive hotel had been remodeled a couple of years ago and featured, without doubt, the most attractive interior of any commercial building on the island. More importantly to me, it had the most pleasant, friendly staff of any hotel I had visited.

I stopped at Bert's along the way to get a cup of coffee. When the Tides had flown the Holiday Inn flag, it had a complimentary coffee bar for its guests. I had expanded the definition of *guests* to include residents who lived nearby and was a frequent visitor to the coffee bar, a tradition I had started during my first visit to Folly Beach years earlier. Probably because of freeloaders like me, the hotel had realized that free coffee didn't have a very high profit margin, so it ended the tradition.

I walked through the front door and said hi to Diane, the night clerk. She had just started in her job during my first visit and always had a good thing to say to all who entered her domain. She was in her mid-twenties, with a great personality and a warm smile accentuated by an overbite. She was attractive even with her less-than-trim figure.

She had a way of cheering up the most fatigued and cranky guests who arrived after a long drive or a night on the town.

We shared early-morning pleasantries, and I moved around the corner to one of the seats along the corridor that faced the pool. The sun lifted its head over the horizon, the Atlantic, and the pier.

I either was deep in thought or drifted off to sleep, because I didn't know anyone was near until a hand rested on the shoulder. I fumbled my Styrofoam cup and nearly spilled coffee in my lap.

"I didn't mean to startle you," said the pleasant voice of Cindy Ash.

She stood at my side in her Folly Beach Department of Public Safety uniform.

"Guess I was drifting," I said and looked up at her. "On duty?"

"No." She shook her head and rolled her eyes. "I come over here every few days to wash my uniform in the pool. Jump in with it on; flail around for a while." She pirouetted. "Think it looks good, don't you?"

"Clean and dripped dry," I said and laughed. Larry was a lucky man; he could stand more humor in his life. "How's the wedding planning?"

Cindy looked around as she lowered herself into the chair facing me. "Slow as chilled molasses," she said and shook her head. "Can you get all your good citizens to stop needing nails, saws, and paint? I can't get Larry out of his danged store long enough to plan and go shopping."

Smart man, I thought and then nodded. "Don't think I have that much influence with the other residents, but I promise not to need to nail, saw, or paint anything until after the wedding."

"Thanks—that's one small step for weddingkind. Speaking of weddings, when are you and Amber getting hitched?"

That was a question I had heard more and more lately. The question was asked frequently, but the answer was still elusive. I had been single for the last quarter of a century; had led—until moving to Folly—a quiet, some would say boring, existence. I was set in my ways and had always been uncomfortable around kids. Sure, I had more fun with Amber than since I don't know when; I cared about her deeply. But she was nearly twenty years my junior and had a son who was younger than many of my shoes. Did I love her? Could I adjust? Could …

"Hmm, hmm ... Chris, I didn't mean to fling you into a stupor," said Cindy as she nudged my leg with her foot. "Was an easy question. Let me help; the answer could range from 'this afternoon' to 'February twenty-ninth next leap year' to 'never.'"

I smiled. "How about no idea—if ever?" Under the smile was a mass of truth.

"Not much of a limb you climbed out on," she said. "Knowing you, that's all I'm going to get. You do know that you're the only one of you two who has cold feet?"

I continued to smile and gave her a tiny nod. "Anything new on the murder?" Changing the subject was one of my most utilized tools of deflection.

Cindy laughed. "Guess our chick-talk is over," she said. The smile waned. "Your buddy Sean looks good for it. I hear he and Long had a couple of near knock-down arguments the week before Long bit the marsh. Sean has quite a temper, I'm told. The stolen money gives him a strong motive. Yeah, and there's the hanky-panky with Long's wife." Cindy looked up and down the corridor. "Add to that, do you know he has a boat that would have provided easy transportation to the marsh?"

I nodded, since Charles and I had learned about his fleet last evening. "Think he'll be arrested?"

"Ah, good question—there's the problem. We have nothing to tie him to the murder; nothing forensic; no weapon; we can't pin down the time of death to within the lifecycle of a mosquito, so there's no way to prove or disprove an alibi. We'll need more to put the cuffs on him."

"Are you and the sheriff's office working any better together?" I asked.

There had historically been friction between the Charleston County sheriff's office and the Folly Beach Department of Public Safety. Homicides were investigated by detectives from the sheriff's office. The local department was seasonally understaffed and did not have the budget for an investigative arm, but it had a good feel for the pulse of the community and could provide invaluable information in the investigative process. Prior to Brian Newman's near-fatal heart attack, the relationship between the two departments was at a high point. Additionally, Detective Lawson had been assigned to murders that occurred on the island. She had taken full advantage of the eyes and ears of the local police.

"Sure," said Cindy. "We're as tight as Osama Bin Laden and Barack Obama."

"Guess Chief King's helping too," I said. My tongue rattled around in my cheek.

"Yeah right. We find Mr. Long in *our* marsh, and you know what our *Acting* Chief King talks, and talks, and talks about in all our meetings?"

"What?"

"Public inebriation, speeding—speeding to him means two miles an hour over the limit, and the crime that must be far worse than beheading kittens."

"That being?"

She yanked on her left ear. "Noise!"

"Why are these heinous crimes so important now?"

"Simple," she said and looked over my shoulder and out at the Folly pier. "Trickle down. Those new yuppies on the island, or whatever the new rich twits who are buying and building all the mansions are called nowadays, are screaming about a little trash or people actually having fun on the beach near their Taj Mahals. They dump on Mayor Amato; the mayor craps on Acting Chief King; he shares the bowel movement with us lowly officers; and guess who we poop on?" Cindy paused, looked up and down the corridor again, and giggled. "We're out there giving tickets for loud farts!"

I laughed and offered to get her coffee from the restaurant. She nodded, and I stretched and walked to Blu, the hotel's upscale eatery. She was still staring at the pier when I returned; she thanked me and said she was on patrol and then leaned back in the chair. Flagrant farters were safe for a few more minutes.

"Is that why the mayor wants to force out Chief Newman?"

"You got it," she said. "Newman's a great chief because he knows what's important and lets us have discretion to do what's right. Are we too lenient? Sure, at times, but doesn't it make more sense to help one of our citizens, or vacationers, home rather than haul him off to jail if he wobbles a little while walking down the street—not driving, not endangering anyone? Acting Chief King wants those 'hardened criminals' in jail, and probably in front of a firing squad."

"Think the mayor'll succeed?"

"Don't know," she said. "I do know that every member of the department hopes not—every member except Acting Chief King." She stood, straightened the crease in her uniform slacks, and said she needed to get back to work.

I thanked her for stopping. "Before you go," I said, "do you think Sean Aker killed Tony Long?"

She slowly shook her head. "I have no idea. What I do know is someone did. If it wasn't Sean, then who?"

Who indeed? I thought.

Chapter 24

It was still early, and the sun hadn't heated the air to an intolerable level. I waved to Diane, who was at the desk with a big yawn on her face, and walked to the east end of the hotel and across a small parking area to the pier. Along with the Morris Island lighthouse, the Edwin S. Taylor Fishing Pier held the distinction of being one of the iconic signature features of Folly Beach. Charles's penchant for useless trivia was wearing off on me, since I remembered that the pier was more than a thousand feet long and twenty-five feet wide and extended out over the Atlantic at twenty-three feet above sea level. Regardless of its no-reason-to-remember vital statistics, the pier held special meaning for me; it was where I went when I needed to relax, think through issues, or get a unique, panoramic view of Folly Beach. I had taken hundreds of photographs from the impressive structure over the years, but could never quite capture a marketable image. It didn't stop me from trying. Several early-morning fishermen stood along the wooden railings. The pungent smell of bait and freshly caught fish filled the air as I walked to the Atlantic end of the landmark.

I sat on one of the stationary wooden benches that dotted the walkway and took a deep breath. I looked back toward the Tides and watched three little girls laugh and scream as they separated from their parents and high-stepped in the rolling surf, twenty-three feet below. The parents followed at a much slower pace and carried aluminum beach chairs and umbrellas in their left hands and Styrofoam coffee cups in their right.

The white-capped waves provided all the amusement the children needed. The hypnotic rhythms and sounds of the powerful waves as they slapped against the beach met the relaxation needs of adults.

The area directly to the left of the pier was always the most densely populated spot on the expansive, wide beach. The nine-story hotel and its neighbor to the west, the Charleston Oceanfront Villas, a large, four-story, modern condo complex, ensured that the beach in front of them always had plenty of vacationers.

I wasn't interested in capturing the perfect photograph today; I needed to decide if I was really committed to going down the path with Charles. What made him think he could find a killer if the police couldn't? For that matter, what made him think he could be a detective? I had told him that I would help; but what did that mean? Why should I get involved? My life was not in danger, and neither was that of anyone else I knew. I was an acquaintance of Sean; by no stretch would I consider him a close friend.

Then there was the most frightening option—that Sean had murdered his law partner. He definitely had motive. I had seen his temper first-hand last night; and he was only talking about Tony. He had easy access to the marsh, owned a boat that would easily navigate the watery maze. He was comfortable on the water and had lived here long enough to know his way around the mysterious, winding tidal creeks. Had Charles's friendship with Sean clouded his objectivity? And if Sean was the killer, how would he react if we got close? Were we in danger?

I spent most of my adult life working for a large, international health care company that prided itself on making logical, well-thought-out, prudent decisions. I fit in well with that corporate culture. Every nerve in me told me that not only should I refuse to get involved, but I should also do whatever possible to ensure that Charles didn't either. So why was I here trying to figure out how we could find out more about the crime and what we could do to solve it?

I was reluctant to admit it, but the answer was simple. Charles Fowler was my friend; he had helped me overcome my boring life and to look at the world with new glasses—rose-colored at times, but new nonetheless. He had helped me to be befriended by folks I never would have met in my previous life even if they were my next-door neighbors.

Now he had asked for my help, and come hell or high homicide, he would get it. Besides, I might be able to keep him from getting killed in the process.

With that decision out of the way, I made the mistake of thinking about Cindy's question about Amber and me. I pondered the options; all I concluded was that I needed three aspirins. My head throbbed.

"About time you showed up," said Charles. He was leaning on the gallery wall closest to the back room. His cane pointed at my face, and an orange beaver stared at me from his white, long-sleeved T-shirt. "California Institute of Technology" was written above the goofy-looking water rodent.

I had learned years ago not to comment on his T-shirt collection. My silence about his near-endless supply of sportswear irritated him, but that was preferable to hearing about his shirts if I commented. Unfortunately, others were slow to learn the lesson, so I had to put up with his narrative on each mascot when someone asked.

I looked around the empty room. "Have you been able to handle the crowds without me?"

"That's not the point," he said. The cane was still aimed at my head. "Have a question for you."

I cocked my head to the right, took off my Tilley, and took it to the back room. Asking him what the question was would have been wasted words.

He followed me back, tapping his cane on the worn, wooden floors as he walked. "Who do I need to ask about getting my detective's license, or whatever I need to detect?"

I looked at him and shook my head. "If you had a therapist, I would suggest you ask her—find out where you and reality parted company."

"Cute," he said and tapped the floor harder. "I'm serious."

"Really, Charles, what makes you think you could be a P.I.?"

"I know almost everything there is to know," he said. "I've read all about Kinsey Millhone, Stephanie Plum, Alex Cross, Spenser, and that pipe-smoking guy Sherlock Holmes ... know all their techniques, how they solve crimes ..."

I held the palm of my right hand in his face. "They're all fictional characters, Charles. They're not real."

"Yeah, so?"

I tried to frown, but couldn't help but smile. "So, never mind. I give up. I don't know, but would guess that there are some state regulations or a licensing process. You could check with Brian Newman; he might know. Or Google it." I shook my head. "Shouldn't a detective be able to find out something like that—hint, hint? I still think you should start with therapy."

The bell over the front door interrupted our less-than-sane conversation.

"Yo, be anyone here?" came a familiar voice from the other room.

"Dude interruptus," said Charles. He then went to the refrigerator and took out a root beer we kept for the rare appearances of the aging surfer. "Back here, Dude."

Dude walked through the door to the back room and then turned back to the gallery. "Where be peeps?"

Charles handed Dude his drink. "Flew the coop, Dude; flew the coop," said Charles.

"Left the pictures," said Dude. He still looked around the gallery.

"Don't remind me," I said.

"Not here to inventory," said Dude. "Marsh voyage give you big-time detectives clues?"

"See?" said Charles. "Dude knows a detective when he sees one."

He doesn't know a complete sentence when he sees one, much less a detective, I thought.

Charles explained that the trip had been helpful, but there weren't any glaring clues or smoking guns, and that we did enjoy meeting Mel.

"So after you saved Mel's life, how did you become friends?" asked Charles.

"Opposites extract, something like that; cause and effect," said Dude. "Think it's Karmann Ghia—Hindu, you know."

Charles impressed me by not interrupting Dude's flow with a detailed explanation about what Dude was trying to say. I thought about the first Volkswagen I had owned and how much I had wished it were a Karmann Ghia and not a faded, rusting bug. It wasn't to be.

Dude plopped down in the one of the wooden chairs beside the table, waved for us to sit, and continued, "Mad Man Melster and the

Dudester rendezvous each full moon at Loggerhead's Beach Grill. Have a beer or seventeen; he cuss Dudester; Dudester diss Mad Man." He paused and took a sip of root beer. "Enough about Mad Mel. Who offed the shyster?"

"Haven't quite figured it out," said Charles. He put his right foot in the chair, leaned his elbows across the elevated knee, and looked at Dude like he was going to impart great wisdom. "But I don't think it was Sean."

"Don't think or don't want to think it be he?" said Dude as he looked at Charles's foot in the chair.

Wisdom was in the air, but not emanating from Charles.

Dude waited for an answer, but when Charles was slow to respond, he continued. "Law Partner S be Barnieing with Partner T, right?"

I looked at Charles for a translation. He returned my gaze and shrugged. "What's that mean, Dude?" I finally asked.

He turned to me with a look of amazement. "'Barnie' be get in fight with someone; duh."

Surely I wasn't the dumbest person he had ever talked with; he just acted like I was.

"Yes, Dude, Partner S, Sean, did have a few fights with Partner T, Tony," said Charles. "But they were just business disagreements."

Dude slowly stood and walked back to the door leading to the gallery, looked around the room, and then turned his attention back to the Charles and me. "Sean not off Tony, the corpse. Okay, who did?"

I definitely understood that question and looked at Charles for an answer and not a translation. After all, he had read Robert Parker and Janet Evanovich.

Charles walked to the door to see what Dude had been looking at in the gallery, shook his head, and mumbled something like "Nothing from this planet" and then picked up his cane. He put the cane on the table and sat back down.

"My list, not in alphabetical or any other order, would be Mrs. Long, Connie, for getting fed up with the jerk or to have Sean all to herself; Conroy Elder, the guy who Tony *done wrong*; the Mafia, always good candidates; and if Tony would steal from his own partner, there had to be others; we just haven't detected who they are yet."

Dude shook his head. "'Bout got it wrapped up, seems like." He headed for the door and turned and gave Charles the peace sign.

"Whoa," said Charles. He followed Dude to the door. "Is Mel gay?"

"DADT," said Dude.

Chapter 25

Amber had to take Jason to a baseball game on James Island and wouldn't be back until late. She and I, along with a growing batch of friends, had become regulars at the open mike night at GB's Bar. Country Cal was the featured entertainer most weekends, and GB's country-stocked jukebox provided a continuous flow of country gems the rest of the week, except Tuesdays.

I liked Tuesdays' atmosphere the best; it was for the same reason some people go to NASCAR races—to see wrecks. About a dozen "singers" paraded across the stage each week to sing their hearts and dreams out. The quality of the performers ranged from Cal, who actually had a hit record, although it was popular nearly a half-century ago, to a couple of guys who had the talent but who hadn't gotten their big break, to a half-dozen or so whose biggest break came once a week at GB's, to Heather, who crammed more off-key notes into a song than there are atoms in a pound of plutonium. GB's weekly event was a microcosm of Folly Beach. It was varied, quirky, artistic, and hopeful, with a layer of gritty sand around the edges.

Humidity was still over the top, and I was anxious to enter the air-conditioned comfort of the country music bar. GB's was less than a block off Center Street, across the street from the recently expanded fire department, and no more than four blocks from home. I stepped inside the door to catch my breath and let my eyes get accustomed to the dimly lit building; most of the illumination came from neon beer signs over the bar that dominated the right side of the structure. I pulled my shirt away from my sweaty back.

"Hey, Chris. Welcome," said a baby-faced, rotund man who came out from the behind the bar to greet me. With his stooped shoulders and grease-slicked, muddy-gray hair, Greg Brile looked in his fifties but was several years younger. "Your friends are already over there." He nodded toward a round table on the other side of the room. "White wine?"

There was something comforting in knowing that the owner of the bar knew my drink of choice; I also wondered, in weaker moments, if the comfort masked a journey toward Alcoholics Anonymous. With the self-diagnosis out of the way, I headed to the table that Charles had commandeered.

Beach-bar-bohemian would describe GB's. The smell of frying onions and stale beer permeated the atmosphere; the onion smell was fresh, while the stale beer aroma was deeply embedded in the cheap, dark-brown, threadbare carpet. Southern Baptists could hold a two-week revival in GB's and the smell would be just as strong after the last amen.

All dozen tables were occupied, and the four stools at the chest-high bar were holding more weight than their small, round seats were designed for. Beer bottles in various stages of full dotted the tabletops.

Charles, as usual, bemoaned the fact that I hadn't arrived earlier; as usual, I ignored him and grabbed the chair he had saved for me. Heather was on the other side of him and leaning on his shoulder. She was decked out in her Tuesday night stage outfit: a bright-yellow, sequined blouse, a floor-length, kelly-green skirt, and her signature wide-brimmed straw hat. I didn't have any firsthand knowledge about her undergarments, but knew the same outerwear had appeared each Tuesday evening on GB's stage for the last nine months. Her highly inadequate singing voice accompanied her as well.

Greg arrived at the table with my drink before I had a chance to see who was performing. He set the glass in front of me and then looked at Heather and held up his index finger. "One, sweet lady," he said and then turned his attention to the couples at the table behind us.

Heather's smile vanished. "You said maybe … never mind." She looked at the ceiling. Greg was already out of earshot.

Charles reached over and covered her trembling right hand.

"He told me he might let me sing two songs tonight," she said loud enough for Charles and me to hear. "Curses on him."

She leaned closer to Charles and said something, but I couldn't hear what it was. Her words were drowned out by a guitar riff coming from two near-antique speakers on the small, raised wooden stage at the far end of the room. A singer who looked to be to be in his early twenties followed the riff with the first verse of "All My Exes Live in Texas," the George Strait hit. The kid was no George Strait, but he wasn't a Heather either, so most of the patrons paid attention, and two couples sauntered to the twelve-by-twenty-foot, laminate-covered dance floor in front of the stage.

Charles waved his cane in the air and got the attention of Colleen, the waitress who had shared a Harley with Harley the other night. She hurried to the table—more to stop Charles from poking someone's eye out with the cane than to provide outstanding service. Charles ordered a couple more beers, and Colleen headed toward the bar. Her hands visibly shook.

"She's in a cranky mood tonight," said Charles as he watched her walk away. "More nervous than usual."

I was surprised. Colleen was my favorite waitress at GB's. She was always jittery and looked like she didn't have enough muscles in her body to keep her upright, but was friendly and seemed to know what we wanted before we ordered.

"Cranky, shaky, bad *chi,*" said Heather. "Gregory'll do that to you." She pushed away from Charles and grabbed her new guitar from the case that leaned against the dark green wall beside the table. "Think I'll sing a second song and see what Mr. GB has to say about that." She grabbed her guitar and headed toward the stage.

I was equally concerned what the customers might think of it, especially the ones with beer bottles and seated within throwing distance of the stage.

The George Strait want-to-be finished and thanked his "fans" as Heather bounded up onto the small stage. Before he could get his guitar in its case on the corner of the stage, Heather began her rendition Patsy Cline's "Sweet Dreams."

My friend and iconoclastic Realtor, Bob Howard, had once called Heather's version of "Sweet Dreams" "Sour Nightmares." Fortunately for both of them, she was warbling onstage at the time and didn't hear him.

Charles's first serious exposure to country music had come within the last year, and he still had little positive to say about the indigenous American genre. Heather's voice fit about every stereotype he had, but because of their growing relationship, he spent most of the time while she was onstage gritting his teeth; it appeared to be a smile to Heather. He looked over at me during her third verse. "Heather has a unique vocal style," he said.

Dude couldn't have said it better.

Heather finished her song with a flourish and a stage bow. Another "girl singer," as Greg called the female entertainers, stood stage left and waited to replace Heather at the mike. Instead of walking offstage, Heather strummed her guitar and began her "unique vocal style" on "Coal Miner's Daughter."

I grimaced and looked for Greg; I could picture him with a shepherd's hook reaching for her neck to yank her offstage. It was Heather's lucky night; the bar owner wasn't attacking the stage with his hook. He was probably afraid to come out of the kitchen for fear that he might strangle Charles's favorite "girl singer."

The instant she finished the song, Heather rushed offstage—no bow, hardly a wide grin. Perhaps she hoped that Greg couldn't count to two. What Heather lacked in the vocal department, she made up for with her enthusiasm and love for life. She beamed as she returned to the table. Charles stood, applauded, and then pulled the chair out for her.

Colleen arrived at the table with another round of beers and a wine for me as soon as Heather had settled. "Seen Harley lately?" asked Charles.

Colleen looked at him and frowned. "No," she said and put a beer in front of Charles. She turned to Heather. "Two songs; good for you, baby girl." She rushed from the table without saying anything else.

Heather elbowed Charles and tilted her head toward the bar. "Strong, macho Charles," she said. "Will you protect me if ol' Gregory comes over to whoop-up on me?"

Charles looked toward the bar, where Cal and Greg were in deep conversation. "No problem," said Charles, "Chris'll take care of Greg; I'll escort you out."

I was ready to tell Charles that if there was any fighting, he would be the one with bruised fists, when the ear-splitting noise of wailing sirens from one of the fire engines across the street bounced off GB's dark green walls. When the second engine added to the sound pollution, I knew it was for more than a dog caught in the surf.

I didn't realize how much more at the time.

Chapter 26

Country Cal settled in behind the baseball-sized, silver mike and strummed the first few notes of his first, and only, hit, "The End of Her Story." No one listened. Three couples at the tables closest to the door rushed out to the sidewalk. I heard muffled shouts from outside. Someone yelled for one truck to set up on Center Street, the other to go around to the side of the building.

Excitement outside our line of vision was all it took for Charles to follow the couples to the door. I followed on Charles's heels. A police cruiser had blocked the street in front of the combination city hall and fire station. Officer Spencer, one of Folly's finest, and youngest, public safety officers, blocked the street in front of GB's and rerouted cars away from city hall, waving bystanders to our side of the road and away from the action. It was past sunset, but I could still see clouds of black smoke billowing into the air from the other side of city hall. The blue LED lights from the cruiser's light bar bounced off the side of city hall; reflections of flames danced in the smoke.

I motioned for Charles to sneak across the street with me; we scurried behind Spencer, who was distracted by drivers who resisted his rerouting. We walked around the back of the fire station and faced the rear of the burning building. Flames pushed out the second-floor rear windows of the weathered, wooden, two-story structure that inched up against the municipal building. City hall and its attached fire station formed the long side of an *L* with the flame-engulfed structure. The fire escape door flapped open from the fire's pressure; smoke and flames spewed out.

Charles and I moved to the back of the city hall parking lot and were directly behind the center of attention. The first-floor door was closed, and it didn't appear that flames had reached the lower shop.

"Hear that?" asked Charles. He pointed his cane at the first-floor door.

"What?" I said. All I heard were the crackling of the fire and shouts of firefighters from the front of the building.

Charles had already started to move closer to the burning structure.

"Somebody's in there."

We were some twenty feet from the building, and the heat felt like I was sticking my head in an open oven. Burning embers floated around my head. Two embers landed on my shirt sleeve, and I quickly brushed them off before I became part of the fire.

Charles was oblivious to everything around him and continued to walk toward the door. Before I could yell, he reached for the knob.

Shouts continued from the front of the building, and I still didn't hear anything from inside.

He looked over his shoulder at me. "Give me a hand." He grabbed the knob and put his right foot on the frame and yanked. Nothing happened.

I was about five feet behind him when I heard a muffled explosion and looked up. The entire second-floor door frame and door were engulfed in flames. The explosion had ripped the wooden frame from the building.

I ducked and yelled, "Get back!"

Charles was focused on the locked door and ignored everything except the knob.

The flaming wooden door and frame bounced off the steel-grated, second-floor fire escape and over the edge. I lunged for Charles and grabbed him around the waist. He let go of the knob.

"What the ..." he muttered.

I pulled him a few feet away from the building before I tripped on a smoldering board and fell backward. I hit the pavement hard, and Charles landed on me. Pain shot through my left leg.

The heavy, flaming door crashed to the pavement. Sparks and embers shot in all directions. Charles had been in the exact spot where the door landed.

"You okay?" I asked. I pulled my legs from under him. Sharp pain radiated to my thigh, but I didn't think anything was broken.

Charles turned to see where I was. "Yeah. I guess." He slowly moved to a sitting position and stared at the broken, burning door at his feet. He turned back toward me and then back to the burning door. "Thanks," he said without elaboration.

I slowly pushed myself to my feet and tested my legs; both worked. Charles did the same. He grabbed his cane and hat. They had hit the parking lot farther from the flames than we had. My Tilley had managed to stay on my head the entire time.

Burning embers floated lazily through the air around us; heat from the inferno was more intense than ever.

This time, I didn't have to tell Charles to move away from the building. We hobbled to the other side of the lot, away from the flames. I struggled to catch my breath and bent over and rested my hands on my knees. Charles stared at the first-floor door.

I pointed to a fire truck that had carefully inched into the lot where we were. Two firefighters were pulling the heavy hoses off the truck and setting up to fight the blaze from the rear.

"Tell them you heard something," I said.

Charles nodded and then took a deep breath. He leaned on his cane—one of the few times it served a real purpose. He nodded a second time and slowly hobbled toward the truck.

Folly Beach had a skeleton crew of firefighters, and its public safety officers served a dual role—sworn law enforcement officials and when needed, firefighters. Tonight they were definitely needed.

I still had trouble breathing and looked around for somewhere to sit. The parking lot was my best option, and I lowered myself to the surface.

Charles had gotten the attention of one of the firefighters and was pointing his cane at the first floor door and waving his other arm in the air. The second firefighter joined the conversation and grabbed a fire axe from the truck and hurried to the door. He pointed for Charles to stay by the truck. His partner aimed the hose at the second floor while the axe-wielding firefighter attacked the door.

It took a couple of well-placed swings, and the pick-shaped pointed edge of the axe shattered the door's lock. The door swung open.

Charles leaned against the fire engine. His eyes never left the door.

The first responder pulled the door the rest of the way open. A small cloud of smoke rolled out from the top of the doorway, and a grateful, black-and-brown German shepherd bounded out.

Charles broke into a huge smile and darted toward the dog. He seemed to have forgotten his injuries and direction to stay by the truck. I think he was happier to have saved the dog than he would have been to rescue a church choir. He was on his knees hugging his new best friend.

I turned back to the burning structure and wondered what the odds were that the cause of the fire in the heavily engulfed building was accidental. After all, the sole occupant of the second floor was the Aker and Long Law Office.

A white Crown Vic with its blue LED emergency lights flashing slid around the corner into the small lot; it almost hit the fire apparatus. Charles and his new canine friend realized that they weren't in the safest place and hobbled toward me. A police-officer-turned-firefighter yelled at his colleague to be more careful but clearly needed the extra set of hands to help with the heavy, cumbersome hoses. Most of their efforts were focused on another small building behind the law offices and city hall. The firefighters kept a constant stream of water on the buildings to keep them safe from the flames and airborne embers. Charles, his new friend, and I stood under the roof of a carport in the back corner of the lot and away from the action. The appreciative canine panted as if it had run from downtown Charleston. We watched the harried activities unfold and tried to blend into the scenery.

A tall, trim lady ran around the corner and looked at us. "Thank God! There you are," she screamed.

I didn't recognize her and doubted she was that excited to see Charles or me. I was right. She was focused on the tail-wagging German shepherd that Charles still had his arms around.

"Rex, Rex ... Thank God ... Oh, Rex," she said. Tears filled her eyes, and she stooped to kiss the dog.

After a few more tears, "Thank God," and "Rex, oh Rex," we learned that she owned the candy store and that Rex was her "soul mate" and "night watchdog." She usually left him overnight in the small office in the rear. "To guard my loot," she said. No one would have known he was there from the front of the store.

The orange-and-red flames began to die down. They were replaced by a cloud of thick, black smoke. After Rex and his owner left, we both sat on the lot and out of the way. I was exhausted, and I suspected Charles wasn't far behind.

Officer/Firefighter Cindy Ash scampered around the building to help the crew in the parking lot. I could only imagine how many people had gathered in front of the building along Center Street. I wondered how many of them would have enjoyed watching the dog rescue and near-death experience Charles and I had and, thank God, lived through. This was the most entertainment to hit the beach in years.

I was relieved that the fire was out, the dog was saved, Charles and I had avoided major injuries, and the excitement was over.

I was also badly mistaken.

Chapter 27

I was about to suggest to Charles that we join the masses along Center Street when a black, unmarked Crown Vic slowly pulled in the lot. "Oh, oh," said Charles. He pointed his cane at the car. "The King has arrived."

The King was the acting director of public safety, Clarence King. Unlike Brian Newman, who was comfortable enough with himself to often wear civilian clothing while on duty, Acting Chief King was always in uniform—a uniform that was two sizes too small for his burly body. He was shaped like a manatee, but wasn't nearly as attractive.

Keep you eyes on the fire, Acting Chief, I wished. *Don't turn around.*

Another wish not answered. Instead of focusing on the heavily damaged building or his crew like any good chief would do, he looked over his right shoulder directly at Charles and me. The general consensus of his department, and anyone else who knew his professional skills, was that he was evil incarnate. I shouldn't have been surprised that he failed to do what a good leader would do.

"I thought I saw you slugs when I pulled in," he said. He slammed his car door and made a beeline for us. The scowl on his face was illuminated by the parking lot light on a pole in front of our not-so-successful hiding place. An inch-long scar over his left eye looked like an exclamation point to his unhappiness.

Charles smiled. "Hi, Chief King."

I had learned over the years to recognize the sincerity level of Charles's smiles. If Chief King knew what I knew about the greeting, he would have pulled his gun and shot my friend.

"Wipe that grin off your face," said King. He was out of breath and looked like he would burst the buttons on his shirt as he gasped for air. He paused to catch his breath, but unfortunately for us, he was still breathing. "What the hell are you two doing on city property?" His right hand rested on the butt of his firearm.

There weren't many people in all my years that I'd come to hate, but Chief King was close to crossing that line.

"We were over at GB's and heard the commotion," I said. "We walked over to see what was going on. One of your officers blocked everyone from going to Center Street, so we came here. Didn't want to get in the way."

I didn't see anything good about mentioning the dog rescue and thought my explanation sounded good. The acting chief must not have. "What do you troublemakers know about the fire? Any witnesses to you being in GB's?"

"Several people saw us," said Charles. He still smiled but wasn't working as hard to make it look real. "Check with Colleen, the waitress. We still have an unpaid tab. She'll tell you we were there."

"Hmm," he said. "I told you before that if I catch you meddling in police business again, you'll be spending a big part of the rest of your miserable life behind bars." He turned toward the fire, hesitated, and then turned back to us. "If I find that you know anything about this, you'll pray for only jail time."

He turned and started walking toward the fire engine and then stopped, turned back to the carport, and shouted, "Get off *my* property. Now!"

"Pleasant," said Charles. "How come you didn't remind him that your taxes pay his salary?"

Instead of wasting words with an answer, I started to walk the few yards to Erie Avenue and around the corner on Center Street to the front of the fire-ravaged building. My legs hurt with each step, and Charles sported a noticeable limp.

I was right about a crowd. Two backup units from James Island had arrived and were trying to maneuver around the mass of bystanders. A ladder truck, the newest addition to Folly's public safety arsenal, displayed its unique talent and allowed the firefighters access to areas of the building that they were previously unable to reach. The police were stretched thin and struggled to keep the curious onlookers on the opposite side of the street. There must have been a couple hundred or more vacationers and residents milling around; many carried plastic cups, a possible violation of the law, but I doubted the police had time to make sure that none of the cups contained adult beverages. There were a few familiar faces, but the one that got my attention belonged to Marlene, Sean's receptionist. She stood directly across from her building with her small dog cradled in her arms. Her husband stood beside her with his arm wrapped around her waist.

When I got closer, I could see tears streaming down her cheeks. The temperature was still in the eighties, but she trembled. We exchanged strained pleasantries, and then I asked her if anyone had been in the building. Charles quickly became engrossed in a conversation with Aaron, something about how to rebuild the building. Charles was trolling for paying part-time work.

Marlene looked at me, but it appeared that she was having a difficult time focusing. "I don't think there was anyone in there," she said. "Someone said the candy store closed about fifteen minutes before the fire. It was empty."

I didn't mention the candy store's night watchdog.

She squeezed her dog so tightly that I was afraid she would hurt the pooch. "I don't think I started it."

That surprised me. "Why would anyone think you did?" I asked. I reached over and petted the shih tzu. She lessened her grip on the poor canine. It sniffed my fingers and cocked its head as if to say, "Who have you been petting?"

"I was the last in there." She nodded toward the building. "Sean was gone; he left about two." She paused. "I closed up at five like I normally do. I know it was five because Aaron wanted us to go out on the boat and was irritated when I said I couldn't leave even though Sean wasn't there." She looked around. "I kept thinking he would come back; he usually doesn't leave that early, and he didn't tell me where he was going." She paused again and looked back at the building. "I think I turned the coffee off."

Charles had finished his conversation with Aaron and listened over my shoulder. "Would it be hard for someone to get in?" he asked.

"Not really. A couple of times, I forgot my key and opened the lock with my credit card. The fire escape door's just as easy. We keep all our papers in locked cabinets because it's so easy to break in." She looked at Charles, and her eyes opened wider. "Do you think someone set the fire?"

"No idea," said Charles. "Just something to think about."

I was no expert, but it looked like most of the fire damage was limited to the second floor, the law office.

"Did Sean have keys to Tony's filing cabinets?" I asked, but not sure why.

"No," said Marlene. "Neither did I. I asked him several times if he didn't think I should have keys in case of an emergency. He didn't get hostile but made it clear that that wasn't going to happen." She hesitated and looked around. "They weren't those big, old, safe-like cabinets," she said and hesitated again. "It wouldn't have been hard to open them."

Cindy Ash worked her way through the crowd. Her hair was frazzled—helmet hair—and her shoulders were covered with ashes. The smell of beer was strong from three college students standing beside us who had been staggering to stay vertical. They held plastic cups and enjoyed themselves way too much. Cindy gave them a nasty look but turned her attention to us.

"Mrs. Ryle," she said in her most sympathetic voice, "the chief would like to talk to you. Could you please come with me?" Cindy was already clearing a path for Marlene and Aaron. They wisely agreed to follow her.

I turned to Charles. "Do you remember if anyone said they found Tony's keys on his body?"

"Good question," said Charles. He tapped his cane on the sidewalk. "Maybe I'll let you join my detective agency."

What a deal, I thought and then quickly changed it to, *What was the deal?*

Chapter 28

Pancakes, burritos, biscuits, and rumors were served in heaping helpings at the Dog the next morning.

"Tony Long's killer torched the law office to cover his tracks."

"The secretary was sick of putting up with lawyers and set the fire."

"A power surge caused it, and every building on Folly Beach could go up in flames any minute."

"A body was found in the rubble."

"Two bodies were found in the office."

"Three bodies were shot through the head and found under Tony Long's desk."

Followed by a favorite of several diners, "God finally wised up and did what he should have done to lawyers long ago."

And I heard all of this in the first hour the restaurant was open. I must confess that I wasn't much different from the others who hung out in the best breakfast spot on the island. I had arrived as soon as the doors opened to hear what was being said about the conflagration. I was seated at my favorite table, and Amber had already decided what I wanted to eat. She had placed a cup of fresh fruit parfait with fruit, granola, and yogurt in front of me, accompanied by a smile. Her concern for my healthy diet far exceeded mine. What she decided that I wanted would have ranked fourteenth on the Dog's thirteen-item breakfast menu. Just because Amber was right didn't make her right. I returned her smile and said, "Thank you."

I was eavesdropping on a couple at the next table speculating on the cause of the fire when Dude Sloan skipped through the door. He was dressed in his surf shop uniform, the multi-colored, tie-dyed T-shirt with a peace symbol on the front. He waved a rolled-up copy of *Astronomy* magazine over his head. I assumed that was what it was, since it was the only periodical I had ever seen him read.

He spotted me in my customary spot against the opposite wall and headed my way. "Yo, Chrisster, get hot chocolate at candy melt?" he asked as he pulled up a chair and dropped his magazine on the table.

I went out on a limb and guessed that he referred to the fire over the candy store. Pain shot down my left leg at the thought of the flaming door tumbling toward Charles and me. I forced a smile and said, "Nope. Were you there?"

He waved his right arm in the air. "Flat-out fine flames. Smoke signals." He moved his arm back and forth in front of him. "Folly's finest fire fighters fighting fires." He hesitated, lowered his hand, and rested his elbows on the table. "Who could miss it?"

That was one of the longest statements I had heard him make—and to a yes-or-no question. I laughed. Amber wasn't nearly as concerned about Dude's weight and delivered an order of French toast with extra butter along with a cup of hot tea—his favorites. The inviting smell of the French toast tempted me to steal a bite when Dude, and especially Amber, weren't looking.

"So what do you think happened?" I asked as he attacked his French toast with abandon.

"First thought be Martians," he mumbled. "But not—they flew out Sunday." He took another bite. "Must be cat that kilt lawyer. Must be other barrister—Sean."

"Why Sean?"

"See him at bonfire?" asked Dude.

"No, did you?"

"Negative."

"So why him?"

"Your gallery be blazing; you be there. Be biting nails, pacing, destraught. Right?" He continued before I could figure out if there was a question to answer. "Barrister not there." He held out his hands and tilted his head. "See, he be flamethrower."

Dude could be right, flawed logic aside. It seemed that all clues pointed to Sean. I didn't want it to be him; but wanting meant zip. I wished Dude had made a better case for the Martians. And then I leaned back in my chair, looked at the granola in front of me, listened to the rumors swirl around the room, and watched Dude attack his French toast like he hadn't eaten since arriving on this planet. This was surreal.

At the time, I didn't realize how quickly I would move from surreal to breath-catching, terrifying, real.

Chapter 29

The rest of the day was anticlimactic after breakfast with Dude at the rumor mill. Charles had left a note in the gallery saying that he had a real, paying job for the day with Marlene's husband. It was a relief knowing that he could make some money; hopefully it would soften his transition from sales manager at the gallery to ... whatever. Local residents, and even a few vacationers, came in to share stories about the fire; the cash register sat untouched in the corner. I wondered if Sean knew more about Mrs. Klein's estate, but I felt bad about his tribulations and didn't want to ask.

Amber wanted me to go with her to her son's Babe Ruth League baseball game. It wasn't my idea of fun, but I couldn't come up with a good reason not to go. It could be a welcome diversion after the fire.

I arrived a little before six. She lived on the second floor in a building that faced Center Street. She was in the second of six small, identical apartments. The view wasn't spectacular, but the location was in easy walking distance of her work and every business on the island.

Jason was decked out in his uniform; the number seven was stenciled on back of the white shirt and "Tigers" proudly displayed on the front. His red-and-white cap was cocked sideways on his head. He was walking along the narrow, wooden walkway in front of the apartments.

"Looks like you're ready," I said.

Talking to a teenager for me was about as simple as carrying on a coherent conversation with Dude.

"Yeah," he said. "Mom'll be out in a minute. She's primping." He walked toward me and stopped. "Mr. Landrum, I have a question." He hesitated and then walked back to the far end of the walk and stopped in front of the last apartment.

I followed. When I got near the door, I heard a television blaring and felt the walkway vibrate from the thunderous volume.

Jason looked down at the walk and back up to me. His hands nervously played with his cap and then his belt. "Mom tells me not to be nosy," he said. I barely heard his words. The television continued to blare. He nodded toward the door and cupped his hands around his mouth. "Television's been that loud all day." He nodded toward the room. "The lady who lives there is always real quiet." He hesitated again. He looked around; his eyes darted from me to the railing overlooking the building and back to the door. "I never hear anything from there. I come up these steps all the time."

There was a set of stairs at each end of the walkway. The stairs closest to Amber's apartment were the most convenient to Center Street, but the back stairs led directly to the parking lot.

"Have you seen her today?" I asked.

"Umm ... no, just heard the television."

Jason was clearly concerned, and I didn't want to simply tell him not to worry about it. I asked myself *WWCD*—What Would Charles Do? For him, it would be a no-brainer. I knocked on the door. I didn't get a response to my first knock; no surprise, considering the decibels that blared out of the television. I knocked harder.

The door wasn't latched and opened about an inch the second time my fist struck it. The sound of the television doubled. The intense noise didn't bother me nearly as much as a pungent odor, a smell I had encountered way too often since moving to Folly Beach—the distinct, nauseating smell of death.

I stepped back, took a deep breath to regain my composure, and turned to Jason, who was inches behind me. "Go to your apartment and call the police. Tell them where I am and stay with your mom until I get there."

He glanced at the slightly opened door and then back to me. He didn't say a word and charged down the walk like he was trying to outrun a throw to first base.

I raised my elbow and slowly pushed the door with it enough to see in. The floor lamp sitting by a gray vinyl couch was on, and there was a small television in the corner. A local weather-person was talking about the chance of overnight storms. I peeked behind the door and didn't see anything. Amber's nearly identical apartment was always immaculate, or as much as it could be with a teenager living in it. This one was a disaster. Newspapers were strewn over the couch and on the floor; a pair of tennis shoes was on a small, plastic table by the couch, and it looked like the carpet hadn't been cleaned since Jimmy Carter was president.

I yelled "Hello?" over the blaring television. No answer. I slowly walked toward the back, and I wondered how I would explain being there if the resident stepped out of the shower and hadn't heard me. From the smell, I knew I was kidding myself.

I reluctantly looked in the bedroom; my worst fears were confirmed. I wouldn't have to worry how the resident would react.

She was dead. And it wasn't just any she; it was Colleen, the waitress from GB's.

Bile rose from the pit of my stomach. I turned to see how close I was to the bathroom toilet if I needed it. I pinched my nose and took a deep breath through my mouth; I calmed slightly, but the smell of human excrement made matters worse.

Colleen was lying diagonally across the unmade bed. Her head was cocked toward me and off the pillow. She had on the same slacks I remembered her wearing at GB's last night. Her black shirt with the GB's logo was on the floor beside the bed; a black, no-frills bra contrasted dramatically with her ivory, lifeless body. Her flat, rubber-soled, black work shoes were still on her feet. A frayed, lightweight, pink robe was neatly draped over a chair in the corner.

A hypodermic needle protruded from her left arm.

I stepped back and tried to catch my breath. I had nearly succeeded when a bloodcurdling scream filled the putrid air. I tripped on the corner of the bed and caught myself before landing on the deadly syringe.

Jason was in the bedroom doorway; his hands were clasped on his cheeks. He was as white as the sheets on the bed. Tears filled his eyes. He wouldn't have been trembling more if he had been standing on an iceberg.

I moved from the bed and hugged him as tightly as I could.

"I'm ... I'm sorry, Mr. Landrum," he mumbled through his tears. "I just wanted to see what was going on—I'm sorry."

I continued to squeeze him. His tears continued to fall.

I looked back over my shoulder at the bed. There was nothing I could do for Colleen. I didn't believe I had touched anything, but was so shaken that I wasn't certain. I carefully nudged Jason through the living room to the front door. He had regained some composure and was shaking less by the time we reached his apartment door. Amber met us at the door and took one look at her son and stepped back. I gave her a twenty-second overview and asked her to take Jason and to call the police.

She didn't ask any questions and ushered her son toward the couch. I headed back to Colleen's apartment to wait for the police. I didn't have to wait long. I heard a siren burst and heard a Folly Beach cruiser skid to a halt in the gravel lot behind the building. It was fewer than five minutes since I left Amber's apartment. I was relieved to see Officer Spencer; I was afraid it would be Acting Chief King—the one person who could make my nightmarish evening worse.

I gave Spencer a summary of what little I knew. He asked me to stay on the walkway as he went in the apartment. Cindy Ash was next to arrive; my luck was holding. I repeated my story and she followed Spencer into the building.

I looked over the balcony and noticed that a small crowd had gathered. Snapper Jack's Restaurant was nearby, and patrons on the rooftop bar had a clear view of the apartment and the arrival of the police. A handful of people stood in the gravel lot below and stared up at me.

Cindy came out first and was talking on her hand-held radio. She nudged me in the direction of Amber's apartment. "You may want to go in with Amber," she said in a tone that wasn't a suggestion. "King is on his way. It might not be good if you're the first person he sees. I'll have someone come over and take your statement."

My legs wobbled, and I grabbed the wooden railing on the short walk to Amber's. She had been watching out the window and opened the door before I knocked.

Jason was on the couch; his head rested on a pillow. Amber backpedaled and sat beside him after opening the door. I went to the kitchen and got a glass of water; my mouth was dry, but I was afraid to drink anything stronger—eating was the last thing on my mind.

I repeated to Amber what I had found, although I knew Jason would have told her most of it. My breathing was back to normal, but I couldn't get the smell, real or imagined, from my mind. I told them that Colleen had waited on us last night. Amber said she didn't know her well and that about the only time she saw her was at GB's. Colleen worked late and didn't get in until Amber was asleep. Jason said she always spoke to him and "seemed friendly."

The door shook as a fist pounded on it. I nearly fell off the couch; my nerves were shot. Amber jumped but only stared at the door. Jason asked if she wanted him to get it. She said no and told him to go to his room. He didn't argue. It could never be good news with someone knocking that hard; I reluctantly opened it.

"Where's the kid?" bellowed Chief King. His face was red, and his hands balled into fists. If looks could kill, my funeral would be in three days. "Get him in here. Now!"

Amber was holding the back of my shirt. "Why do you want Jason, Chief King?" she asked. She smiled, but her eyes didn't get with the program. She was livid.

"No problem, Amber," said the chief. "I just have a couple of questions for him."

Amber had waited on the chief many times and was on fairly good terms with him—at least civil terms; more than I could say for most people.

Jason had moved from his room to the center of the living room. King saw him. "Could you step outside a couple of minutes, young man?" asked the chief. He stepped out of the way so Jason could exit.

"Do I need a lawyer, Mom?" he asked. He shifted his gaze between Amber and the chief.

"No, hon. I'm going with you," she said. "The chief just wants to ask what you found." She turned and stared at the chief. "Isn't that right?"

He gave a paltry smile and nodded.

Jason and Amber weren't gone for more than five minutes. Jason tiptoed back into the apartment; his mom stood between him and the chief. King stuck his head around the corner and looked at me. His scowl was as big as ever.

"The kid saved your ass," he growled. "Buy him some ice cream." He moved back and then slammed the door.

Jason decided his team could survive the game without him. Amber suggested that we stay right where we were and call out for a pizza. I agreed, since I wasn't sure I was calm enough to drive. Jason shared that the chief wanted to know what had made me knock on Colleen's door and whether I had been there before Jason. He said he had told the chief, "the truth, the whole truth, and nothing but the truth."

Amber nodded agreement and hugged her courageous son.

That was the last we spoke of what had occurred fewer than fifty feet from where we sat. I did notice that Jason was never more than a couple of inches away from his mom and the security of the couch the entire time. I caught him staring at the front door several times; fear was evident in his eyes. The sight of poor Colleen lying on her bed, needle in her arm, stayed with me much longer.

Chapter 30

Conversation the next morning at the Dog was equally divided between the locals, who hashed, and rehashed, the fire and Colleen's death, and the vacationers, who, from their perspective, debated an equally serious topic: what time to go to the beach. Once again, I was the first to arrive at my table of choice. Amber quickly arrived with my coffee. Her eyes were red, so I asked if she was okay. She mumbled about not getting any sleep and added that Jason had been up most of the night. She headed to another table, and it struck me that the redness might be from tears. I hoped I was wrong.

I was accustomed to seeing Charles or Dude or occasionally Larry walk through the door and head to my table, but I was surprised to see Country Cal, someone who seldom frequented the Dog. I was more surprised when he looked around the room and then headed toward me. He wasn't wearing his stage garb—an aging, rhinestone coat and an off-white, hair-wax-grease-stained, classic Stetson—but new jeans and a red polo shirt. His spine was slightly curved from spending nearly fifty years leaning over a mike stand made for someone shorter than Cal's six-foot-three frame. He had already celebrated his sixty-sixth birthday, but years on the road living out of an old Cadillac Eldorado had taken their toll—he looked older.

Cal stopped about a foot from the table and gave me his big, toothy stage smile. "Mind if I join ya?"

I pointed to the empty seat. I liked Cal. We had met last year when he was suspected of killing several people from the boardinghouse where he lived. Charles and I had spent a great deal of time with him and even took a trip to Kentucky and learned way more than we wanted to about every venue along the route in which he had performed.

Cal folded his trim body into the seat and reached toward his head and then quickly pulled his hand back when he realized that his Stetson wasn't on its normal resting spot. He then raised his right hand and turned to the center of the restaurant. I had seen the maneuver several times; it was effective in bars when Cal wanted a beer but was wasted in the Dog. He lowered his hand but kept his stage smile aimed toward Amber, who finally noticed him and returned to the table.

He turned to me after she left with his order. "Hear about poor, ol' Colleen?"

I told him that not only had I heard, but I had also found the body.

"Oh geez," he said. "That had to be terrible. She was such a nice kid."

To Cal, anyone under the Social Security Administration's retirement age was a kid. "Was she into drugs?" I asked. I remembered how Cindy had speculated about Colleen's drug use when we talked about how thin—more accurately, emaciated—she was and how nervous she appeared.

Cal looked down at the table and then slowly looked my way. "Yeah. She went down the same road that I did a zillion years ago." He hesitated. "She knew about my past and told me about a month ago that she'd finally kicked the habit. She was happier than I'd seen her." Cal smiled. "She attributed it to love." He leaned back in the chair. "Guess who she was in love with?"

"Harley," I guessed. At least, that's who she had shared a motorcycle with the other night.

Cal tapped his hand on the table. "Oh," said Cal. "Should have known you'd know that, with you being a detective and all."

I ignored his detective comment. "Do you think she was off drugs?"

"For a while, maybe," he said. "Took me a couple of years to boot the devil out. My parents were alcoholics, and they tried year after year to stop drinking—never did. Not saying Colleen didn't succeed; it's a lot harder than people think."

"I know she was at work until the fire started," I said. "What about the rest of the night?"

"Let me think," said Cal. He rubbed his chin. "It was hectic after the fire. Most of the singers—using that term loosely—left, and I filled in with a few more songs. Good old Greg didn't want to deprive any of his customers of music to drink by. Sadder the song, more tears in the beer, and more beer. Yeah, I remember her there until it closed at twoish; she had to clean up after that. Why?"

"Just curious. Think she left with Harley?"

"That's a lot of thinking this early," he said. "No idea; didn't see him."

"Hmm! Hmm!" said Charles as he tapped his cane on the painted concrete floor. He had magically appeared by the table and stared down at Cal.

I looked at my watch and smiled. Cal was in Charles's self-appointed seat. "Late again," I said.

"Hmm," he repeated and grabbed one of the two vacant chairs at the table and plopped down like a pouting ten-year-old. He looked at me and then back to Cal. "Want to change seats?"

And he called me a creature of habit.

Cal said he would do Charles one better; he would leave. "You can have both of them," said Cal as he unfurled his tall frame and bowed toward Charles.

"Hmm," said Charles, for the third time, as Cal headed to the door. He moved to the chair Cal had vacated and sighed. Charles was back in his comfort zone.

Cal tipped his imaginary Stetson at Amber as he passed her near the exit. He tipped his air-hat once more and sidestepped to avoid running into Cindy Ash as she opened the heavy front door. She grinned at the grand, bordering on silly, gesture and headed directly to our table.

"Morning," I said. "Have a seat; Charles'll let you have his if you want."

She looked at me like I was a grasshopper and sat in one of the empty chairs. Charles grinned and asked her how Larry was.

Charles swore that he could tell from the early-morning glow on Cindy's face whether she had spent the night at Larry's rather than in her small room at Mariner's Breeze.

She turned a shade of red just shy of tomato soup and mumbled, "Fine." Before Charles could pursue his line of questioning, she continued, "I wanted you to know that the fire was arson."

"Wow," said Charles, forgetting about where Cindy had spent the night. "You sure?"

"The techs from Charleston's Explosive Devices Unit confirmed it this morning; my contact there called me. There's no doubt. They found evidence of an accelerant in three or four places in the suite."

Amber brought Cindy a mug of coffee and asked if she wanted anything to eat. Cindy declined and said she was on a diet and wanted to lose ten pounds by the wedding. Amber stared at me and said she wished other people would try to lose some weight. I was an advocate of the denial approach to many problems; she must have been talking about Charles.

"Do they think Sean set it?" I asked.

"No," said Charles sharply. Cindy didn't answer. "Why would he? If he wanted anything destroyed, all he had to do was take it, shred it, and be done with it. No, he didn't start the fire."

Good point, but I remembered what Marlene had said about each attorney having a key to his, and only his, filing cabinet. But she had also said that the cabinets were anything but burglarproof.

"Anything new on Colleen?" I asked.

"Not that I know," she said and turned toward the door. Ever since Acting Chief King had been appointed by our misguided mayor, he had treated Charles and me as pariahs and looked down, way down, on Cindy by association. "Still looks like a simple drug overdose." She excused herself and headed to work.

Charles looked into his mug and then at his left palm. I thought he might read a passage from it—the influence of Heather. He finally spoke. "Did I tell you about the first time I met Sean?"

I often tune Charles out, so I wasn't certain. "Don't believe so," I said.

"Didn't think I did." He maintained the gaze at his palm. "He'd just moved here and opened his law office. I'd been around for several years and worked a couple of days a week for a builder; did mostly remodeling. It paid cash—lowered my tax bracket ... well, anyway, we were working on a house by the Washout." He paused as Amber refilled our mugs. "Where was I?"

"Remodeling a house by the Washout?" I prompted.

"Yeah, well, the builder had the naïve owner, a fellow from Virginia, pay half down on the job—several thousand, a ton of money back then. That's when I learned that the guy was a fly-by-night operator ... he flew. Poof! Gone. Guess who was the only person left on Folly Beach who had worked on the job?"

"Guy named Charles?" I asked.

"Bingo," he said and pointed to me. "Maybe bunko."

"So what happened?"

"I heard the cops were after me. Didn't know what to do, so I walked up the stairs to the new attorney in town. Sean had just passed the bar, had student loans out the as—wallet. He was hungry as a starving shark in a cornfield for paying business."

I didn't have that many years left, so I had to move the story along. "And then what?"

"Then ..." he said and huffed. "I had seventeen dollars and thirty-five cents in my pocket, and in my bank account, in my IRA, and in my off-shore accounts ... and ..."

When will I learn not to rush him?

"Okay, okay," I said

Charles grinned and continued, "Sean listened to my sad story and told me his fees. No wonder lawyers have two American homes and three European cars. Well, I told him that I could pay for about seven minutes of his time." Charles smiled at the memory. "Sean laughed—a good sign, I thought. He looked toward his empty reception area and then said he was holding a grand opening sale and asked me for a dollar."

I stared at Charles, afraid to say anything.

"Well," he continued, "to make a long story short—"

"Too late," I interrupted.

He rolled his eyes. "Anyway, he met with the cops, talked to the prosecutor, and spoke to the homeowner. He got them to not charge me with anything ... not even turn me over to the feds for tax evasion ... all if I ratted on my former employer."

Charles looked back into his mug. "Chris," he mumbled, "anyone who would be that nice to a total stranger—a broke, looking-like-a-bum stranger—couldn't be a killer. He simply can't."

I nodded, but wasn't sure the logic was foolproof.

To the police, Colleen's death was a "simple overdose," and Sean "simply can't be the killer."

But nothing was *simple* on Folly.

Chapter 31

We left the Dog, and I was faced with the dilemma that I had faced on a recurring basis over the last few months: open the gallery or find an excuse—any excuse—not to. Charles wanted to check on Harley. There was my excuse *du jour*.

Mariner's Breeze Bed and Breakfast was on Sandbar Lane, within sight of Charles's apartment and the Sandbar Seafood and Steak Restaurant. The main—and possibly only—redeeming feature of the dilapidated B&B was that it sat on premium real estate; it backed up to the marsh and the Folly River. The aging, two-story wood building fit in well on Folly Beach. Paint peeled in large chunks from the formerly white exterior. A permanent *Rooms Available* wood sign was precariously attached at a forty-five-degree angle to a bracket by the front door. Half of the roof had been patched, and several shingles were twisted and broken on the other half.

There was a small gravel-and-shell parking lot in front and seven more spaces on the side. Harley's motorcycle wasn't in either lot, but Charles insisted on checking anyway. I said, "Okay," since it beat opening the gallery and listening to the doorbell not ring.

True to the axiom "Where Harley's Harley goes, so goes Harley," no one answered Charles's knock.

"We should have called first," I said.

"Have his number?" Charles asked.

I did, but it was at the house. I asked if Harley had a cell phone. Charles said he didn't have a clue, but maybe Sean had it. I couldn't figure what that had to do with now; I didn't ask. Charles knocked harder, but with the same results. My mind flashed back to when I had knocked on Colleen's door. A chill ran down my spine. Instead of anyone answering at Harley's, Heather couldn't resist seeing who was knocking on the door across from her apartment. She flung her door open and broke into a big grin when she saw Charles. He reciprocated.

Heather was in massage garb and had her purse over her shoulder and her straw hat in hand. Charles, being the detective that he was, asked if she was headed to work. She said Millie's had called a half hour earlier with a request from a customer, Conroy Elder, who was demanding an "emergency massage." He was flying to Baltimore, and he wanted to be loose for the flight.

Charles looked at me. "Isn't that the guy Marlene said fought with Long?"

I nodded.

Heather closed the door and pointed for us to walk with her down the steps. "Wouldn't surprise me," she said. "Elder is the most uptight client I've had. I need twice as long to loosen him up as my other clients." She started down the steps, and we followed. "His inner turbulence is much stronger than is healthy. I don't care how rich he is—he won't enjoy it when he dies from a frozen ticker."

We reached the parking area, and Heather put on her oversized hat. "What'd you need with Harley?"

"Just wanted to see if he was okay," said Charles as he matched her step for step. Heather didn't have a car and walked toward Millie's, about a quarter of a mile away. "I guess he was close to Colleen."

Heather stopped. "Close enough to make the building shake like it was in the middle of an earthquake about three times a week." She grinned at Charles and then turned to me. "If you catch my drift."

I wrinkled my nose. "When did you see him last?" I wanted her to talk but wasn't about to follow her to Millie's.

She reached the end of the street and leaned against the stop sign. "Night of the fire; he was in the crowd across the street from the action. Haven't seen him since; his cycle hasn't been here. Gotta go; don't want to keep Mr. Tense tight."

Charles offered her a ride, but she said she needed to decompress her body and awaken her *chi* before taking on "The Rock." Charles, the gentlemen, then said he would walk with her and that I could probably find my way back without him.

Two phone messages greeted me at the gallery. One was from my landlord, who wanted to offer to lower the rent and extend my lease for another year. The building had stood vacant for more than a year when Bob Howard conned me into renting it; the landlord desperately wanted to keep me there. If the landlord wanted me that much, he should have lowered the rent before I told him I was not renewing the lease. I deleted the message.

The second message was from Marlene. Sean had asked her to contact Charles, Harley, and me to meet him the next morning at nine o'clock at the Tides. He had rented one of the hotel's meeting rooms to work out of until he found a better alternative. It would be several months before his burned-out space was rebuilt. She also said she had talked to Harley, which answered the question about Sean having his cell number. I returned the call and said I'd be there and would tell Charles when I saw him. Marlene didn't tell me what it was about, and I didn't ask. Since the three of us were invited, I assumed it was to discuss the will.

Chapter 32

I looked down at Colleen on her bed with the deadly needle stuck in her arm, and then I shifted to Amber with a terrified look on her face as someone pounded on her door. That was enough to jolt me awake. I rubbed my eyes and realized that the horrible dream was more fact than fantasy. I had no interest in going back to sleep, even though it was well before sunrise and the meeting with Sean wasn't for four hours. I quickly showered and dressed, not because I was in a hurry but because I wanted to do anything to avoid thinking about the nightmare I had awakened from—the nightmare I had lived the last few days.

The Mr. Coffee machine sputtered through the last drops of brew, and I sat at the small kitchen table and stared at—well, stared at nothing. I had moved to Folly Beach so I could live out my mostly routine life in an environment with a mild climate and idyllic ocean, with a few good friends, to pursue my passion for photography and with any luck, sell enough of my photographs to fend off poverty.

Here I was, exactly where I wanted to be—the ocean two blocks away, with more friends than I ever had in Kentucky—and I sat here thinking of death, murder, fire, and if I gave in to my more depressing thoughts, rapidly heading to the natural conclusion of my life.

Nothing good came from sitting in the kitchen, staring at the wall, and moving closer to depression. I grabbed my Nikon and the one piece of photographic equipment I hated, a tripod, and headed toward the center of town.

A tattoo-covered arm on a young, unshaven construction worker held the door open for me, and I entered Bert's Market, Folly's iconic grocery, which specialized in everything from beer to bait and prided itself on never closing. The early-bird worker took a bite of apple, yawned, and showed teeth that would be a perfect *before* photo in a dentist's newspaper ad.

My house was within a nine-iron shot of Bert's, and over the years, I had spent more time in the store than some of its employees. The Tides' revised complimentary coffee policy encouraged me to take took advantage of Bert's twenty-four-seven coffee urn with the handwritten note taped above it that displayed one of my favorite words, *free*. Clint, one of the night clerks, was stocking the cigarette rack behind the counter, and two customers hovered near the processed breakfast food rack. From their disheveled appearance, they could have still been out for a night on the town or headed to a job on a Charleston street corner holding a cardboard sign announcing "Will work for food!"

Clint was one of the wannabes who sang each Tuesday at GB's. He was always pleasant at the store but seldom said more than what was necessary to complete the transaction. I was surprised when he stopped stocking the cigarette rack and walked over to me at the coffee urn.

He gazed at the concrete floor. His jet-black, six-inch-long, curly beard was pushed against his Bert's T-shirt. He hesitantly said, "Good morning."

I looked at him and nodded.

"Terrible about Colleen," he said and looked at me for a response.

"Sure is," I said. "Did you know her?"

He looked over toward the other two customers. They were on the far side and talking to Eric, another of Bert's unique employees, whose substantial beard made Clint's look like he had simply forgotten to shave that morning. Eric won the hair-length competition locks down. They were out of hearing range. "We sort of dated for a while," continued Clint. He paused again.

I wanted to ask what *sort of dated* meant, but since this was the most he had ever said to me other than the cost of whatever I was buying, I chose to move the conversation at his pace.

"Thought we had something going," he said and poured himself a cup of coffee. "Then that biker bloke made a move and swept her off her cute feet." Clint smiled. "My Ford Pinto couldn't compete with his big ol' Harley phallic symbol."

What could? I thought. I nodded.

He surprised me when he continued, "I feel bad, though. I thought she'd kicked the drugs. She told me she'd been clean since Christmas. She was real proud of that. Had a fairly shaded past, you know." He sipped his coffee and gazed at the other two customers, who were near the back of store.

I didn't know about her past and was certain that Charles would shun me for days if I didn't ask. "Shaded how?"

"Umm … well, I guess it's okay to tell you since she's … she's gone."

He paused and stared at the floor and then toward the front door. "She came over here from Atlanta. Umm, she was, let's say, a working girl." Clint smiled. "She jokingly called herself the not-so-happy hooker."

"Oh," I said. After all, it was early, and my profound words were still asleep.

"Well," continued Clint, "she came here to leave that life behind." He continued to stare toward the door. "She was happier here than ever."

He was near tears, so I didn't say anything.

Clint shook his head and finally said, "Think Harley kicked her off the wagon?"

"No idea," I said. I remembered that Cal thought she was clean, but that Cindy wasn't sure. Neither apparently knew about her "career" in Atlanta.

"You know, if Harley did lead her astray, it happened in the last week," said Clint, who was clearly in need of someone to talk to.

"Why?"

"The other open-mike night—not the night of the fire, but the week before—I was outside GB's having a smoke when she came out and looked down the street. She said she was looking for Harley." Clint maintained his gaze at the other two customers, but continued, "I asked, all friendly-like, how she was doing. She said great; said she was still off the hard stuff. She said she was overjoyed about her new life."

"Don't guess that meant booze?" I said.

"Nope, coke—still off it."

The two men finally made their grocery selections, and Clint headed to the register. Three more customers arrived and got in line behind the first two; Eric manned the second register. I walked to the exit, held up my Styrofoam cup in mock salute, and thanked Clint. He nodded and continued to ring up the purchases.

I walked to the pier and set my tripod up halfway to the end of the long walkway. I attached the Nikon and pointed it to the east over the Atlantic. The slightest glimmer of natural light reflected off the low, dark clouds near the horizon. While a bit jaded, I was still optimistic that someday I would capture the perfect sunrise photograph. I was a good photographer, and occasionally thought better than good, but I lacked the one characteristic that was necessary for me to be consistently better—patience.

I practiced patience, but all that resulted was me asking myself questions—difficult, frightening, and confusing questions.

Did good guy Sean kill his partner? If he didn't, who did? Did Sean set his office on fire? If he didn't, who did? Did Colleen die of an accidental overdose? Was it suicide? Did someone kill her? Could it have something to do with Long's murder? If it did, what could be the connection? Or could it be related to her secret past in Atlanta? Was meddling in the murder or murders worth risking my relationship with Amber over?

Of all the questions, I only answered one with certainty. Today would not be the day for the perfect sunrise photograph; raindrops started bouncing off my Tilley and my delicate camera perched confidently on the tripod. I quickly covered the camera, grabbed the tripod, and headed to the Tides before the rain intensified. I was exhausted, and it was only seven a.m.

Chapter 33

I was startled awake for the second time this morning, this time by a homemade cane, wielded by one Charles Fowler. It smacked my right knee. I had fallen asleep in the hotel's corridor, slumped in one of the lounge chairs that overlooked the pool and the pier. It was not the first time I had snoozed there, and Charles was quick to remind me of that. It was ten minutes before our scheduled meeting with Sean Aker.

After my initial "Ouch," I asked Charles whether Harley was there.

"No, he's late," said Charles.

I wasn't worried. Any concerns I might have had were answered when I heard the low, pulsating rumble of Harley's bike pull under the covered entrance to the hotel. I suspected it generated an early wake-up call for several guests.

The sour look on Harley's unshaven face was enough for Charles not to mention that he was late—late in Charles Standard Time. "Where is he?" asked Harley. His voice bellowed to all corners of the modern lobby.

Charles and I stood in front of the check-in counter. Behind us were steel free-floating steps that led to the next level. Charles grinned at Harley and nodded toward the stairs. "Up there, I suppose," he said. It was a good guess, since all the meeting rooms were on the mezzanine.

"Come on," grumbled Harley as he walked to the sisal-covered stairs and grabbed the handrail. The stairs were not only functional, but also provided a designer highlight to the lobby. The handrails were laced with vertical, brown wooden pieces shaped like sea oats—one of the many special features of the recently renovated hotel.

We followed Harley to the wide corridor at the top of the stairs. "Well, now where?" he continued to grumble. Undoubtedly, he would rather be anywhere but here.

I wasn't nearly the detective Charles was, but a computer-generated paper sign taped on the door of the second meeting room that read "Aker and Long, Lawyers" seemed like a clue. The note didn't have the panache of the florescent orange surfboard that had announced the firm to anyone who walked along Center Street, but it was effective. I didn't know whether Aker was behind the door, but was certain Mr. Long wasn't.

Marlene greeted us with a smile and shared that not only was Mr. Long not there, but Sean also hadn't arrived. The room was a typical hotel conference room, with tan-cushioned stack chairs slid against the back wall and two round folding banquet tables near the door but placed on opposite sides of the open space.

"When's he getting here?" asked Harley before Marlene finished her offer to go downstairs and get us coffee.

"Any minute, I hope," she said. She looked over at me and shrugged, a gesture I interpreted as, "What's he so cranky about?"

I said we would wait in the large, wide corridor that all the meeting rooms opened to. Harley was more surly than usual, and I didn't want to expose Marlene to any fits that he might feel the need to throw. He had already established that law offices were not his favorite hangout, even if they were in a beachfront resort hotel.

Harley plopped his compact body down in one of the dark-brown wicker chairs near a window opening onto a panoramic view of the ocean.

Charles grabbed another chair and moved it beside our nervous friend. "Harley," said Charles, who was looking out at the backlit waves, "I was sorry to hear about Colleen. Were you two close?"

Charles was not only expressing sympathy but also beginning a fishing expedition. I grabbed a chair and moved it close to the two of them.

"Getting close," he replied. "I really liked her; she was fun." Harley followed Charles's gaze out the window.

Charles waited as long as his impatient curiosity would let him. "Was she back on drugs? Hear she had kicked it for a while."

I was glad that I hadn't had time to tell him about Colleen's other less-than-legal activity.

"Looks that way, don't it?" he said.

It looked that way, I thought. But looks are deceiving on Folly Beach. "When was the last time you saw her?" I asked.

"Hell, don't know for sure," said Harley. He looked at me and then at Charles. "Sometime before the big ol' fire, I guess. Been out of town."

"Where?" asked Charles.

I was afraid Harley would think we were tag-teaming him, but was anxious to hear his answer. Especially after Heather told us she had seen him outside the law office as it went up in flames.

Harley gave Charles a scowl. "Here and there," he said.

Sean arrived before Charles could handcuff Harley to a table, point a high-powered lamp at his face, and continue the interrogation. Harley would have been seriously conflicted if he had realized that he was saved by a lawyer.

Sean mumbled an apology and waved us into his temporary office. He asked Marlene to go downstairs and get us coffee without asking if we wanted any. It struck me that he wasn't comfortable with her hearing whatever he had to say.

I expressed condolences about the office and asked if he had heard what happened.

"Nobody's saying," he said. "I feel horrible but really lucky." He paused and shook his head. "Marlene and I were lucky. We'd just left right before it started." He shook his head again. "Lucky, really lucky."

I glanced at Charles. His head was cocked to the left. He had caught the discrepancy between Sean's version and Marlene's. Marlene had said that Sean left much earlier.

I didn't share that it was arson.

"Enough about that, fellows," said Sean. "Let me get to the point. You must have a busy day, and I don't want to waste your time."

What did he know about our day that I didn't know? Instead of asking "busy doing what?," the three of us nodded; Harley nodded and grunted.

"I'm about ninety percent through Mrs. Klein's paperwork," said Sean. He shook his head. "What a mess." He took a manila folder out of a briefcase and placed it in front of him on the banquet table. He fiddled with the tab as he talked. "I believe there are two certificates of deposit left that I haven't quite figured out, but they're fairly small. I can't tell if she cashed them or they're still out there." He hesitated and looked at each of us and then opened the folder. "It looks like her husband had done a pretty good job of managing money. He wasn't wealthy, but managed it well."

"How much?" asked Harley. He leaned from side to side in his chair as if he had hemorrhoids. He stared at the folder and then at Sean.

Sean ignored the question. "I took the liberty of talking to a real estate appraiser from Charleston and then two developers who contacted me when they found out I was handling the estate. I have two cash offers." He tapped his palm on the folder. "Now remember, Mrs. Klein still had a mortgage, so not all of the sale price would go to the estate."

Harley pushed his elbows down on the chair arms. I thought he was going to spring out of the chair and grab either the folder or Sean's throat. "How much?" he repeated.

Marlene opened the door behind us. She balanced three cups of coffee. As soon as she heard Harley bark, she eased back out.

"Let me get to the bottom line," said the wise attorney. "I'll go over the details later if you want them."

"Good," said Harley.

"It looks like after attorney fees, taxes, filing fees, on and on, the three of you should net about one-point-five million."

Charles looked at Sean. His eyes bulged. "Gulp."

I said, "Wow."

And Harley blinked; he looked down at the folder and then up at Sean. "Can I get mine today?"

Sean started to laugh but masked it with a cough when he realized that Harley was serious. Harley stared at the folder like there were three checks in it for five hundred thousand each. Sean explained that the investments and savings could be made liquid in a few days, but that any proceeds from the property would have to wait until the sale closing. Harley wanted to know how quickly the closing could be scheduled. Sean did his best to explain the timeline on selling the property and Mrs. Klein's stocks and the tedious process of closing the estate. Bottom line, it could be up to nine months before everything was settled. Harley looked at Sean like he had just keyed the side of his motorcycle.

Finally, we agreed to let Sean do whatever was necessary to speed it up and use his best judgment on the various complexities of the process. He did say he could cash the certificates of deposit and close some of the stock accounts and free up a hundred thousand dollars or so within a week. The rest would take time.

Harley brusquely responded, "Get to it."

We shook hands all around and left the temporary office. Marlene was in the corridor in one of the chairs we had been sitting in before Sean had arrived. Three cups of coffee were getting cold beside her on the ocean-blue-and-tan-striped carpet. Harley glanced her way and then bounded down the stairs. He gave us a half-wave bye.

Charles and I walked slowly to the front door. The electric door opened, and we stepped out into the morning humidity.

"You noticed that Harley didn't answer your question about where he had been." I said. "We know he was at the fire; he seems to have forgotten."

"Yeah," said Charles. "I also noticed that Sean lied to us about when he left the office the day of the fire."

"Marlene told us that he left at two," I said. "Sean said they'd left together; around five if Marlene was correct."

"So what?" asked Charles.

"So what, indeed," I said.

Harley roared out of the parking lot and turned right on Arctic Avenue.

Charles watched the brake light on Harley's cycle as he swerved to avoid a young boy on the way to the beach. "Forgotten, right. As President Johnson once said about Richard Nixon, 'I may not know much, but I know chicken shit from chicken soup.'"

Chapter 34

Charles spent just shy of a nanosecond longer talking about Harley and Sean's misstatements before his mind and mouth catapulted to the inheritance. Had I heard what Sean said about a half million dollars for Charles? Would I repeat what Sean said to make sure Charles had heard it correctly? Charles said he was "wealthy beyond comprehension," pondered the need for a "financial guru," and gave out a guttural "wow" that could be heard by nearly everyone in the eastern time zone. He then remembered that he had to make a delivery for Dude and peddled away on his Schwinn. How quickly the wealthy can fall.

I tried not to think about the money. I hadn't seen a penny and felt bad that Mrs. Klein hadn't had any family and had to leave her legacy, and money, to three near-strangers who did what anyone would have done to save her from Hurricane Greta. Besides, I kept thinking about Harley's reaction. Why was he so anxious to get his money and leave Folly Beach? Coupling that with his relationship with the late Colleen, I was getting a weird feeling. And why would Sean have lied about something as inconsequential as when he had left the office? Had Marlene lied to us? And could she be a suspect?

I wouldn't have hesitated to talk to Brian Newman about Harley and maybe about Sean, but never with Acting Chief King—my death-wish wasn't that strong. I was on less-than-positive terms with Detective Burton, the primary on the Long case, so that left Detective Lawson. I reached her on her cell and began to tell her about Harley. She interrupted and said she would rather not talk on the phone and asked if I could meet her; she was starved. I suggested we meet at Al's Bar and

Gourmet Grill, a restaurant where we had met before; but she said she wouldn't have time and suggested McDonald's on Folly Road.

The restaurant was ten minutes from the house, so I opened the gallery with more enthusiasm than I had in months. I looked at the walls and the displayed photos and smiled. I should be able to keep it open. But did I want to? If Charles were not in the equation, what would I do?

Time nearly got away from me; fortunately, traffic headed toward Charleston was light, and the traffic lights were kind. I pulled into the McDonald's just a couple minutes late—or in Charles Standard Time, twelve minutes late. Karen was at a small window table with a Big Mac, large fries, and soft drink spread out in front of her. She was runner-thin, so full-time detecting must burn a lot of calories. She apologized for not waiting, said that she didn't have much time. I sat rather than heading for the growing lines at the counter; I'd eat later.

She was dressed in work garb: an off-white blouse and navy pantsuit. She had the unmistakable aura of a law enforcement official, albeit a lovely one.

"So, why do I have the pleasure of a visit? What about Harley?" she asked. She smiled and leaned back in the tiny swivel-chair; but I knew, despite the casual look, that time was our enemy.

"I hate to bother you about this," I said. "It may not mean anything, but you're the only one I could come to."

I told her about Harley's relationship with Colleen and how anxious he was to "get out of Dodge"—or in this case, Folly. I shared what I had heard about Colleen kicking drugs and how it seemed suspicious that she would overdose. And finally, how Harley had denied being around the night of the fire when Heather said she had seen him in the crowd.

I didn't share the time discrepancy about when Sean had left the office.

Karen reminded me how I had described Heather as being a bit nutty. Would she be credible? Could she have been mistaken about seeing Harley? I told her the more I was around Heather, the less nutty she seemed.

Karen took a bite of her burger and grinned. "Knowing your friends, you have an elevated nut-tolerance." Her grin disappeared. "Do you think Harley had something to do with Colleen's death? Just because he was in town doesn't mean he started the fire."

"I have no idea," I confessed. "It all seems strange. It's crossed my mind that he might be connected to Long's murder. But really, no idea."

Karen looked around the restaurant and then at the ceiling. "It's a big stretch to think a biker, with no ties to anyone here, would kill a lawyer, burn another lawyer's office, and then kill his own girlfriend."

"All true; I agree," I said after feeling foolish for the lack of motives in my analysis. "But I saw how uncomfortable he was the first time we were in Sean's office and then how he reacted this morning."

"I'm not saying you're wrong; just that on the surface, it doesn't make sense."

"You're right," I said. "Now that I say it, I agree."

"Tell you what," she said as she began clearing the wrappers off the table, "I'll share this with the sheriff and Detective Burton. They may scoff, but they'll have the information."

We stood, and I offered to walk her to the car. She smiled, said that wasn't necessary and that I should get lunch. She asked about Amber, and I mumbled, "Fine." Karen gave me a peck on the cheek and then headed out. Not quite the most professional exit gesture, but it felt good. I was also relieved. Even if I was terribly off-base, I had shared my concerns about Harley with the "proper authorities," something others—mainly the "proper authorities"—had reminded me to do since I arrived on Folly Beach. I had done all I could do.

Or had I?

Chapter 35

Before the traumatic events surrounding the fire and Colleen's tragic death, Amber and I had planned to have supper tonight at the Sandbar Seafood and Steak Restaurant. Jason was going to spend the night with Samuel, a friend from school, and Amber looked forward to a night out.

She waited for me on the sidewalk in front of her apartment building. I was always amazed how great she looked after a long day on her feet at the Dog. She wore a turquoise short-sleeved blouse and white shorts. Her hair, tied back when she was at work, flowed over her shoulders. She hopped in the car as soon as it stopped; to delay would have resulted in a horn honk from the driver behind me. Amber usually leaned over to kiss my cheek, but this time she just patted my right thigh and pulled on her shoulder harness.

The restaurant was in the same rambling buildings that housed Charles's small apartment. The well-known dining spot had been in and out of operation since the late 1950s and was one of the island's few out-of-the-way restaurants and had the reputation of having one of the best menus. It also featured a panoramic view of the Folly River and sunset.

On the short ride to the Sandbar, I asked Amber about work, whether Jason was still going to be away overnight, and how he was adjusting after the trauma of the other night. She gave one- or two-word answers—not a good sign. She sat erect and silent.

The parking lot was nearly empty when we arrived. We had beaten the crowd and were rewarded with a prime table beside the large windows that faced a small pond with the Folly River in the background. Amber continued her one-person crusade to get me to eat more healthily, so I let her order. My main contribution was to request a bottle of mid-priced Chardonnay. I avoided the word *broiled* if *fried* was nearby; Amber didn't give me a chance to utter the evil five-letter word. Broiled flounder with red rice and fat-free dressing on a house salad would be my dining fare. I didn't argue, especially since she appeared tenser than I had seen her in years, maybe since I'd met her. I tried to lighten the mood and told her that Charles was trying to cut back on unhealthy food and the last time we were together, he'd ordered raw onions and asked if they had celery he could dip in a bowl of chocolate syrup. I thought the story deserved more than a distracted smile—not tonight.

The salads arrived, her glass of wine disappeared, and I saw progress. She had shared a couple of items of gossip from the Dog and actually laughed when I told her about Charles caning me awake at the Tides.

The waitress slid the boring broiled fish in front of me, and then I told Amber about the meeting with Sean and the will and that I was thinking about keeping the gallery open. She said she was happy about for me, but her eyes told a sadder story. I finally garnered the courage to ask what was wrong. It wasn't my first mistake of the day, but it surely was my biggest.

Amber took a bite and then looked out at the river and the sun as it descended behind the trees. Her lack of reaction made me wonder if she had heard me. A minute later, I had my answer.

"It's nice that Cindy and Larry are getting married," she said, and continued to stare out the window. "They're cute together; made for each other, I think." She paused, looked back at her wineglass, and took a sip. "Chris, why do you have to get involved in all the dirty, horrible stuff that happens? Why? You could get killed." She looked me in the eyes; tears formed in hers. "I had a husband run out on me, and it took years to get over it. I can't put Jason through losing someone like that. I can't."

I followed her segue from Cindy and Larry to Jason. It was a path she had started down before but had never been as blunt about our relationship. She had never said it directly to me, but I knew—from my gut and comments by our friends—that she wanted to get married. In my weaker—or stronger, depending upon your perspective—moments,

I wanted that too; but I couldn't get around doubts about our age difference, the thought of bringing a teenager into my home, and my selfish, stuck-in-my-ways attitude about my style of life.

"Amber, sometimes it doesn't make sense, but I get involved when my friends are involved. I know I've told you this before, but I've never had friends like I have here."

She wiped a tear out of her right eye with the back of her hand and then interrupted. "Jason hasn't slept hardly any since you exposed him to that terrible scene." Her hand gripped the fork like it was trying to escape. "He wakes up screaming—two, three in the morning. He's terrified." She put the fork on the table and stared into my eyes. "My God, Chris. He's twelve and having nightmares! Your friends are more important than Jason? More important than me?" she said sharply.

"No, but ..."

"But what?" She banged her palm down on the table. "Butting into a murder of a lawyer you hardly knew ... trying to dig up dirt on a biker you barely know ... and then exposing my son to a dead drug addict ... all those things are more important than our relationship? If you think that, hell with you!"

I reached across the table for her hand. She pulled it away like she'd grabbed a rattlesnake. "Amber, you know they're not more important than you."

"Then prove it," she said. The tears continued down her cheeks. She wadded her napkin and threw it on her barely touched entrée. "Leave the filthy, dangerous police work to the cops. Walk away from whatever happened with Long, the waitress, and that damned biker."

She abruptly slid her chair back and stood. The couple at the table next to ours were turned to us but pretended to look at the sunset. "I'm ready to go home," said Amber. There was no doubt that she meant it.

Chapter 36

"Was she serious?" asked Charles.

We sat under a palmetto tree on the small patio that also served as the entrance to Kirby's Café on Hudson, which until recently had been Li'l Mama's, another of Folly's quaint and rustic restaurants, located in a two-story building off Center Street. They didn't have celery or chocolate syrup for Charles and were fresh out of anything broiled, or so I assumed, so we shared a cheese pizza for our Saturday lunch and Landrum Gallery staff meeting.

I had shared bits and pieces from last night's abbreviated meal with Amber. I was prone to divulge less than Charles hoped for, but gave him a good feel for her mood. "Yeah, she was pretty upset. You know how much her life revolves around Jason. She believes I put him in danger."

"It's not all about Jason; she doesn't want to get hurt again," said Charles. "She loves you too much just to say adios. You'll see." He stuffed another bite of pizza in his mouth and mumbled, "Maybe."

I felt hope until Charles got to the pizza-infused "maybe." Our uplifting discussion was interrupted by Country Cal, who ambled around the corner of Center Street and pointed at us. "There you are," he said as he reached the low, red, wooden railing that separated the outdoor dining from the parking spaces. He gasped for breath and was more stooped than usual. Charles waved him to our table. Cal caught his breath and pulled out the empty plastic chair and picked up a slice of pizza. "I've been looking all over for you," he said after taking the first bite. "Did you know you aren't at the gallery, or at the Dog, or Rita's, or home, or ..."

Charles raised both hands above his head. "Whoa," he said, "before you name seventy-nine more places where we aren't, you found the one where we are—adjust. What's so important to search the universe for us?"

Cal grinned at Charles and then aimed his patented stage smile at the lady who was cleaning a recently vacated table. "Could I get what he has to drink?" he asked and pointed to Charles's beer.

The woman gave an equally oversized smile to Cal and pointed at the door. "Sure, hon, hop right up and go in there and order yourself one."

She looked like she could bench press Cal, so he lowered the wattage of his smile, but still headed inside. "Well worth the price of admission," said Charles as Cal opened the door. It was cloudy, so we weren't in direct sunlight. There was no reason to be in a hurry. I got more curious as to why Cal actually had tried to find us at a few of our regular hangouts, if not quite the rest of the universe, as Charles said.

Cal's beer was half gone by the time he folded his tall frame back into the chair. "You two are sharper than the average prairie dog," he said. "I need your advice."

I felt certain that that must have been a compliment in Cal's native Texas, so I nodded. Charles moved closer to the table, placed his elbows on the surface, and looked at Cal. He wasn't used to being asked for advice and wanted to be ready.

"Greg Brile asked me to be a partner in GB's. What do you think?"

"I think we need more information," said Charles.

I gave a bigger nod.

Cal looked around to the other tables. Only two were occupied, and they were on the opposite side of the patio. "Okay," he said, "here goes." He reached in the back pocket of his cutoff jeans and pulled out a piece of blue-lined notebook paper. It looked like the tablet paper I used to practice the alphabet on in the first grade. "Knew you'd want it all; my memory's not quite as good as it was. I took notes." He looked down at the paper and turned it upside-down and began reading as if he hadn't seen the words before. "I was over at GB's the other night, and Greg asked if he could talk to me—outside. I figured he was either going to say he couldn't pay me any more to play on the weekends, or maybe to give me a big raise, or ..."

"What did he want?" asked my impatient tablemate.

"Let me grab another beer," said Cal. He didn't wait for an answer and was headed for the door. He was back before I could figure out whom he'd pointed to when he told the lady inside to put the beer on someone's tab. I suspected that I knew.

Cal returned to his chair and continued, "Okay, here goes—again. Greg said that he was getting too old to spend all his time in GB's and had had his eye on me for a year or so. He called me reliable, sort-of-talented, and said I got along with most everyone. I bristled a bit at the 'sort-of-talented' remark, but figured he wasn't a big fan of country music and had a tin ear when it came to quality country crooning. Well, anyway, he said he'd give me a percentage of the business and it wouldn't cost me a red cent." Cal stared into his near-empty second beer bottle. "He knew I didn't have any cash, red or otherwise, to buy my way into GB's."

"What's the catch?" asked Charles.

"Don't think there's one. I'd have to sing on weekends for what he's paying me now and be there two other nights a week so he'd have more time off."

"That's all?" I asked.

"Well, sort of. On those nights when I'm not singing, I'd be bartender, and bouncer, and in charge of the staff; and, oh yeah, take the money and balance the books."

"Do you know how to do that?" I asked. I'd put money on already knowing the answer.

"Nary a lick," he said.

"That's not much," said Charles.

"What do you think about the offer?" I asked.

"Mixed feelings, my friends, mixed feelings." Cal leaned back in the plastic chair and rubbed his hands through his long, gray hair. "First, it made me feel good that someone thought I could do more than just sing; gave me a moment of pride, to be sure. Second, it would give me a way to earn some money and put down solid roots here; I don't want to leave. And whatever the percent is, it'd be the first thing I'd own that won't fit in my car."

"Negatives?" asked Charles.

"Shoot," he said with a grin, "I've never managed anything in my life; have trouble managing myself. My freedom will go out the window. I've spent my whole life bopping up on stage, sharing a few tunes, and then hightailing it out of town. Didn't have to worry about cleaning up, paying the help, counting the dough, throwing out the drunks, anything except finding the road out of town. Can't screw up too much that way."

"When does he want to know?" I asked.

"'Soon,' he said. Not sure what that means, but I need to know. It's driving me crazy." Cal reached for his bottle of beer and noticed it was empty; he set it aside and grabbed Charles's bottle and took a drink.

Charles started to grab the bottle but pulled his hand back. "How well do you know him?

Excellent question, I thought.

The sound of a large diesel food-delivery truck stepped on Cal's answer, so I asked him to repeat it. The strong smell of burnt diesel fuel filled the air.

"How well does anyone know anyone?" said Cal, for a second time.

Charles waved his hand in front of his face like he could fan away the diesel aroma and then shook his head. "I didn't ask for a philosophy lesson," said Charles. "Do you trust Greg?"

"Sure," he replied. He looked at Charles and then to me. "He's let me sing whenever I wanted to, paid me for my weekend gigs in cash—makes life simpler that way, you know. Nope, no reason not to trust him."

"How's the bar doing?" I asked. "I'd heard it was on the verge of bankruptcy last year before he changed the format to country."

Cal smiled. "Asked Greg that exact question yesterday. Wanted him to think I knew what I was talking about." He leaned back in his chair and folded his arms in front of him.

"Well," said Charles, "what'd he say?"

"Said I could come in and check the books and stuff before I decided."

"Would you know what you were looking for?" I asked.

"Not a clue," said Cal. "I figured that if he made the offer, he must not have anything to hide."

I didn't want to clutter Cal's decision-making process, so I didn't tell him that was one of the effective techniques of a con artist. I suspected that Greg knew that Cal would be clueless about the high finances of a bar, especially since much of the business is in cash—hard to trace, hard to account for.

"So what should I do?" asked Cal. He looked at Charles and then turned to me.

I took that as my turn to answer. "Cal," I said, "it's your call. I don't know enough about GB's to have an opinion. Greg seems like a nice guy, but I only see him dealing with customers, where he has to be nice. I don't know anything about the finances, although the bar seems to do a brisk business. Bottom line, I guess, is that since it won't cost you anything to get in, I don't see where you have much to lose."

Cal nodded but didn't respond. He cocked his head toward Charles.

"Sounds like a job for CDA, the Charles's Detective Agency," said Charles. "I could do a forensic analysis of GB's books ..."

"Uh," Cal tried to interrupt.

Charles gave him a sideways glance. "Could interview his employees, check all his legal-like filings ..."

Cal raised his right hand to stop Charles; he then leaned forward in his chair. "Mr. Detective," he said, "I don't know a lot about anything but singing, but it seems to me that a new business—the CDA, for example—should start out with something a bit smaller." He paused and held his palm over his forehead. "I've got it: how about investigating the theft of some kid's tricycle? Or how about finding out who's been taking two newspapers from that box over at the hotel and only paying for one?"

Charles had been well-accustomed to rejection throughout his life of leisure and handled Cal's rebuff without violence. He snarled. "Okay," he said, "don't come crawling to me when old Greg does you wrong."

"I appreciate your concern," said Cal. "I will ask to see all paperwork; I can be pretty good at pretending. Remember, I've sung my hit song just over three zillion times and can still act like I'm enjoying it every time." He strummed an air guitar and hummed a few bars. "Know how sick of that song I get?"

I could guess, but chose not to. Charles was still irritated that Cal had rejected his services. He frowned.

Cal took the last bite of his adopted pizza and said he needed to run. "Got to head to the library and find a book on bookkeeping. Thanks for all your *helpful* advice."

I suspected he leaned toward sarcasm with that last remark.

Charles watched Cal go around the corner. "*Bookkeeping for Dummies* will be a graduate course for our crooner."

And that was spoken by someone who actually thought he could do a forensic analysis of GB's books. I spent another hour and listened to Charles talk about his newfound wealth, or as he put it, "loads of lucre." He first said he would be able to retire, but after three seconds of thought, ruled that option out, since he hadn't been on anyone's payroll since he moved to Folly Beach. Then he said he would rent a big office, hire a sexy, long-legged secretary, open the Charles's Detective Agency, put his feet up on a big mahogany desk, and bank wadded-up copy paper off the wood-paneled wall into a trash can. Then he conceded that Cal's recent rebuke might make him reevaluate his business plan. And then he said that if I would use some of my "load of lucre" to keep Landrum Gallery open, he *might* consider staying on as sales manager.

I told him I would think about it but wasn't ready to decide. It wasn't the answer he wanted, but he seemed to accept it for now; at least I didn't say the gallery was history.

Charles had agreed to man the gallery while I ran a few errands; a trip to the grocery was first on my list. Saturday afternoon in-season was a busy time for the Piggly Wiggly, a large chain grocery on Folly Road a couple of miles off-island. Most vacationers spent an hour or so their first day at the beach in the store stocking for their time on Folly Beach, and it was the grocery of choice for most locals. Today was no exception, and I had to park closer to the road than to the building. I would normally do most of my grocery shopping at Bert's, less than a hundred feet from my house, but decided a ride would do me good.

"Hey Chris, did they let you off the island?"

I turned and was pleased to see Brian Newman push a cart up behind me. He stood more erect that I had seen in a long time; color was back in his face, and unless you knew about his health problems, you would think that he was in perfect shape.

I stopped, angled my cart off to the side of the aisle, and shook his hand. His grip was as strong as he appeared to be.

"I heard something about you yesterday," he said. His face didn't give anything away. Many years in law enforcement had paid off. "Rumor has it that you and you-know-who are nosing into the Long killing." He continued to stare at me.

Before I could confirm or deny the rumor, I was saved by the smiling, attractive face of Brian's daughter, who had walked up behind him and put her arms around his waist. "Are you keeping Dad from grocery shopping?" she said.

"Yep," I said and returned her smile. "He was struggling with deciding on which of the seventy-three choices of Oreos to get. Men shouldn't be subjected to those kind of decisions."

Karen balled her hand into a fist and playfully hit my arm. "Don't give him an out; I just was getting him trained to do grocery shopping," she said and hit me again. "Men!"

Brian clearly had heard enough about grocery shopping. "I was telling Chris about the rumor that he was butting in the Long case." Brian gave me a more hardened police stare. "And I was telling him that *if* the rumor was true, he should butt out and leave the policing to the police. Isn't that right, Chris?"

"That's what he said." I suspect that both highly trained, experienced law-enforcement officials noticed that I hadn't said *yea* or *nay* to the rumor. And after all, wasn't it Brian who shared all his investigative secrets with Charles?

We visited a couple more minutes and talked about the weather and how crowded the store was before Karen pointed into their cart and said they needed to get to Brian's condo before his ice cream melted. They headed toward the check-out line, and I walked toward the wine and beer department. I was surprised a moment later when Karen tapped me on the shoulder.

"Can you meet me in about a half hour?" she asked and looked back down the aisle to make sure her dad hadn't seen her.

"Sure," I said.

"How about Kronic Coffee?"

"I'll be there."

She nodded and grabbed a bottle of wine and rushed to the front of the store. The coffee shop was in the opposite direction from home, so I put my chilled bottle of wine back in the cooler and wandered around the store—more accurately, wandered and wondered. What could Karen possibly want that she didn't want her dad to hear?

Chapter 37

Kronic Coffee was a locally owned shop located in a tiny strip center on Folly Road a few miles from the beach. The attractive, yellow, teal-trimmed building had become a popular hangout for locals and provided wireless Internet access and comfortable leather seating inside and a couple of outdoor tables for good-weather coffee sipping and conversation. A large, green-white-and-red-striped Italian flag with the word *espresso* printed diagonally across it was proudly displayed on the porch.

Karen's car wasn't in the lot, so I ordered coffee and then grabbed the table under the flag before someone else took it. No sooner had I taken my first sip when the dark-blue, unmarked detective's car turned in and parked on the opposite side of the property. Her long, confident gait as she crossed the parking lot made her look like the athlete I knew she had been.

"Hmm, started drinking without me," she said. A sly grin alleviated any doubts about the seriousness of her comment. She removed her pantsuit jacket, carefully draped it on the back of a chair, and strolled inside to get a drink.

"How do you think Dad's doing?" she asked when she returned.

"Looked great to me," I said. What I really thought was that there was absolutely no reason he shouldn't be back on the job.

"He's still a little weak, but blames it on age," she said. "Not being able to go to work is eating at him more than anything; I think that's why his energy is low—just sitting, sitting and pouting." She paused and smiled at a little girl trying to open the door. The child's mother stood back to let her daughter open it by herself. "Doing nothing will wear you out more than work."

I nodded, but still wondered why she wanted to meet me. I doubted it was to talk about Brian's recovery and his frustrations. I didn't have to wait much longer.

"There're a couple of things I wanted to let you know about," she said and then took a long sip of iced coffee. "I didn't want to say anything in front of Dad—you know he doesn't want you nosing in the case."

He had made that perfectly clear, and I assumed his daughter, the detective, felt the same way. "You agree with him?" I asked.

She stared at me and then looked down into her coffee cup. "Yeah, well, of course." She looked back up at me and grinned. "I should. But I know you. It doesn't matter what cops think; you're involved. Besides," she paused and giggled, "you have a better record than us at solving murders."

I returned her smile. "You also know those were pure luck: being at the wrong place at the wrong time. I have no interest in treading on police business."

She shook her head but continued to smile. "Whatever," she said. "The point is, a friend of yours is close to being arrested for murdering his law partner. There's no way to keep you out of it."

"But," I said.

Karen raised her cup toward my face. "I have no idea if Aker killed Long, didn't know either other than by sight. It's not my case, but let me put it this way: if it was my case, I wouldn't rifle in on one suspect like our guys are. I told the sheriff what you said about Harley; he told me he'd 'take it under advisement,' sheriff-speak for he'll ignore it."

"Sorry to hear that," I said.

"To be honest, that pissed me off. I also know the sheriff is leaning on his former deputy, your acting chief. So, an idiot's running the show—you didn't hear that." She gripped her drink so tightly that if the cup had been made out of Styrofoam, it would have been in pieces all over the table and I'd have been running for towels to clean the coffee up.

"Are they going to arrest Sean?"

"The only reason they haven't is his hot-shot attorney."

"Abe Fox?" I asked.

"Yeah. Sean's on a short leash, and if my source is correct, he's under constant surveillance." Karen looked at the other table, where the young mother and her daughter talked about not being able to go to the beach until the dad got off work; they weren't paying attention to our conversation. Karen continued, "On top of liking Sean for his partner's death, the medical examiner says Colleen's death is suspicious."

"Why?" I asked. I suspected something, but it was only a suspicion.

"They found bruising on her upper arm that didn't have anything to do with the overdose. Speculation is that she may have been held down and then injected."

"Her death, accidental or otherwise, couldn't have anything to do with Long, could it?" I asked. Now I was really confused.

"I don't see a connection, but again, I'm not involved in the case and haven't seen the file. But there is something strange … Shee, Chris, I don't know why I'm telling you this."

I gave her my best you-can-trust-me smile and remained silent.

"Okay, here's what's strange." She looked up at the Italian flag and then back at me. "I ran all the databases for anything on your buddy Harley McLowry, and nothing negative appeared."

"Isn't that good?"

"It would be if he existed."

"Huh?" I asked, far less than articulately.

"About four years ago, he popped up having a plumber's license, driver's license, a couple of speeding tickets, even a DUI a couple of years ago. But before then, there's nothing, zip, zilch. It's like he arrived here from some other planet."

"Maybe the one Dude's from."

"Not funny, Chris, not funny."

Another common reaction lately.

"So what's it mean?" I asked.

"Don't know, but at best, it's strange. I'm still digging."

"What about Long's wife? Weren't there rumors about her having an affair with Sean?"

"Verified," said Karen. "In the sheriff's mind, that's another nail in his proverbial coffin."

"What about her doing it?" I asked. "Sean may not know about it. Where was she the night of the fire?"

Karen swirled the coffee around in the mug. "Good question. Better than the dicks on the case have asked. I'll check."

"Thought you weren't on the case," I said.

"I'm not. Enough murder talk; been back to Al's lately?"

Al's Bar and Gourmet Grill was a hole-in-the-wall restaurant near the hospital in Charleston. I had introduced Karen to the best hamburger in the universe when Brian was in the critical care unit last year. She and I ran into each other several times when I was visiting my favorite police chief and she was visiting her dad. It was during these meals over burgers, fries, beer, and wine that I got to know the softer side of the tough, hard-nosed detective. I was glad to be there for her to lean on during her traumas.

We talked some about Al and his hamburgers and joked about my friend Bob Howard, another frequent patron of Al's and the person who had introduced me to the out-of-the-way hidden gem.

She then asked about Amber. I was tempted to tell her about the apprehension and distress that Amber was having about my looking at the death of Long and how upset she had been after I found Colleen's body, but hesitated when Karen looked at her watch. She said time had slipped away and she was late for a meeting. Before she left, she walked around the table and kissed me on the forehead and reached for my right hand and gave it a squeeze. "Be careful, and please don't tell anyone we had this conversation."

I sighed, leaned back in the green, metal chair, and watched her pull out of the parking lot and turn toward Charleston.

Chapter 38

I haven't visited all the cities in the country, but have been to my fair share. Charleston is, without doubt, one of the most beautiful. It's a perfect combination of being relatively small, having more drop-dead gorgeous gardens on both private and public properties per capita than most anywhere, and boasting more stately mansions per block than any city I'd visited. It made a walk through its historic areas a delight most anytime. Sunday morning in the early summer was, for my money, the best walk to take. A slow saunter along the Battery and up and down the narrow streets south of Broad Street had always provided me with fantastic views and an opportunity to stop, watch, and think without anyone thinking anything unusual about it. Hordes of tourists lugged cameras, backpacks, and usually a small child or two and were everywhere. They snooped into back yards of the gentry, admired the multicolored doors that fronted many of the houses, and suffered from mansion-envy.

I found a rare empty parking space along the Battery wall near White Point Gardens, the stunning public area at the southern tip of Charleston. It was one of the few places where the city fathers hadn't managed to stick parking meters or signs reminding visitors that parking was limited to residents and short-term opportunities. I grabbed my camera and climbed eight steps to the elevated, concrete walkway that overlooked the bay. I gazed out on the fog-shrouded, Charleston Harbor and could barely see Fort Sumter, the historic location of the first shots fired during the Civil War. The ubiquitous tour busses and carriages that crisscrossed the lower portion of the city had not yet begun their daily rounds, and only a handful of locals were on the walkway.

A couple of dogs yapped on the other side of East Battery Street, and one dog-walker commanded his canine to "poo-poo so we can get home-zee." I smiled and wondered if the dog was fluent in traditional American cute-speak.

A border collie brushed against my leg. It was dragging its octogenarian owner behind it. The dog was on the trail of a squirrel but took time to allow me to pet it. Dogs, unlike cats, can be kind like that.

The owner gave me a nod of appreciation for slowing his rambunctious canine and commented on how great a morning it was turning out to be. "Beautiful mornings around here are about as predictable at the rise and fall of the tides," he added.

I told him I agreed. The dog soon lost interest in its owner's mundane discussion with me and pulled on its leash. The squirrel had a head start, but that wasn't going to stop the one-track-mind collie.

The early-morning philosopher caught his breath and slowly shuffled away, pulled by his much-younger and enthusiastic dog. His comment about the predictable tides rattled something loose from the back of my mind, something that had bothered me since our visit to the marsh near Secessionville. There was no doubt that the person who dumped Long's body had been familiar with the streams through the marsh; it would have been difficult for a stranger to have found the secluded spot. But on the other hand, the killer had not intended for the body to be found—or if it was found, it would have been so long after the crime that the natural elements, or the scavengers of the marsh, would have made the body unrecognizable.

The killer had either left the body too close to the shore or dumped it at low tide so that when the first high tide rolled in, the body floated toward the stream. High tide could be some six feet higher than low tide. Someone intimately familiar with the tides would not have made that mistake, would have been more careful to ensure that Tony's body wouldn't have floated so close to the waterline that the unsuspecting family from New Jersey had their day, and possibly entire vacation, ruined. In other words, the killer messed up.

Sean Aker owned two boats and spent most of his spare time on the one that was anchored in the Folly River. He knew the idiosyncrasies of the area waterways, marshes, and tides. If Sean didn't want a body found, it wouldn't have been.

I couldn't take it to the bank, or especially to the witness stand, but in my mind, Sean was off the hook.

So, if not Sean, who? And if Colleen had been murdered, who killed her? And why? Could it have a connection to Long's murder?

Murder had a way of screwing up what should have been a pleasant walk through the opulent streets in one of America's most beautiful cities. I headed home with no photos and a camera bag full of unanswered questions.

Chapter 39

Charles was determined to spend some of his newfound wealth and planned to take Heather, Amber, and me to supper Tuesday at Bowen's Island Restaurant and then to GB's for open-mike night. I was touched by his generosity, even though I knew he hadn't received any of inheritance and I would have to pick up the tab. Charles would call it a loan. And since his only working mode of transportation was a bicycle, I would also get to drive us to the restaurant, which was located off Folly Beach. It was the thought that counted, and Charles was never short on thoughts. Occasionally, one made sense.

Amber was her usual prompt self and met me on the sidewalk in front of her building when I pulled to the curb five minutes early. She slid into the front seat and looked my way and asked how I was. She wasn't smiling. We exchanged some small talk, and when I reached over to take her hand, she pulled it away. Charles's apartment was only a minute from Amber's, but on the short ride filled with silence, it seemed like thirty.

Heather stood patiently by the stairs at the bed and breakfast; Charles paced in front of the building.

"Late," he said.

Not the kind of welcome I needed after the silent treatment from Amber. "Early!" I grumbled. "Hop in."

Charles knew that it was still a few minutes before the time he had told me to be here, but expected me to be early. He lowered his head and gave me a quizzical look from under the brim of his hat. I knew he wondered where I had left my good mood. I wasn't about to discuss it with him now. Heather, the eternal optimist, radiated a huge grin and was oblivious to tension in the car. She asked if I'd pop the trunk so she could stow her guitar case.

"Don't want to have to come back here to get it on the way to GB's—can't be late for my gig," she said.

How many prayers would be answered if Heather didn't make it to GB's? I wondered.

I pulled out of Sandbar Lane, peeked in the rearview mirror, and smiled—my first since I had left Amber's apartment. Charles wore a long-sleeved black T-shirt with a cow skull and "Charlie Daniels Band" on the front, his hat cocked to the left so it wouldn't hit Heather's large straw hat, and his right arm around her shoulder.

Heather carried the conversation for the two-mile drive up Folly Road to the turn-off to Bowen's Island Road. In fact, Heather was the only one who spoke during the uncomfortable ride.

The road to Bowen's Island Restaurant began beside the early phases of a condo development and on paved roadway, which quickly gave way to a gravel road, then to a mixed gravel-shell-and-dirt, pothole-marked adventure. The restaurant was at the end of the three-quarters-of-a-mile-long lane. First-time visitors were often convinced that they had taken a wrong turn somewhere. The restaurant has a storied history and was about four years older than me. If not for a devastating fire a few years ago, that past would be readily apparent. Waist-high, rolling hills of oyster shells surrounded the parking area, and the surface was shell-covered. If there were such a thing as an oyster factory, we would have been standing in the middle of it.

We beat most of the crowd and parked in the lot closest to the building and entered the newest structure on the sprawling complex of buildings, docks, and oyster shell mini-mountains, which was the wooden dining room that replaced the rustic structure that had burned. The building was new, but the furnishings were anything but. Mismatched tables and chairs were haphazardly spread throughout the dining room. We commandeered one of the large communal tables in the center of the room and left Amber and Heather to hold it for us, and Charles and I walked back downstairs and stood in line to order from the limited fish menu. We returned to the table with a large hole in the center with a bucket underneath to throw the oyster shells in. Since oysters were out of season, the hole remained unused. We sat at one end of the long table, knowing that we would have to share it with anyone who wanted to be friendly. The freshest fish to be found anywhere and the opportunity to talk to total strangers were the two reasons Charles had chosen the steeped-in-character restaurant. Fish was not my favorite food and talking to strangers low on my priority list, so these were the same reasons I had never joined the Bowen's Island fan club.

Amber sat on the other side of Heather and began a conversation about Heather's hat and how hard it was for her to find "just the right one." Charles was fascinated by a father and his two young boys dangling fishing poles off the small pier behind the building and wondered out loud if the kids would grow up to be firemen or nuclear physicists.

I looked at him and said, "Firemen."

Charles nodded and with an equally straight face said, "That's what I thought."

It reminded me of my early conversations with my quirky friend. I also realized it was his way of helping me get my mind off Amber and the tension that had permeated the ride over.

The parking lot quickly filled, and the restaurant was nearly full. The locals knew about the outstanding meals, and vacationers returned year after year. Many felt they hadn't had their vacation until they had spent an evening experiencing the culinary fare and rustic ambiance of the unique restaurant.

Charles interrupted his fortune-telling about the young fishermen and elbowed me in the ribs. "Umm," he said and then nodded toward a couple who had zeroed in on the other end of our table. He then leaned closer and whispered, "That's Conroy Elder."

I remembered what Marlene had said about Elder and Long's heated discussions and how Elder had accused Long of cheating him out of oodles of money. I tried to be inconspicuous and turned to get a better view of our new tablemate.

Elder was tall, maybe six foot five or six, appeared to be in his late forties or early fifties, and looked as out of place in the iconic restaurant as Charles would be in the Supreme Court chambers. He had a buzz haircut a lot like some of my high school classmates; his black-framed, Buddy Holly-style glasses were from the same era. A mousy-looking lady with him was about twenty years his junior, thin, and had spiked, shoe-polish-glistening black hair.

Charles whispered, "Daughter."

I responded, "Wife."

Charles came back with, "Mistress."

Before I responded with "daughter of his mistress," Charles had leapt to his feet, stood over Elder's plate, and invited him and whomever to join us at our end of the table.

Heather had been oblivious to Charles's and my conversation and finally noticed Elder. "Hey. Hi, Mr. Elder, how was your trip to Baltimore?"

He looked at Heather and seemed confused; he had never seen her when she wasn't in her massage uniform, and her wide-brimmed hat had to be a major distraction.

"Oh," said Elder, who finally had a glimmer of recognition in his eyes. "Hi, umm, umm ..."

"Heather," she said, giving him a break.

Charles was still standing behind Elder. "You two know each other," said Charles. "So you will join us, won't you?"

I began to sense surrender rather than desire on Elder's face. His wife/daughter/mistress looked at him and said, "Sure, why not?"

"While you are figuring this out, I'm going for drinks," said Amber. She smiled, but I knew it was her work smile. Heather jumped up and said she would help with the drinks.

Elder slid his plate toward our end of the table. His gold Rolex glistened in the sunlight that washed through the nearby window. He rubbed his hands on his tan linen shorts so they wouldn't get caught on a splinter from the chair and then introduced us to Samantha, his wife. That answered one question. I'd venture to guess that it wouldn't be Charles's last.

Charles told the Elders that he had often seen them around town and that's why he'd invited them to join us. I knew Charles had seen Conroy perhaps once, and I doubted he had ever seen his wife. Elder mumbled something about thinking he recognized Charles and thanked him for the invitation.

"I may have seen you in Aker and Long," continued Charles with his imaginary story. "I'm in there every once in a while on estate-planning business."

I bit my lower lip not to laugh.

"Could be," said Elder.

Before Charles could continue the interrogation—under the guise of friendly, neighborly conversation—Amber and Heather returned with the second round of drinks. Introductions were repeated for the newcomers.

Charles turned to Heather. "I was telling Conroy that I remembered seeing him at the law office." She hesitated, giggled, and then turned to Elder.

Charles was on a roll and didn't want Heather to distract Elder. "I think I heard you and Tony splitting a few profanities a few weeks back," he said. "Heck, I've often wanted to cuss out my attorney, but never had the nerve."

Elder blinked and quickly looked away from Charles and toward Heather like he wanted her to bail him out. He regained his smile. "Oh," he said, "that must have been when Tony and I were talking about our fishing trip." He shook his head and grinned. "We were joking about the one that got away and how big it was. I may have cussed a bit when I said he was about as big a liar as the size of the fish he fabricated."

"Could be," said Charles. "So you and Tony were good friends?"

"Not close. More like fishing buddies; and he did some of my legal work. It sure was sad about what happened."

"Terrible," said Charles. He continued to stare at Elder. "Who do you think killed him?"

"Heavens. I have no idea," said Elder. He leaned closer to Charles. "I hear he had mob friends, but don't know that for sure."

"Like Mafia?" asked Charles, although he already knew the answer. "Wow."

"You never can tell about those people, you know. I do know that he was on his phone a lot when we were trying to silently commune with nature, or at least I was. He seemed to be involved in a lot of deals, but I never knew who he talked to. Lawyers!"

Charles looked around the table, smiled at Mrs. Elder, and pointed at the double order of fries in front of the group. "Eat up; enough sad talk," he said.

Apparently, Charles had given up on sneaking a confession out of our guest.

By now, the room was packed. Amber had loosened a bit and actually spoke to me. Elder offered to buy the next round, and he and Samantha walked arm in arm toward the bar.

"Check out his shoes," said Charles as soon as Elder was out of hearing range. "They're python, Ferragamo, nine hundred bucks."

I had no idea how Charles knew that, unless some United States president had a pair. Until Charles's recent inheritance, his net worth would be a flat-screen television shy of nine hundred dollars.

"Think they can walk on water?" asked Heather.

A legitimate question considering the price, I thought.

"Check out his tanned legs," said Amber. "Took a lot of sun-time to get those."

"Out of a bottle," said Heather. "Learn a lot working in a spa."

I leaned back in my chair. I had no interest in his tan or overpriced shoes, regardless of what reptile they used to slither around on. I did wonder if he believed we were dumb enough to fall for his fish tale.

I pulled back to the table when Heather asked Amber if she thought Elder's wife was too young for him. My effort to hear went for naught; Amber leaned over to Heather and whispered something. Heather rolled her eyes and said, "Good point," and then looked at Charles and over at me. Not even Charles had the courage to ask what Amber had said.

Conroy and Samantha set our drinks on the table but didn't sit. "Sorry to have to leave," said Conroy. "I forgot we're to be on Tradd Street at a cocktail party. Good talking to you." He looked at Heather. "I'll be sure to ask for you at Millie's the next time I need a massage."

Conroy and Samantha headed to the door before I could stand and offer an appropriate goodbye.

"Hard to keep up with all those Charleston cocktail parties," said Charles. He stared at the door through which the Elders had just exited.

"Right," I said.

Chapter 40

Amber mumbled that she needed to get home, since she had to be at work early. Charles tried to talk her into riding up Ashley Avenue with us to get a "gander" at Conroy Elder's house; he said we'd drop her off at her apartment on our way to GB's. She said, "No thank you," in the same voice I had heard her use many times when a more amorous customer had asked her for more than the check. She was pissed, politely; I didn't try to sway her into going with us. My heart wanted to keep her in the car; my head and foot knew braking at her apartment was the right thing to do.

"So," I said after I pulled away from Amber's apartment and turned left on East Ashley Avenue and headed toward the Washout, "anyone know where Elder lives?"

"Pull in here—I'll ask," said Charles as we approached Bert's Market.

I swung into one of the rare empty parking spots in front of the grocery. Charles hopped out before I had put the car in park. It took him less than two minutes to get his question answered. "Past the Washout; then about halfway to the old coast guard station," he said as he got in the front seat, leaving Heather in back to be chauffeured.

The Washout was well known as one of the best surfing areas along the Eastern Seaboard and was about two miles east of Center Street at the most narrow section of Folly Beach. Hurricane Hugo had remodeled most of this area of the beach when it rolled through more than twenty years ago, and many of the houses along this desolate strip were replacement structures—replacements and much larger than their predecessors; much larger and had price tags that ended in the word *million*.

The sun rapidly sank over the marsh behind us, but there still weren't any vacant parking spaces in the metered berm along the ocean side of the road. Surfers of all shapes, sizes, genders, races, and socioeconomic levels rushed to catch the last boss waves before dark.

My navigator tried to catch house numbers once we passed the mass of surfers. I had long suspected that Charles needed glasses but decided if he didn't mind squint lines on his face, it was his call.

"There it is," he said and pointed to the large, elevated three-story house we had passed.

I hit the brakes and wished that I had talked him into glasses after all. I slowly pulled into a drive a hundred yards past Elder's McMansion, waited for a steady stream of vehicles to pass, and then pulled back on the street.

Elder's humble abode stood out like a porcupine at a nudists' colony. It dwarfed its neighbors in pure mass and quality of exterior finishes, and by a multiple of millions in value. He clearly didn't want his mode of transportation to feel slighted; a white-on-white Bentley convertible was backed into the drive. Its wide, distinct grille and four large headlights smugly stared at the nightly parade of hand-painted mini-vans, Volkswagen beetles, and Dodge four-by-four pickup trucks that had infiltrated the automotive stock on the island. Elder's Ferragamo shoes began to seem cheap.

Charles asked if I wanted to stop and request that our new friend give us his financial statement. I rolled my eyes and continued toward the center of town. He also wondered what the Elders had driven to their cocktail party in Charleston; I treated it as a rhetorical question and didn't comment. Heather summed it up best when she said that twenty-four caret gold *chi* wasn't as strong as the good ol' American-made forged-steel kind. I couldn't explain it to anyone, but got her point. I was thankful she didn't try to sing it.

I took my first sip of wine, looked around the near-full bar, and thought what a difference a week made. Seven nights earlier, Colleen had served my drink of choice, and the members of the City of Folly Beach fire department were sitting around bored, prepared for a disaster while wishing they never would have to face one. I had struggled with the need to close Landrum Gallery without hurting Charles any more than I already had, while at the same time, Amber and I were getting along fabulously.

Now Colleen was dead and Sean Akers' law office was literally in ashes, as might be my relationship with Amber. The only saving grace was the knowledge that through the generosity of a cantankerous old lady, Charles and I would have enough money to not worry about feeding my costly hobby—the gallery.

Charles tapped me on the knee before I had a chance to ride more hills and valleys on my rollercoaster ride down short-term-memory lane. Laughter and the usual Tuesday night sounds inside GB's didn't sound quite as festive as usual. I got a whiff of the charred wood from the fire each time the door opened.

"So," he said as he tapped me a second time, "Now that you're rich, am I going to get a big raise?"

Heather was walking toward the bandstand to "entertain" the crowd with her one allotted song, so Charles could spend a minute or so talking to his driver, boss, and depressed friend.

"'Bout time we got a hot chick up there," yelled a man at the next table.

He had been making comments ever since we came in and took the last empty table in GB's. Each comment was louder than the one it followed. He was alone at the four-top table, but there were enough empty beer bottles spread around it for a small army. Either his friends had deserted him, or he was in no condition to move.

I leaned into Charles so he could hear me. "Rich, right," I said. "Before long, Mr. Elder'll be borrowing money from me." I tried to smile but my facial muscles weren't up to it.

Charles watched Heather tune her guitar on the corner of the stage but leaned closer to me. "Speaking of Elder, think he killed Long?"

"His version of the cussing match between him and Long sure differed from Marlene's," I said. "After seeing his house, if he felt Long screwed him out of a deal with his business, we have to be talking big bucks; he's not a petty-cash kind of guy."

Charles still watched Heather, who was almost to the mike. "If Long helped drive him to the poorhouse, he was going in a mighty nice ride; I'd put him at the top ..."

Charles's last few words were swallowed by Heather's rendition of "Faded Love."

Her warbling wasn't the only thing depressing about the song.

Charles stopped talking and gave his full attention to the stage. A quick glance around the room told me that he was the only one. Three minutes—three long minutes—later, Heather finished the sad song and took a big stage-bow to the round of applause from Charles—Charles and the drunken, slovenly, rude vacationer at the next table, who had spent the last half hour asking everyone around him when Garth Brooks was singing.

"Take it off; take it off, cowgirl—you sure as hell ain't a singer," continued the drunken heckler. His eyes rolled toward the ceiling. "Hell with you anyway. You'll never compete with cute Colleen. She understood … She …"

Greg had moved in behind him and slowly reached out and took a handful of the man's loose shirt and pulled him back against the chair. Greg's smile never faded, but he told the disruptive visitor that he would recommend he find another bar, and find it fast.

The confused slob turned and looked up at Greg. "Who the …"

He wisely didn't finish the sentence and was sober enough to see that the man pinning him to his chair was serious. "Okee-dokee," he slurred and stumbled to his feet.

I wasn't a big enough hypocrite to applaud Heather's massacring of a pleasant, albeit depressing, song, but was ready to give Greg a standing ovation. I was close to throwing the unwelcome nuisance out the door myself. I probably was spared a black eye or worse when the patron managed to find the door on his own. I had my hands full enough trying to keep Charles from jumping into the fray.

Greg turned to our table and wiped his hands together like he was slapping off dust. "Ah," he said, "the fun and frivolity of owning a bar. He's been in a few times the last three weeks. Just to see Colleen, I think. Name's Dillon something or other. Not a bad fellow when he's sober." Greg stared at the door. "Thought we'd seen the last of him now that poor Colleen's gone."

"What's going on?" asked Heather. She had leaned her guitar case against the wall and put her arm around Charles.

"Nothing," he said. "Just talking to Greg."

Greg turned to Heather. "Fine job, little girl. 'Cept, I got a crow to pick with you."

"Pick away, Greg—pick away," she said as she removed her large straw hat, moved her half-empty beer bottle out of the way, and set the hat in the middle of the table.

"Heard you sung two songs last week," said Greg as he shook his head. "What's the rule?" He pointed his index finger at Heather. I was afraid he was going to hand her a notebook and pencil and have her write the answer in it.

Heather put her index finger on her right hand on the side of her nose and rolled her eyes toward the ceiling, paused, and then said, "One song ... but remember, you said ..."

Greg looked down at her. "Little girl, I believe I said maybe ... maybe ain't a yes."

"Ain't a no either," said Heather.

I couldn't argue with that, but didn't think arguing with the person who controlled access to the stage was a wise move.

Greg's face broke into a big smile. He put his burly left arm around Heather and hugged. "One means one," he said and unwound his arm from Heather's waist. "Next drink's on me." He nodded. "Y'all come back," he said as he left the table.

Charles's right arm replaced Greg's around Heather's waist. He nudged her back in her chair and grabbed his cane and pointed it toward the bar. I could take a hint and started to the bar to replenish our liquids. Before I got too far from the table, I heard Charles say to Heather, "As President Johnson said about Gerald Ford, 'He's so dumb he can't fart and chew gum at the same time.'"

He had been referring to Greg—I assumed.

Chapter 41

Al's Bar and Gourmet Grill was a block off Calhoun Street, the main road from Folly to the center of Charleston. It was three blocks from one of Charleston's modern hospitals; the only thing modern about Al's was a forty-year-old jukebox. The hole-in-the-wall bar shared a concrete block building with a Laundromat. Al's jukebox was newer than the washers and dryers next door.

Illumination in Al's was provided by Budweiser and Budweiser Light neon signs behind the bar and the cheerful eyes of Al, the bar's seventy-something owner, barkeeper, cook, waiter, and cleaning crew.

Bob Howard had agreed to meet me at Al's if I bought lunch—solid and liquid—and would tell him how I wasn't going to get involved in the murders of Long and Colleen. My fingers were crossed when I agreed.

Traffic on Folly Road and Calhoun Street was surprisingly light, and I arrived at Al's thirty minutes early. I was still surprised that Bob wasn't already there with a head start on one of Al's "world famous," according to my Realtor friend, cheeseburgers, and a brew from Milwaukee.

"Lordy, lordy," boomed a voice from behind the bar as I walked through the paint-peeling front door and went from light to dark. "The boy's still alive."

Al, slowed by arthritic knees and a hard life, walked around the bar and met me in the middle of the room. He gave me his biggest smile; his coffee-stained teeth barely contrasted with his skin, which was somewhere between light black and dark brown. He wrapped his frail, thin arm around me and gave a tight squeeze. My eyes slowly adjusted to the dark room, and I noticed we were the only people there.

"You bring hurricanes, then fires, then crossbows, and then killers," he said as he stepped back and looked me in the eye. "If locusts start swarming, don't you come back in here. I got enough trouble just getting out of bed." He broke into another ear-to-ear grin. "You meeting Bubba Bob or that sweet-looking little detective lady?" he asked and looked back at the door.

I told him Bob, and he said he was sorry; he pointed to the only booth in the building and said for me to have a seat and he'd bring me a glass of his finest boxed wine. I took my usual side of the booth, saving the wider space on the other side for Bob. Al and Bob had been friends for years, although to the outsider it would have been nearly impossible to tell why. Bob had never heard the phrase "politically correct," and if he had, he would have told whoever used it where to shove it. To him citizens of other countries were Spics, Towelheads, Japs, Wetbacks, damned this, damned that, and worse. Al told me that Bob had made progress. He said that those of the gay persuasion were now called queers and not fags. And according to Al, the greatest leap into the twenty-first century was when Bob stopped referring to Al by the *N* word and progressed to "Afo-rican-Americano"—which showed not only racial sensitivity, but also Bob's fluency in near-Spanish.

Despite their many differences, Al and Bob were close and took great pleasure in insulting each other. Al had christened his sole booth Bubba Bob's Booth and had salted his jukebox with traditional country music to meet Bob's musical tastes. Al's black patrons—who constituted approximately 99 percent of his business—continually grumbled about the selections, but Al simple told them not to push the button if they didn't want to hear George Jones, Roy Acuff, or Patsy Cline.

"Where the hell's my cheeseburger?" yelled the customer who just doubled the number of patrons as he squeezed his way through the door. He was six feet tall and half that wide. He wore a blue-and-white, flowery Hawaiian shirt over tattered red shorts that raveled at the bottom of each leg. His four-day-old, scruffy beard was as disheveled as his white-and-green tennis shoes. He answered to Bob Howard, the best Realtor with the second largest of the three small island realty firms on Folly Beach.

Bob stopped as the door closed behind him, like he was waiting for applause. None was forthcoming, so he ambled toward the booth and ungracefully scooted in where the table was three feet from the bench seat. I had to push on the table to keep Bob from cutting me in half when he shoved it to get in.

"Yo, old man," he said and gave Al a halfhearted smile. "Two cheeseburgers and a quadruple order of fries—couple of Buds to start." He then acted like he saw me for the first time. "My dear, sweet Aunt Louise is heartbroken over the untimely death of her friend, Margaret Klein. For some reason—only God could know why—Aunt Louise has taken a fancy to you."

"Smart lady," I said.

Bob slowly shook his head and then continued, "Whatever. She told me she couldn't stand it if something happened to your damned scrawny ass. Now she tells me that the rumor is you're meddling in more murders on that damned murder-a-week island where you live." He paused and took the napkin from under the fork on the table, unfolded it, and then stuck the corner of it in his shirt collar. He straightened it out across his ample stomach and looked back at me. "Now, you hear me—if you go and get yourself killed and break my dear, sweet aunt's one and only heart, I'll dig you up, yank you out of your cheap coffin, and wring your damned neck."

I choose not to comment on his statement about an eighty-six-year-old's death being untimely or how little I'd care about my neck after I was already in ground. I merely grinned.

He smirked, maintained eye contact with me, and yelled, "Where the hell is my lunch? Old man, get the food out here before the guy who's paying gets himself dead."

"Yeah, yeah, yeah," said Al. He slowly made his way around the empty tables with a tray with Bob's lunch—feast—and my lonely little cheeseburger. Al set the tray on the table and pulled one of the chairs from the nearby table and cautiously lowered his body into it.

The comforting aroma of the burgers added a couple of hundred calories to my system before I took a bite. Bob's massive plate of fries added more.

"Where'd she hear I was chasing a killer?" I asked. Bob already had his mouth stuffed with fries, so I had to get my words in while I could.

"How the hell would I know?" he mumbled. A piece of fry fell from the side of his mouth. "She hasn't figured out how to work a ballpoint pen yet but knows her way around a phone and police scanner with the best of them. Doesn't matter how she heard; it's true, isn't it?" He raised his right hand, stuck the palm in my face, and stuffed another fry into his mouth with his left hand. "Don't answer. I know you are—no damned need to lie about it."

Al had been sitting quietly and sipping on the beer he had added to our tray of food. "So, Chris, who killed the shyster?"

Despite Bob's bluster, I knew he would have filled Al in on the goings-on with the death of Long, the fire, and probably the murder of Colleen.

"The cops think it's his partner, Sean Aker," I said.

Bob tapped his beer bottle on the table; he had been out of the conversation for two sentences and felt neglected. "Damn it, Chris, Al didn't ask who the cops think it was. He knows they're too stupid to have half a guess; them getting it right's beyond all odds."

Al gave Bob a dirty look; fortunately, there weren't any law enforcement officials in Al's, so Al didn't have to deny Bob's absurd claim. "Think the Aker guy did it?"

"I hope not," I said. "He's a friend of Charles and seems like a good guy." I nodded left and then right. "But he's the most likely suspect."

"Not much of a damned reason for him not to be the killer; if you ask me," said Bob. "Who else?"

"Harley McLowry, for one," I said. "Don't know why, but he's mighty nervous around Sean, and he dated Colleen."

Bob had met Harley a couple of times after Hurricane Greta.

"Wouldn't be surprised," said Bob. "Who else?"

"A guy named Conrad Elder; rich guy who had been fighting with Long about some business deal gone south. I'd like it to be him."

Bob raised both arms in the air. "Well, hell's bells, Chris," said Bob, "that does it; he's the one. Al, go call the cops."

Another customer strolled in, and Al pushed up on the table to stand and muttered, "Just when it's getting good," and slowly walked to the front of the bar to wait on the new arrival. He had to lean on each table along the way.

"Damned unfair," mumbled Bob as he watched Al's painful walk to the front. "Damned unfair," he repeated and shook his head.

I nodded agreement and then said, "Got a favor to ask."

"Well, of course you do. You better have enough in your pocket to cover another burger and three slices of pie."

I nodded and then continued, "Conroy Elder apparently has boatloads of money; got a mansion out past the Washout; drives a new Bentley; made most of his money in cloud technology up in Baltimore ..."

Bob waved his hand in my face. "What the hell is cloud technology?"

"Doesn't matter," I said. "It's Internet related."

"Don't have a clue, do you?"

"Nope," I confessed with a smile. "Whatever it is, he made a bunch and thinks Tony Long screwed him out of more."

"And," said Bob as he leaned back in the booth—no easy accomplishment considering his size—and put both arms behind his head, "you want good ol' Bob to come in and save your frickin' bacon—again."

"You don't have to save anything; just check on his real estate holdings and see if you can find anything strange about him, either here or in Baltimore."

"I thought you and that half-baked friend of yours were the big-assed detectives. What do you need me for?"

"Will you or not?" I asked.

"Hell, yes; I always do, don't I?"

"Yes, and thanks," I said.

"You're more fun than selling overpriced condos I have to hawk to keep Betty in bobbles."

Betty is Bob's charming wife, who has the patience of, well, anyone who would put up with Bob. In other words, she's one of a kind.

"While you're at it and in such a generous mood," I said, "my buddy Cal has a chance to become partners with Greg Brile, the guy who owns GB's Bar. Could you check Brile's finances? I'd heard that he was near bankruptcy when GB's was called Greg's: Home of Rowdy Rock. I'd hate for Cal to get messed over somehow in the deal."

"Damn, Chris," said Bob, "want me to find a cure for cancer and solve the national debt while I'm at it?"

I smiled. "If you have time ... but first, check out Elder and Brile. That'll be enough for today. I can't afford that much food."

With business out of the way, Bob and I spent the rest of his feasting talking about country music, a topic we did have in common, and I listened to him tell me why I should invest my newfound wealth in real estate. And—surprise, surprise—he knew an excellent Realtor I should use. I told him I was thinking about using the money to keep Landrum Gallery open. He thought that was a "damned stupid" idea; how, he wondered, was he going to find another sucker to rent the gallery if it wasn't vacant? Finally, he belched and said he couldn't stuff any more of Al's famous cheeseburgers into his stomach.

I watched Bob walk to the door. Before he left, he swung the plastic bag holding the extra two desserts I had had to buy for Betty. It hit Al in the side. "Out of my way, old man," he said. We all express love in different ways.

I didn't want Al to have to make the torturous trip back to the booth, so I took the money to the bar. As I headed out the door and back into the light, I heard Al ask, "When are you going to bring that cute lady cop back to see me again?"

Karen and I had not been back to Al's since her dad was released from the hospital several months ago. *Good question, Al,* I thought. *Good question.*

The sound of Roger Miller singing "When Two Worlds Collide" filled the bar as I pushed the door and walked back into the sunshine.

Wouldn't it be great to only have two worlds colliding? I mused.

Chapter 42

"The answer man is in da house," blurted Bob as he plowed his way though the gallery door. Words like *hello, good morning,* and *how are you* weren't in his everyday vocabulary—neither were *diet* and *I'll pay.* And neither was the concept of being cool—"in da house"!

Two potential customers were flipping through a bin of matted photographs and pivoted to see who, or what, had entered. Bob grinned at them; his four-day beard was now in its fifth day, and he wore the same Hawaiian shirt from the day before. The potential customers had seen enough—enough photos and enough of the street person bellowing nonsense. They scooted out the door.

Bob nodded to the opening that separated the gallery from the back room. "Any cheesecake back there?"

I pointed to the front window. "The Lost Dog Café's that way," I said, as I stated a fact that Mr. Howard knew quite well.

"Good idea," he said. "I'll let you buy brunch."

I had gotten so good at ignoring comments from my friends that I had been accused of going deaf. I didn't repudiate it. I ignored Bob; practice makes perfect.

The Realtor beat me to the back room and the refrigerator in the corner. He was surprisingly light on his feet when food was involved. Bob grabbed a Pepsi and then a bag of Doritos from the counter. "Have some," I said after he had already helped himself to the food and drink and had plopped down in the rickety wooden chair at the table. I exhaled once he was settled and the chair was still in one piece.

"Thanks a hell of a lot," he said as he ripped open the chip bag. "Sending me on a wild-goose chase in Baltimore about some rain-fog-cloudy technology—whatever the hell that is." He paused his rant and took a gulp of the drink. "I was on the phone all yesterday afternoon calling everyone I knew in Baltimore to find out about your Mr. Elder. Damned wild-goose chase."

"And how many people do you know in Baltimore?"

"One—now," he said. "Had to call a Realtor I know in Washington, who called someone he knows in Baltimore, who called someone who knew Elder, who called me—collect." He stopped and glared at me. "He asked what I wanted to know."

Why did I ask? I wondered. "What did you learn?"

"Chill, wild-goose-chase initiator. I'm getting there." He turned to the refrigerator and pointed.

I sighed, then went to get him another drink, a fairly low price for information—if he ever got around to giving me any.

He mumbled something that I translated as *thank you*; it wasn't, but was as close as he'd get. "First," he said as he held his index finger in the air, "Elder is legit. He has tons of money and even pays taxes." Bob added his middle finger to the index finger. "Second, he's into stuff. He lives in a five-million-dollar pad in Baltimore's ritziest area and has a fleet of exotic cars, none made in the good US of A. His cloudy company is a damned goldmine. When it rains, it pours."

"So, there's nothing to suggest he's the murderer?" I said. I didn't hide my disappointment.

"Didn't say that, did I?" said Bob as he raised the third finger to stand tall beside the other two. "Third, the mystery moves back down our way. My new bud in Baltimore told me to call a friend of his in Charleston, South Carolina, and ask about Isle of Palms." He leaned back in his chair and smiled. "That's the Isle of Palms that's less than a twenty-five-mile drive from this dingy gallery."

Bob was on a roll, right up there with eating as one of his most favorite activities; so I didn't interrupt.

"After a call, left message, returned call, left message, a return call, and yippee, talking to a real person, I learned that your Mr. Elder has a good reason to hate your marsh-murdered shyster. Anything else to eat?" Bob had finished the Doritos, held the empty bag in the air, and looked back to the counter.

"No. So why'd Elder hate Long?"

"Long story—hee, hee. Here's the short version: Elder and a local partner wanted to build a big-ass condo development on Isle of Palms; zoning Nazis said hell, *nein;* Elder greased some palms on Isle of Palms; the local partner split with Elder."

"Who's the local ..."

"In time," he interrupted. "The local partner then found a loophole in the law and got permits for the development; Elder got the shaft— elevator not included. Long represented Elder; didn't find the loophole but found hole in local cemetery. Rumor is the grease cost Elder nearly a mil."

"Yow, that's big bucks," I said.

Bob stared at me until he knew I was going to shut up, and then continued, "Losing the development cost him about seven mil. I reckon, even for him, that was real money. Did Elder kill Long? No damned idea." Bob took a deep breath. "Let's go eat."

Thank goodness for the short version. I didn't fully understand everything Bob had said, but it clearly didn't rule Elder out. If he was as wealthy as Bob said, I didn't see enough incentive to want Long dead.

"Bob, who's the local partner? Would he have any reason to want Long dead?"

"Knew you'd get back to that," he said. "It's a woman. Last name was something memorable like Smith; first name just as rare—June or Jane. Could be Jan. She definitely wouldn't have any reason to want Long dead. Hell, Long made her millions. Long was the best thing since sliced chocolate meringue pie." He pushed himself out of the chair. "Speaking of pie, let's go."

"One more thing," I said as I looked at my watch; it was only ten a.m. "Learn anything about Greg Brile?"

Bob huffed and puffed and then sat back down. "Damn, Chris. Do I look like Wock-O-Pee-De-Yoo?"

I smiled at the Duke University graduate—a recently uncovered fact and a total shock to all who knew Mr. Howard. "So, what did you learn?"

He smiled back at me. "Good news for your singing buddy. His soon-to-be partner is flush. Before he changed his format to country— the only kind of real music—Brile was going under. He wisely changed from a rock bar to country; took on a couple of investors; tricked enough stupid vacationers into thinking GB's stood for Garth Brooks, and business soared. Yep, good news for Country Cal." Bob then grabbed the edge of the table and rolled his head. "I'm about to collapse … starvation's setting in. Now can we go eat?"

I seriously doubted that starvation would appear on Mr. Howard's death certificate, but rather than chance it, and so as not to have to listen to him complain more, I waved toward the door. *Dog, here we come.*

Chapter 43

Stuffed was the best word to describe how I felt after an hour in the Dog with Bob. And I only had pancakes. To Bob, brunch meant breakfast *plus* lunch—he squeezed in three cinnamon rolls between a double order of pancakes and society street French toast.

I hadn't seen Larry for a few days, and his store was only three blocks from the Dog, so I took the opportunity to walk off some of my brunch. Pewter Hardware was located in a tiny, shell-pink building near the post office. Its gravel driveway held only a handful of cars, but if it were any larger, the drivers wouldn't fit in the store at one time. But like the five-foot-tall owner, its size was deceptive. Neither Bert's Market nor Pewter Hardware could compete in size with the big-box groceries or home improvement stores off-island; but a rule of thumb on Folly was, if you couldn't get it at Bert's or Pewter, you didn't need it.

Brandon, Larry's only full-time employee, greeted me and said that Larry was out back but should be in soon. Brandon had worked for Larry for a couple of years and knew that the odds of me needing something from a hardware store were slim to nonexistent. I was there to see the owner.

"Looking for a whatchamacallit to fix your doohickey?" said Larry as he came in the back door. He knew that I was as hardware-store-product-challenged as a dust mite. He looked around the empty store and then asked me to help him out front; roughly translated, he wanted to tell me something and didn't want his entire staff of one to hear.

Larry grabbed a case of Cokes from near the back door and nodded for me to get the second one. I picked it up and followed him out the front door to the vending machine.

He unlocked the front of the machine and swung the door open. It was larger than Larry. "I hear Amber's royally pissed at you," he said as he started loading the machine.

"I think it's fear more than anger," I said, more defensively than I had intended. "She's afraid for Jason. I don't blame her. She says he hasn't slept since seeing Colleen's body. I see the hurt and fear in her eyes."

"So what are you doing about it?"

"I've tried to reassure her that they're not in danger ..."

He slammed a Coke into the machine. "You can't say that. You don't know who's in danger and who's not. Look at Colleen; what'd she do? Now she's dead."

I knew Larry was right but didn't know what do about it.

Larry filled the last empty slot in the machine and carefully closed and locked the door. "I know you think the cops are incompetent; if it wasn't for Cindy, I'd agree with you; but it's their job to get this sorted out. Why not let them do it?"

"I don't think they're incompetent," I said. "We're looking at this from different angles. They seem intent on sticking it to Sean; I'm not sure they're right; and truth be known, I'm not sure Chief King knows his head from more southerly parts of his body. Detective Burton is just going through the motions."

"You can see where Amber's coming from, can't you?" said Larry.

I nodded.

"Chris, you know she loves you; give her time. She's afraid and doesn't know what to do. She's lost a lot over her short lifetime; she doesn't want the hurt of losing you. Give her some distance until this is resolved."

It was scary getting love advice from Larry. Until he met Cindy, I didn't know if he even knew what a female was. Before I had to swear on a Coke that I'd give Amber room, Cal walked across the lot. He carried his beat-up, black guitar case, wore a bright-yellow golf shirt over his stooped shoulders, and covered his long, gray hair with his sweat-stained Stetson. He was a sight for all eyes, sore or not.

"Caught you breaking in the Coke machine. Put them up, partner," he said as he stopped and pointed his guitar case at us like a rifle.

Cal didn't know about Larry's checkered past and hadn't hit it off well with him when they had met last year. Their attitude toward each other had improved, but comments like this one only helped rile my vertically-challenged friend.

"Wrong again, Pops," said Larry. His smile barely covered his irritation.

"Glad you're here, Cal," I said, not only because I was glad, but also to try to defuse the rapidly deteriorating conversation. "I learned a couple of things you'll be interested in."

Larry held his shallow smile and said he had work to do inside, picked up the empty Coke boxes, and left us standing in the lot. He didn't say "Bye," or "See you later," but considering the other options, Cal was better off without further comments.

"What's under his saddle?" asked Cal as he watched Larry enter the store.

I put my hand on Cal's elbow and slowly led him away from the front door. "Just tired, I think. Let's get in the shade." We walked across the street and up a mulch-covered path that lead to the small Folly River Park that faced Center Street and the Folly River. It seemed forlorn and empty when it wasn't hosting the monthly art fair. Cal walked toward Center Street and folded his lanky frame on the top concrete step. He delicately set his guitar case on the brick and concrete sides of the three steps. We watched a half-dozen vehicles drive by before either of us spoke.

I told Cal what Bob had learned about the financial stability of GB's. I expected him to be happy about the news, but he frowned. "What's wrong?" I asked.

Cal stared at the road like he was getting paid to take a vehicle count. "Nothing," he uttered.

Even the small lizard that scampered across the step in front of Cal's boot wouldn't have believed him. "What?"

Cal yanked his foot back like he thought the killer five-inch-long lizard was going to bite it off. "Promise you won't tell the cops you heard it from me?"

"Not unless they attach electrodes to my tongue and pour battery acid up my nose," I said. "Or unless I have to," I continued, in a much lower voice.

"Snail spit," said Cal, "I shouldn't be telling you this ... I promised ... I don't know what to do ..."

"What's it about?"

"Shee, don't know for sure ... maybe Colleen's death ... maybe Long ... maybe nothing. I promised." He hesitated and finally looked away from the road. He did an owl impression with his head and finally rested his gaze at me.

"Promised who?" I said. If I took it one bite at a time, I could possibly get the story—eventually.

"Just someone who works at GB's." He rolled his eyes up toward the bill of his Stetson and then looked at the Baptist Church across the street like he'd never seen it before. "Someone that I'm sort of getting close to, if you catch the flow."

I assumed that I did and didn't push. I waited.

Cal hesitated again before giving in to my powerful interrogation techniques. "You didn't hear it from me, okay?" he said.

I nodded, knowing that if push came to shove, I couldn't honor the promise.

"Okay, well, my friend, I'll call her Sally Lou—not really her name, mind you. Last night—okay, maybe it was sometime early this morning—Sally Lou told me that Colleen told her that she had learned something about Long, the lawyer, that could cause some real trouble for someone." Cal took the Stetson off his head and wiped his brow.

I waited for him to continue, but I had learned over the last year that wiping his brow was a punctuation mark slightly shy of an exclamation point. He was done. I tried to assimilate what he had said and was confused over which *her* and *she* had heard *what* and *who* could be in trouble. I asked him to repeat the story.

He looked at me like, *How much clearer could I have made it?* But he finally surrendered to my charm and clarified that Sally Lou, or whoever she was, hadn't done anything except repeat the story to Cal and that Sally Lou had no idea who might be in trouble. He did say that Sally Lou thought that whatever Colleen had learned had come from someone under the influence of hops. According to Cal, the crooner and lyricist, "You know how a few extra sips make customers spill their beer, their guts, and their inhibitions."

I had no idea what the information meant, but it showed a connection between Colleen and Tony Long. I then remembered the encounter the other night with the drunk at GB's.

Cal fidgeted with the torn, aged, leather handle on his guitar case and then renewed his traffic count.

"Chris," he said, "I don't know what to do about Greg's offer. Judy—I mean Sally Lou—thinks I need to stay away from the snake-bit bar. But hell, I could use the money, and it would give me a nice, permanent place to hang my hat." He tapped the bill of his Stetson. "And there are always new audiences; just like being in Branson, Missouri—the star stays put and the tourists come to him. Beats the snot out of the other way around."

"I don't see where you'd be in any danger at GB's," I said. "You've been in there singing most weekends and Tuesdays. Did you ever see Long?"

"A few times, but it could have been more," he said. "I didn't know who he was at first, so I didn't pay attention."

"Was he there with his wife?" I asked.

"Don't think so. I don't know who his wife is, but he was always alone; sat at the bar, threw back a few beers, and then left."

Cal was finally talking, so I'd better get everything I could from him. "How often was Harley there?"

"He usually came in around closing—at first to hit on Colleen, and then after his hits took, he came to take her home, or somewhere else." He refocused on the church but didn't speak.

"What?" I asked.

Cal grinned and then paused and snapped his fingers. "I did see Harley almost get in a knock-down with Chief King once. Don't know what it was about. Think that's a clue?"

I smiled. "Not to me. Was *Acting* Chief King in often?"

"Fairly regularly," said Cal. "I think he was buds with Gregory—if that's possible. I personally think he was in for the free food and beer." He grinned. "Cop comps, Sally Lou called it."

Cal jumped to his feet so fast I looked around for another killer lizard. "Gotta head out, pard. Thanks for the advice."

He was headed down Center Street before it struck me. *What advice?*

Chapter 44

Some of the most enjoyable times I had had on Folly were spent walking around the island with Charles and taking photos. Walking, I admit, is not my favorite activity—I'd put it slightly ahead of a colonoscopy—but when I had a camera in hand and someone to distract me from thinking about the exercise part, it was fun. If nothing else, Charles was a powerful distraction. The extra hole I had recently augured in the end of my belt told me I needed to get back into my earlier routine. After I had imparted phantom advice to Cal, I returned to the gallery, where Charles was anxious to talk about the murder. I told him that was a good idea but he would have to grab his camera and cane and walk with me.

"It's about time," he said and then started looking for his camera.

We locked the door and headed toward the Tides. Other than sharing near-identical headwear, Charles and I would appear to most of the people we encountered as the odd couple. His scruffy beard was about three days behind Bob Howard's; I couldn't stand going a day without shaving. Charles wore a long-sleeved University of Wisconsin T-shirt and raggedy shorts that would be called short-shorts in some circles. I had on a logo-free, dark-green golf shirt and shorts with cuffs that hit just above my knee. Neither of us would have been a candidate for bachelor on any of the mindless reality television shows, but we had been called "decent looking" by some, and "cute as a button" by our biased significant others.

"So, did Harley do it?" he asked. We had reached the corner of Center Street and Arctic Avenue and stood on the sidewalk outside

Rita's patio. Charles abruptly stopped, and I almost stepped on his heel. He pointed his camera at an empty Milk Duds box lodged between the sidewalk and gutter. The subject of many of his photographs mirrored his quirky outlook on things. He snapped the shutter and looked up at me for my response.

"Don't know," I said. "He would have had opportunity with Colleen—access to her apartment, she would have trusted him, and he's strong enough to restrain her to inject drugs. But what's his motive for killing Long?"

"Remember how nervous he was when we went to see Sean?" said Charles. He had photographed the mangled candy box from every angle and moved down Arctic, away from downtown. "'Taint normal.'"

"Harley doesn't strike me as someone who would be comfortable in a lawyer's office. You're right about him being embarrassingly uncomfortable."

"You bet I am."

"But so what? What's the motive?" I stopped and waited.

"He's hiding something. He's a plumber but hardly ever works; disappears for days at a time; and talks about his past about as much as you do. Not only hiding something, but unhealthy … I say unhealthy." Charles nodded at me and looked across the road. He waited for an electrician's panel truck with a surfboard on top to pass and then skipped across the street to the beach side. His cane tapped the pavement as he went.

The smell of the salty surf in the humid air and the low roar of the rolling waves gave me a sense of security and peace, a feeling I knew was deceptive. We had walked a couple of blocks before stopping in a vacant lot that held remnants of a concrete foundation and partial floor of the hurricane-demolished boardinghouse, the Edge—the house where Mrs. Klein had lorded over a generally dysfunctional group of tenants that included Harley, Cal, Heather, and even Cindy Ash.

Charles grinned and hopped on a large piece of concrete and started looking around. His photographic eye and point of view saw photo ops in every direction—trash was everywhere: newspapers, a rubber inner tube, a deflated, colorful, striped beach ball, and beer cans. So many photos, so little time, for my artistic friend.

I apparently didn't have Charles's flair for art, so I headed to the wooden steps that led to the public beach walkway, wiped sand off a step, and sat. There were several sunbathers on the beach, and a dozen or so kids splashed in the waves; the nearest person to us was thirty yards away.

"What about Conroy Elder?" yelled Charles. His eyes were on the unique subject matter, but his mind was still in detective mode.

"If Marlene was right about how angry he was with Long, he lied to us about his fish story," I said. "Long may have messed him over and cost him a lot of money, but if he's as rich as Bob says, I can't see him killing his attorney."

"I think I want him to be guilty because of his reptile shoes, inhumane amount of wealth, and ... and I just don't like him."

"I think the cops will need more than that to hold him," I said.

"Okay," said Charles. He flung the camera strap over his shoulder and came to the steps. "How about Long's wife, Connie?" He held up his right palm toward me. "Before you answer, get this: I ran into council member Marc Salmon in front of Planet Follywood this morning. I was doing some detecting, and Marc is a good source of information; the law of averages says that some of it's accurate." He waved his cane in the air; my interpretation was that when it waved one direction, the information was true; the opposite direction, false. Or he could have been practicing to be a drum major.

"Well," he continued, "the conversation got around to the untimely death of Tony Long and then leapt to a discussion about Tony's wife. Marc tried about seven ways to tell me that Connie was having an affair with Sean, without using the word *affair*. I pretended I didn't know anything about it—course, if that was true, I'd be the only person in town who didn't. Anyway, Marc told me that he suspected Connie."

"Anything other than the obvious?" I asked.

"Glad you asked. Marc said that Connie's dad was a US Park Service ranger, and for several years before Connie ran off with Tony Long, she lived with her dad at Everglades National Park. Marc said she was a tomboy and good with boats, guns, and other outdoor stuff."

"Like hunting down a lawyer, killing him, and then taking him out in the marsh and dumping him for the marsh-critters to feast on?"

"Like, yeah," said Charles. He leaned his cane on the rail beside me, fanned his head with his hat, and then sighed. "Now to the biggie. What about the five-hundred-pound shark in the fishbowl?"

"Referring to Sean?"

"Like, yeah," he said for the second time in thirty seconds. "He had motive, or motives: the seventy-five grand Tony stole … their business conflicts … the affair with Connie." Charles paused and looked toward Folly Pier which majestically stood a few hundred yards to our right. "He had means; we know he has that little dinghy and two real boats—the small real boat could have easily been used to haul Tony into the marsh. And using our tax dollars, the military gave him the skills to kill."

With the amount of tax dollars Charles had paid in his lifetime, the military wouldn't have had enough money to train Sean to peel a potato, much less kill someone, but I let it slide. *And he lied to us about when he left his office the night of the fire,* I thought.

"Charles, you know him better than I do. Do you think he did it?"

Charles picked up a small shell from the sand near the dune and threw it toward the surf. He turned back toward me. "Chris, I don't want it to be Sean. I've known him for a long time and really like him. I didn't think it was at first, I really didn't, and … well, I didn't. But now, yeah, I sort of think he did. I keep remembering his little temper tantrums and keep rolling over in my head the stuff I just mentioned, plus he lied to us. You know, the police think he did; they can't always be wrong. Can they?"

"If they were sure, they'd have him in jail," I said. No sooner had the words left my mouth than I realized how weak a defense it was; not quite as weak as Charles saying the police couldn't always be wrong, but still weak.

Charles shrugged. "I think his hot-shot lawyer is the reason Sean's not in the hoosegow."

I still had doubts, but they were based on little things. Wouldn't Sean have known enough about the tides in the marsh not to have thrown the body where it would be washed into the channel and found that quickly? What motive would he have had to torch his own office, since he had access to everything in it?

I shared with Charles what Cal had learned from his new lady-friend, Sally Lou, about a possible motive for Colleen's murder and how it could be tied to Long's demise.

He patiently listened to my monologue and then shook his head. "Of all the names in the universe, Cal used Sally Lou for an alias?"

You can't slip anything important by my buddy, I thought. "Do you remember ever seeing Sean in GB's?"

"No, and don't remember a Sally Lou either; what's the point?"

"The point is that if Colleen learned something from a customer in GB's that could have caused Long trouble and she was killed because of what she learned, most likely she heard it from the killer. If Sean didn't frequent GB's, the odds are low that it was him."

"Pretty weak," said Charles. "I hope it's true, but I still'd put money on Sean."

I didn't totally disagree with him about the assumption being weak.

Chapter 45

We had spent a lot of time talking about possible suspects, but other than discovering a connection—a weak connection—between the two murders, we didn't know much more than we had when I discovered Colleen's body.

Or did we? I was bothered by something I had heard the other night at GB's; but the more I tried to remember, the further it slipped away. What could Colleen possibly have heard at work that made her such a threat—enough of a threat to kill her? What was Harley afraid of? What was he hiding? Could the two deaths be unrelated and Cal's alias-challenged "friend" have misunderstood what she heard that connected the two? Could Charles and I do what the police with all of their resources and tools had failed to do? Could we find the killer? Why were we risking our lives nosing in?

Before I could come up with answers or more realistically, determine that I didn't have a clue, the phone rang. I barely recognized Amber's voice. I sat in the chair in the back of the gallery.

She sniffled and started her sentence twice before she said, "Give me a second."

I wanted to wrap my arms around her and hold tight, tight enough to squeeze the hurt out of her voice, but said, "Sure."

The sound of plastic striking a hard surface rattled in my ear. I heard her blow her nose and then the rustle of the phone receiver. "Sorry," she whispered. "I thought I could do this without crying."

I held my breath. The only sound I heard was the loud grating of the air conditioner and a couple of vehicles rolling up Center Street.

"Chris, I'm a coward, I know it. You deserve better, but I can't do this in person. Sorry … Here goes. I love you, and have for three years. I didn't want to at times, but I couldn't help it."

"I know—"

She interrupted, "I don't think I can go on dating you. Jason has to be my priority. I … I know it's not your fault and you wouldn't intentionally do anything to hurt him or me. I also know that you won't stop until you find out who killed that lawyer and that girl, or … or you get killed trying." She sniffled. "I'm sorry, Chris; God knows, I'm sorry. Please don't call me back or try to see me. Maybe someday … maybe … I love you."

The line went dead. So did my heart.

I stared at the phone and then lowered my head. I don't know how long it was before I had the energy to stand, and then I felt like I was in a fog. I didn't know if I wanted to yell, cry, curl into a ball and sit in the corner, or shut my eyes tight and pretend the phone had never rung.

Instead, I walked to the front door, turned off the lights, walked out onto the sidewalk, locked the door, and began walking. I nearly tripped over a beagle that was enjoying the sunshine while its owner stood in the middle of the sidewalk talking on a cell phone. I didn't want to cross the street because I would see the Lost Dog Café and think of Amber; I couldn't walk toward the ocean because I'd pass her building—probably where she had called from. I headed away from town on one of the side streets that immediately put me in a residential area—no sidewalks, no vacationers on the streets, no happy, laughing children to make me feel more miserable that I felt. I walked and walked. Unlike the beach or the center of town, many of the residential streets and yards were shaded by canopies of oaks and large palmetto trees.

The sun rapidly bowed toward the horizon behind me, and the trees had already thrown dark shadows. I wandered until I stopped on Hudson Street in front of a sign that echoed my feelings and mood: Dead End. It was an omen; I ignored the warning and continued to the spot where the road ended at the marsh. I paused and caught my breath as I leaned against the red-and-white striped barrier strategically placed to prevent either the most stupid or most inebriated drivers from plowing into the marsh. The warm, red colors from the setting sun reflected off the billowy clouds that hung low over the lush, green spartina grass. The only sound I heard—other than the sloshing of blood pulsating through my arteries—was a flock of birds off in the distance and the happy yapping of a small dog. I pictured its wagging tail as its master ventured into the yard to deliver the evening meal. For a moment, I wished I could be as happy as the dog, or even the birds as they flew in circles over the wetlands.

I considered walking on, but knew the view wouldn't get better, so I lowered myself onto one of the small concrete barriers that marked the end of the road. From the way I felt, the barrier was as much symbolic as real.

I didn't know how long I had moped, pondered, and flat-out became more and more despondent, but the next thing I realized was that it was pitch dark and my phone was ringing.

"Chrisster. Be Dudester," came the familiar voice, breaking me out of my less-than-stellar mood. "We got poop for you; barrel on over."

The next thing I heard was nothing. Dude had hung up. And here I was, at the end of the road: no Heather around to use her psychic ability to tell me where Dude was, no Charles to tell me if Dude's use of *poop* was more significant than what I thought it meant, no clue as to who *we* were. So I did all I knew to do: I hit the Last Call button and crossed my fingers that Dude would answer.

Miracles did happen.

"Dudester, state your need."

"Where are you and who are you with?" I stopped; saying anything else would have been counterproductive.

"Loggerhead's … Mad Melster."

He hung up—again.

I didn't call back. I slowly stood, turned back toward town, realized that the walk was more than I would have chosen, but didn't have a choice. Dude had called me no more than three times in the years I had known him, so I knew if he asked me to join him, there was a good reason. I hoped it wasn't just to shovel poop.

Chapter 46

Loggerhead's Beach Bar was a wooden, one-story, elevated yellow building directly across the street from the Charleston Oceanfront Villas, the largest condo complex on the island. It had begun to rain by the time I arrived at the bar. Water ponded on the parking lot and reflected the blue neon lights that outlined the roof of the elevated bar. The Folly Beach Bluegrass Society invaded Loggerhead's each Thursday evening, and several weeks, weather permitting, they performed on the outdoor patio—"Pickin' on the Patio," according to signs plastered around town.

Tonight's festivities had been forced inside by the rain, but I could still hear guitars and a banjo as I climbed the steps and opened the glass door to the restaurant, bar, pool hall, pinball machine arcade, and weekly gathering spot for fans of bluegrass music. GB's open-mike Tuesdays were liberally cloned from the weekly bluegrass event.

An illuminated, two-tiered bandstand was in the far corner and was bookended by two large Yamaha speakers. A half-dozen guitar and banjo cases sat on the floor to the right of the bandstand, and seven bluegrass musicians leaned into three mikes on the crowded stage. Three of the musicians looked like they had just walked in from the beach, two others wore jeans, and one was dressed in black, with boots and a straw, fedora-style hat. While the group was as varied as could be, their music was great—a significant difference from GB's open mike night. Most of them had gathered every Thursday for the loosely organized Bluegrass Society and were more than familiar with the song selections.

Multi-taskers in the bar could listen to the music, watch baseball on the flat screen television to the left of the stage, and read the Kona Longboard, Yuengling, and Budweiser signs behind the musicians.

The rest of the bar was as crowded as the bandstand. Several natural-stained pine booths were to the left of the stage and were already packed with customers enjoying the typical beach menu. There were only a handful of tables in front of the musicians, and they were full. Seven bar-height, black-vinyl-covered swivel chairs were near the bamboo-faced bar and occupied. Approximately a dozen other patrons edged in among the lucky few who had the chairs.

Dude and Mad Mel were lucky enough, or had arrived early enough, to have commandeered two of the swivel chairs at the far end of the bar, away from the bandstand. They were in deep conversation; their heads almost touched so they could hear over the banjo licks and the lyrics of the bluegrass standard, "Fox on the Run."

Dude didn't see me coming and fell to the side of the barstool when I tapped his shoulder. "Whoa, Chuckster, nearly axed me!"

He was almost on the floor, so I assumed being axed wasn't good.

"Sorry, Dude," I said.

Mel started to laugh but stopped when Dude turned to him and hopped back on the chair. "Hey, Chris," he said. He held out his extra-large hand and gave mine a definitive shake. A bored, middle-aged bartender wearing a spaghetti-strap, yellow tank top and black shorts leaned toward me and then picked up Mel's empty Pabst Blue Ribbon bottle and tapped it on the bar. I took the not-so-subtle hint and ordered white wine. The bartender tapped the bar again, slightly harder than before, and both Mel and Dude nodded for another round. She mouthed a toothy grin and headed to the cooler at the other end of the bar—her sales pitch had succeeded.

"Me ... we ... be glad you shuffled over," said Dude. "Full moon be tonight."

"Reason you two are here. Right?" I said.

"No all-hammerz in you," said Dude. "We ..."

"Enough damned chit-chat," interrupted Mel before Dude could break out in a monologue and utter three or four more words.

Dude's head bobbed between Mel and me. "Mel told me stuff. Me not great detective like you and the Chuckster; wasted words on me;

so, you be called … and," Dude threw both arms in the air. "Ta-da, here you be."

The wine arrived in the nick of time, and I took more than a generous sip. I figured I'd need it. I turned to Mel. He had on the same sleeveless, leather bomber jacket and camo pants he had worn during our marsh escapade. His Semper Fi camouflage fatigue cap was replaced by a dark-brown golf cap with the M&M candy logo in green on the crown. If the letter "m" hadn't made it into the alphabet, Mel would have been lost—or named Nel.

"Okay, here goes," he said and then took a sip of his new Pabst. "I've got a friend … a close friend … who lives with me." Mel looked down at his beer bottle. "My friend's a rock promoter in Charleston." He looked up and grinned. "Handles most of the big tours that hit the Lowcountry, and some of the up-and-comers too—the kind of groups small bars can afford."

"Beach Boys once," interrupted Dude. "'Round, round, get around.' Cool."

Mel gave him a sideways, dirty look and continued, "He's threatened to stick an ice pick in my ear every time he hears I've been listening to Bluegrass music." The smile suddenly disappeared. "Well, anyway, yesterday I told him about our trip to the marsh to check out the dead zone and some of the other characters you guys were talking about."

"Yeah, tell him," said Dude. The peace symbol on his T-shirt glowed in the reflection of the stage lights.

Mel turned his mad-Marine stare on Dude, and then turned back to me. "Yeah, well, my … friend knows nearly every bar owner in Charleston County. He'd be great at reconnaissance. Anyway, he knows Greg Brile. They go back to when Brile had the rock bar; hired some of the cheaper acts that my friend promoted."

An enthusiastic version of "Rocky Top" drowned out Mel's words, but I did catch something about Brile struggling to pay Mel's "friend" his fees and that the "friend" had to make several trips to the bar to collect. The song ended, and most of the group left the stage for a "beer break." My aging, high-note-challenged ears appreciated lack of amplified sound.

"Tell him all," urged Dude.

Mel jerked his head toward Dude. "Damned draft-dodging pinko druggy," he said and then shook his head. "This is my story. Use you own few words when I'm done ... Damned hippy."

Mel pulled a cigar from one of the many pockets in his cut-off field pants, put it in his mouth, and reached for a retro-looking lighter shaped like a pin-up girl from the forties. He looked at the lighter and slammed it back on the bar. "Damned no-smoking rules." He then turned back to me. "Caldwell ... that's my friend ... said that when Greg was a day shy of going under, he found someone who wanted to be his partner—a silent partner, said Caldwell."

Dude held his beer bottle in front of Mel's face. "Who be it? Tell the Chrisster," interrupted Dude.

"Hush, you damned ate-up hippy," said Mel. He pushed the beer bottle out of his face and pointed the unlit cigar at Dude. "I told you I don't know who the partner is; Caldwell doesn't know either, so don't ask."

Dude and Mel showed so much love toward each other that I thought I'd better push the conversation forward or witness a murder—or at the least, a court-martial of Dude by the Marines. "Did your friend, uh, Caldwell, tell you anything that could help?"

"Don't know if it'll help or just be a bum scoop, but he did say that Brile told him that he had found a 'sucker' to buy into the business; said that the sucker was a crooked attorney. Help, I don't know." Mel took off his M&Ms hat and waved it in front of Dude.

Dude smiled. "Imaginary smoke be gone."

"And he didn't have any idea who the attorney was or where he was from?" I asked.

Before Mel answered, Dude said, "Crooked attorney—don't narrow field, do it?"

Considering the entire universe of attorneys, no, I thought. But in my small corner of the world, only one attorney had been murdered in the last couple of weeks; one attorney's office had been torched; and only one attorney had been accused of being crooked—Tony Long.

The conglomeration of musicians had re-gathered on the bandstand and started strumming Bill Monroe's signature song, "Blue Moon of Kentucky." The amplified sound made it nearly impossible to hear whatever few words Dude had tried to say. I leaned over to Mel and asked if Caldwell had shared anything else. I think his answer was no, so I thanked him for the information and patted Dude on the arm and weaved my way through the crowd to the exit. Jamie, a member of the band and one of the society's organizers, nodded to me as I passed the stage. Being recognized is a good feeling—most of the time.

If the crooked attorney was, in fact, the late Tony Long, did that mean Greg Brile should be added to the list of suspects? If Long was the attorney, it still didn't mean that Brile would have had any reason to kill him. What was the motive?

Fortunately, the rain had stopped, so I didn't have to rush home; my legs were still sore from Charles landing on them and already feeling tight for the walking tonight, and besides, I wasn't in a hurry to get home and rehash my conversation with Amber.

Chapter 47

Charles, formerly the paragon of punctuality, had been arriving at the gallery later and later, a trend that coincidentally started about the time he had begun dating Heather. From a few comments in recent months, I suspected the sheets on the bed in his small apartment didn't get nearly as much wear as they had the last couple of decades. Friday mornings were decent for attracting customers—not decent enough to pay the bills, but enough to beat most of the other weekday mornings. I arrived early and cranked up the air conditioner to be ready for the swarm of customers. Charles was nowhere to be seen.

I had poured my first cup of coffee when the bell over the front door rang. I was pleased with myself for being prepared and with a mug of coffee in hand, walked to the door that separated the back room from the gallery, a large customer-service grin on my face.

My smile disappeared as quickly as a shooting star. Harley was at the door, his back turned toward me. A chill ran down my spine as I watched his trembling hand turn the deadbolt. He hadn't seen me, and I quickly calculated my chances of getting to the back door and to freedom before he could reach me—slim if any at all was my alarming conclusion.

What could I grab as a weapon? Where was Charles's cane when I needed it? Where was Charles? What was it about the gallery?

A couple of years ago, I was nearly blown into unrecognizable pieces by a bomb as I sat in this room; and now, Harley, a man whom I would bet on in a wrestling match against a grizzly bear, locked the door on any help that could save me. The adage that "there's nothing to fear but fear itself" had never been more absurd.

Harley turned away from the door and saw me standing in the back corner. He had never been the spitting-image of a GQ model, but he looked more disheveled than usual. His eyes screamed lack of sleep. He had on bib overalls with the strap over his left shoulder unbuttoned. His work boots were mud-splattered. His burly, muscled arms nearly ripped out the seams in his shirt.

"Hi," he said. He took two steps toward me.

I had never heard the simple greeting sound so ominous. He took a pack of Camels from his work-shirt pocket, shook out the unfiltered cigarette, and lit one without taking his eyes off me. It wasn't the time to tell him that I didn't allow smoking in the gallery. I nodded and gave him my best faux smile.

"Got a minute?" he asked.

I hoped he was asking and not telling me that that was all the time I had left. I continued to force a smile and nodded again.

He pointed his beefy index finger toward the back room, and I obediently led him into the room and out of sight of anyone who might look in the plate-glass storefront window. I continued to look around for a weapon, any weapon, but didn't find anything that would even the odds. I sat on one of the rickety chairs at the table, and Harley glanced at the Mr. Coffee on the other side of the room. I didn't fool myself into thinking I could kill him with kindness but asked if he wanted a cup. He didn't answer but walked to the machine and grabbed a Piggly Wiggly mug from the counter. Not sure why, but I saw it as a sign of hope.

He brought the coffee to the table and sat on the opposite side from me. He stared at the pig logo on the cup and then took a sip.

"Let me tell you a story," he began. I hoped it was a long one, and I nodded. "Until nine years ago, I was an accountant—a good accountant, a danged good one. I had a lucrative practice up north."

It took me a moment for what he said to soak in. Of all the things I'd imagined he would say, that was somewhere below the bottom. He took another sip and stared at me—more like stared through me.

"One problem," he continued. "One big problem. I only had one client, the mob. How I got involved is a long story; I won't bore you with it; suffice to say, I got deeper and deeper in places where I shouldn't have been."

I hadn't gotten my hands around what he said but began to feel that today might not be my last day on Folly Beach. The Harley who was speaking didn't sound like the Harley I had known for the last eight months—words like *lucrative* and *suffice* weren't words that I had heard from his lips.

"How did you go from an accountant to a plumber?"

"About nine years ago, I was enjoying a round of golf at a private club I belonged to; beautiful day, nice, warm sunshine. Then I was struck by lightning—actually, something worse. I had been paired with a guy I hadn't seen before; we had just finished putting on the fifteenth green ..." Harley smiled, "I was two up on him." He hesitated again and shook his head. "And then the guy reached in his pocket, and instead of pulling out a tee, he flashed a badge, identified himself as a special agent for the FBI, and said he had an offer I shouldn't refuse."

I didn't know what to say, so I offered him more coffee. I was surprised when he said he'd get it and slowly walked back to the Mr. Coffee.

"The guy said he needed my help and offered me something he thought I'd value—freedom. He said he had enough on me—tapes, video and audio, computer printouts, and photos—to put me away for the rest of my life. I knew he wasn't bluffing."

"And he wanted you to testify against your colleagues?" I asked.

"Affirmative," said Harley.

"And you did, and let me guess, you're now a fine, upstanding member of the elite Witness Protection Program."

Harley grinned. "Technically, it's the Witness Security Program; but yes, that is what I am."

"And you're telling me this because?" I asked. My breathing came more regularly, and I regained hope that I would survive.

"Chris, I've watched you closely ever since we spent time in Hurricane Greta; I watched you when we saved poor Mrs. Klein and me and how you handled the overbearing cops after that. I know your reputation of helping friends and, through skill or dumb luck, catching killers. I've seen how you watched me when I was in the attorney's office; you think

I killed that damned lawyer and ... and Colleen ... my girlfriend." He lowered his head; he was hurting, and I waited for him to continue.

He finally did. "The guys I helped put away have long memories and short fuses. It's not that I don't trust the feds; I do. But when I heard that that damned lawyer, Long, had mob connections, I knew there was a chance someone would recognize me. Sure, my name's different, accountant to plumber is a big leap, but I'm still the same old, big, burly, ugly guy I always was."

"No wonder you didn't want your photo taken for the *Folly Current* after you saved Mrs. Klein," I said.

"Yeah, and then you go dragging me to the damned lawyer's office about her will, making me sit in the same waiting room where the mob could be checking to see who knew their crooked lawyer. All I want to do is hide, and here you are, parading me in front of all sorts of people. Hell, Chris, why not just send a photo of me with an invitation to my coming-out party to my old mailing list?"

Harley stood and walked to the front of the gallery and unlocked the door. I followed him, but instead of him leaving, he slowly walked around the room and looked at the framed photos. "Not bad," he said. "If I wasn't a poor plumber, I might buy a couple."

I elected not to mention that he was no longer poor; Mrs. Klein had seen to that. I knew what he meant.

I snapped my fingers. "The story about being arrested in a bar fight. Was that true?"

His face erupted in a wide grin. "Nah," he said and raised both arms into the air. "Made it up. Good story, I thought."

"Why?"

He continued to smile. "Sounded like something a guy named Harley would do, and it explained my reluctance to be around lawyers."

I returned his smile. "Good job," I conceded.

I had new admiration for his creativity—especially from an accountant.

He abruptly turned back to the door and stopped smiling. "Please, please don't tell anyone about this conversation—not even Charles. My life's in your hands."

He was out the door before I could respond.

I had no reason to doubt his story, but in the back of my mind, I wondered. So what? He could still have killed Long and Colleen. If he had known about Long's mob ties, that could have been the motive I couldn't figure out.

My head hurt—after the last two days, a well-deserved headache.

Chapter 48

Greg Brile had been completely off my radar as a suspect until Mel told me about the conversation he had had with his friend. I wasn't aware of any connection between the cheerful bar owner and Long; Colleen had worked for Brile, but so had many others.

I grabbed a yellow legal pad from the counter next to the Mr. Coffee and began a list of suspects. Seeing it in writing might jar something loose. Despite my misgivings, the number one suspect was still Sean Aker. He had motive, means, and a temper. He had a boat to transport the body into the marsh; his law partner had stolen from him; he was having an affair with Long's wife; there was a history of bad blood between the two; and the police had focused in on him from the beginning. On the left side of the paper, I outlined the reasons he would be the killer. On the right, I listed the reasons he wouldn't. There were only three for innocent, and one of them worthless—Charles's and my hope that he didn't do it. I still couldn't figure out why he would torch his own office, since he already had access and could have removed whatever he didn't want found. And he was familiar with the rise and fall of the tides enough to make sure the body wasn't able to wash to the stream and be found as quickly as it was. But if I were the police, I'd be at his door with handcuffs out.

I shook my head and wondered why I needed to continue the exercise; I slowly walked to the refrigerator, got out a Diet Pepsi, and continued anyway.

I flipped Sean's guilt-ridden page over and started the next sheet with Conrad Elder and listed why he would be guilty; but other than his fight with Long and lying to Charles and me, there wasn't much I could add to the blank page. Sure, with his wealth, he would have access to any boat he wanted, and he definitely had a grudge against Long. But there were more questions than facts. Did he even know Colleen, had he ever been in GB's, and most importantly, with so much money, would he have had sufficient motivation to kill? I didn't spend much time on his page.

That brought me to Connie, Long's wife. A motive would have been pure speculation. Perhaps she wanted a way to permanently eliminate her husband and live happily ever after with Sean; perhaps she just wanted to eliminate her husband—not the first wife to act on that wish. From what Marc Salmon had told Charles, she would have had the means, having been raised around fishing, hunting, marshes, and glades. I wondered if she would have had the strength to lift her husband's dead weight enough to carry him into the debilitating pluff mud and dump the body, but it wouldn't have surprised me. Besides, she could have conned him into the boat ride and killed him where the body was found; no hard lifting required. Her lack of strength would have been a good reason why he was dumped so close to the stream. I put the pen down and stared at the ceiling. Instead of some divine inspiration or insight, all I saw was a burned-out bulb in the overhead florescent fixture.

I sighed, flipped the page, and wrote "Harley McLowry" at the top. Until two hours ago, I would have been more confident with listing the plusses below his name. He had been more than distressed at the Aker and Long offices; he had dated Colleen; without doubt, he could have killed anyone he wanted to—quickly and efficiently—and dumped the body in the marsh; he had no background on record. What he didn't have was a motive for Long's murder.

Since the early-morning visit, the visit that almost sent me to the funeral home, he had dropped near the bottom of my suspects—not completely fallen off the list, just slipped to the bottom.

Dillon, the drunk at GB's Tuesday, seemed to have known Colleen and according to Greg, had begun coming around about the time Long was killed. But even if there was a tenuous connection to Colleen, did he know Long?

Now to the name that jumped to the top of the list with a bullet: Greg Brile. Before my conversation with Mel last night, I had never thought of Brile. But even after having learned that the late Tony Long was allegedly a silent partner in GB's, what else pointed to him as the murderer? Once again, I looked to the burned-out florescent bulb for inspiration; once again, it failed to illuminate. My fall-back plan for inspiration was to grab a new bag of Doritos and stuff two chips in my mouth.

What did I really know about Greg Brile? Very little. If Long was his silent partner, there could be obvious avenues of discord between the two. Brile, like bar owners in resort areas everywhere, often had to serve as a bouncer—wimps need not apply. I remembered how Greg had handled Dillon the other night; he had smiled, but had a death grip on the back of the drunk's shirt. I didn't know if Brile had a boat, but he would have had easy access to several if he didn't own one.

Then the Doritos memory-refresher kicked in. Something had bounced around in my unconscious the other day about our visit to GB's. It was something Greg had said, but I couldn't remember what—until now.

He had jumped on Heather for singing two songs during open-mike night the day of the law office fire. He said that he "heard you sung two songs ..." Greg hadn't been in the bar when Heather massacred twice as many songs as she was permitted. The bar was nearly full, and I remembered that Gregory was in earlier and after Heather's debasement of two great songs. I assumed he was there the entire time. I doubted anyone could swear that he wasn't; GB's was packed, as usual. He had a perfect alibi. And since Colleen worked there, it wouldn't have been too suspicious for him to show up at her apartment. I assumed she had learned something bad from a customer; now I realized it could have been from her boss—his motive for killing her.

I flipped the pages back in the yellow pad and slapped it on the table. *What do I do now?* If Charles were here, he'd say we should "stomp over to GB's, find the murdering, two-faced, egg-sucking sleaze-ball, and beat a confession out of him."

I was more subtle, but still didn't have an answer. There was no way that I would talk to Acting Chief King about my suspicions. If I shared them with Cindy Ash, she would be obligated to go to King. Detective

Braden with the Charleston County sheriff's office was investigating the murders, but he had me pegged as a butting-in trouble-maker; hardly the opening I would have liked. That left Karen Lawson. It wasn't her case, but she trusted me.

I caught myself pacing back and forth in the small back room. I stopped and looked down at the legal pad, took a deep breath, grabbed my cell phone from the table, and punched in her number from the speed-dial menu.

Karen answered on the second ring with a cheerful, "Hi, Chris."

I was glad that she sounded so happy to hear from me, but proceeded to try to ruin her day. I told her what I had learned from Mel, what I had remembered about Greg's conversation at open mike night, and why I thought he had killed Colleen. My explanations were rambling and not in the best order. She listened carefully and asked me to repeat parts of it two and three times. Karen had years of experience listening to witnesses ramble and drift off on tangents, so she understood what I was trying to say.

Finally, she told me not to do anything—said it twice—and that she would take care of it. She ended the conversation with "See you soon." *Interesting*, I thought; I doubted that was something she told all her witnesses.

Chapter 49

Most of the time, I didn't have trouble doing nothing. After all, I had spent most of my life working in a less-than-exciting job, contributing less-than-anything-significant to society. Now I was retired, supposed to enjoy the twilight years—whatever that meant—and doing nothing. Other than stumbling upon a few dangerous glitches since moving here, I had succeeded.

Today wasn't to be one of those days. I was relieved to have handed the Brile situation off to Karen Lawson, but still had a sour feeling in my stomach. I couldn't do anything about the murder, but I couldn't stand back and let Amber walk off into the sunset. It was a little after three, so she should be home from work. *Do I show up at her apartment or call?* I didn't want to inflame the already tense situation by showing up, Tilley in hand. I called.

Her stilted response after hearing who it was was followed by silence; I feared she would hang up. I asked—more accurately, begged—her to meet me for drinks. She finally agreed to meet me on the patio at Rita's. I thanked her and got off the phone before she changed her mind.

I still hadn't heard from Charles and finally remembered that he would be "running an anthill full of errands for the surf shop" and wouldn't be in. He hadn't enlightened me on how many errands were in an anthill, but it should be a lot, I would think.

I had met Amber many times in the last couple of years, but had never been more nervous. I knew it wouldn't be the last time to see her, but could easily be the last opportunity for me to plead my case. Rather than continue to deepen the shoe-worn paths in the gallery's wooden floor, I headed to Rita's and arrived at four-thirty, a half hour before our meeting. The patio was full, and I stood at the outside bar until one of the tables opened. There wasn't a cloud in the sky, and I silently thanked the owner for adding the permanent roof over the patio. Amber walked through the restaurant on her way outside as the waitress brought my glass of wine. I pointed to the glass, and Amber nodded before she got to the table. I ordered one for her.

Her face contrasted with the crispness of her peach-colored shorts and off-white golf shirt. She looked tired, and her eyes reflected a sleepless night; her shoulders slumped, and her smile was forced.

I had rehearsed what I wanted to say on my walk over, and ran through it again while I waited for a table. Now that I was sitting in front of Amber, I was struck with stage fright, with cue cards nowhere in sight.

I tried to apologize and then realized that I didn't even know what I was apologizing for. I started to tell her that Jason wasn't in any danger and then realized I couldn't honestly say that. I almost told her what I had learned about Greg and then remembered that my meddling in a murder was at the root of her fears. Her drink arrived, but she ignored the glass. The waitress asked if we wanted anything to eat, and Amber shook her head. I heard the laughter of little kids but didn't turn my head to see where it was coming from.

I finally looked her in the eyes, shook my head slowly, and said, "I love you, and have for a long time; I don't blame you for what you're doing." I hesitated. "Jason must be your priority. I don't think he's in danger, but I can't promise that. Colleen's murder a few feet from your apartment brought the horror home to you—I understand. I ... I ... Never mind. Thanks for hearing me out." I looked down at my glass but didn't see anything.

Amber put both hands over mine on the table and smiled. "Chris, you know I love you too—have almost since I first saw you in the Dog. I know nothing is permanent—God knows, I know that ... but I'm scared ... I'm scared for Jason ... scared for me ... scared for you. I couldn't take it if something happened to you, and I know you can't back off when a friend's in trouble. To me, that's one of your best traits—and your worst. Maybe ... maybe when things calm down ..."

The ring tone of my cell phone startled both of us. We stared at the phone bouncing in vibrate and ring mode on the table. It reminded me of a cobra preparing to strike. I didn't realize how accurate the analogy was. I shrugged, and Amber's eyes penetrated my skull like a laser beam through a marshmallow.

"Get to Heather's place quick," yelled Charles. He sounded out of breath and desperate.

"Can it wait?" I said and looked at Amber. "How about an hour?"

"How about five minutes?" said Charles. I didn't detect any negotiating in his tone.

"What happened?" I asked.

"Strange," he said. "Something about Greg Brile and Cal."

Amber's eyes hadn't left my face. I could almost see hope slipping from her body. "Okay," I said to Charles. If he hadn't mentioned Brile, I would have said no. Charles didn't know the latest about the bar owner.

I pushed the *end call* button and saw a flicker of sunlight reflected in a tear under Amber's left eye.

She wiped it away and motioned for me to leave. "Go," she said and then sniffled. "I'll be fine. Go."

I knew she wouldn't be fine; neither would I. Unless I woke up and this was all a bad dream, neither would the two of us as a couple.

I walked the short distance to the house and got my car. The temperature was in the high eighties with humidity to match. The sour taste in my mouth matched my mood as I grabbed one of the two empty parking spaces in front of the Mariner's Breeze Bed and Breakfast. Charles was on the front porch and chided me for being late; I pushed past him and knocked on Heather's door.

"Thank God you're here," she said without preamble. She motioned me into her room and left the door open for Charles, who was a step behind. I had never been in Heather's room, but it was as I imagined. A beat-up, red vinyl recliner held a prominent place in the corner with a small manicurist's table beside it with an empty, chrome, picture frame with crystals attached by a thin thread dangling from the top edge. A large, black-and-silver karaoke machine stood near the center of the room with an easel in front of it; sheet music from "Always, Patsy" prominently rested on the makeshift music stand. The door to the closet-sized bedroom was open, and I could see an unmade bed with pink sheets strewn about.

"Tell him what happened," said Charles. He sat in the recliner while Heather bounced from one wall to another.

"Okay," she said and focused on me. "I was getting home from Maggie's—had four massages this afternoon, big, old, hairy-backed guy and three women, sure were hard on these old fingers." She wiggled her fingers at me.

"And?" said Charles.

"Well—" She looked at Charles and gave him a disgusted look for interrupting her massage story and turned back to me. "I unlocked the door." She nodded in the direction of her apartment door. "Then I saw Cal in the hall. I usually try to be friendly-like, so I turned to talk, and there was Greg—you know, the one who wouldn't let me sing two songs—hunkered up close to Cal. I sort of thought he was pushing something in Cal's back, but I could have imagined it. Anyway, Cal looked like someone killed his pet chinchilla, if he had one. Old Greg wasn't much happier."

"Did they say anything?" I asked.

"Didn't give them time to," said Heather. "When I saw the looks on their faces, I eased back into the room and shut the door. Turned the deadbolt too—I was pet-re-fied."

"Then what?" I asked.

"Well, I heard the front door close, so I peeked around the corner. The hall was empty, so I snuck to the front door and looked out. Greg shoved Cal into the front seat of his Toyota, sort of rough-like. They pulled out of the lot, and I called Charles."

"I was home and came right over," said Charles. "Heather told me the story, and I called you. And here we are."

"Think we need to call the police?" asked Heather.

Charles looked at the front door and then at Heather. "To tell them what—Greg and Cal drove off together? Doubt that'll bring out the Calvary and rescue-sniffing dogs."

Charles was right, but we couldn't stand around here and do nothing. I said, "Let's drive around and see if we can find Greg's car."

Heather started out the door. Charles moved between her and the door and held his cane out. "Why don't you wait here?" he said. "Then you can call us if they come back."

Her shoulders slumped, and she shrugged. She wasn't happy with that plan but didn't protest.

Chapter 50

"Now where?" asked Charles.

We were at the corner of Center Street and looked both ways. "Any idea where Greg lives?"

"Nope—off island somewhere, I think."

"That doesn't narrow it down much. Let's go to the bar and see if we get lucky," I said.

"Good line," said Charles.

I snarled at him and turned right on Center Street and drove three blocks and then turned right just past the burnt-out law offices and city hall. Traffic was at its usual summer standstill. We inched along at a frustratingly slow pace.

I was struck by the irony of GB's being across the street from the police department. Traffic was just as heavy in front of the bar, and I had to concentrate to avoid hitting cars stopped in the road waiting for parking spaces to open. Charles looked from side to side hoping to catch a glimpse of the Toyota.

We circled the block twice with several Toyota sightings, but none belonged to the bar owner. "Pull over somewhere, anywhere," said Charles. "Maybe someone in there knows where he is."

The bar wasn't open, and I didn't see any lights in the front window; that wouldn't deter Charles. Two blocks later, I struck pay dirt—an empty, sand-covered parking space. Instead of walking to the front of GB's, Charles headed to the side entrance. The door was slightly ajar, and the smell of stale beer whiffed through the crack along with Conway Twitty's distinctive voice coming from the jukebox. I stood to the left of the door opening, Charles to the right. He pointed his cane at the door and held out his other hand as if to say, "Now what?"

We'd come this far, and I couldn't think of a reason—other than avoiding us getting killed—not to stumble on. "Hello, hello," I said as I pushed the door open. The rusty, steel hinges were nearly as loud as my greeting.

"We're not open. Come back in an hour."

I peeked in the near-dark bar and recognized Nick, one of Greg's bartenders, moving a table to the far side of the room. He slid two chairs under the table and then turned toward Charles and me. "Oh, hi," he said and wiped the sweat from his forehead with a white bar towel he had draped around his neck.

"We know you're not open," I said. "We're looking for Greg."

Charles had already walked around Nick and looked around the corner of the counter. He looked like he was chasing a wayward mouse instead of trying to find Cal and Greg.

Nick looked at Charles and said, "Well, he ain't under there. Fact, I don't know where he's at."

"Seen him today?" I asked and watched Charles continue to check every corner and crevice.

"He was in thirty minutes ago; said something about leaving for a while. Then he was gone."

I glanced at Charles, who was near the restroom door. He looked from Nick to me and then walked closer. "What kind of boat's he got?" asked Charles. He tried to act casual, but his jaw was tight and the words came out harsh.

Nick giggled. "Not quite a yacht; more like one of those squatty little boats with the big-ass motor on its butt. He won't be sailing the ocean blue in it."

Nick didn't know it, but that wasn't the answer we wanted to hear. We thanked him and hurried down the sidewalk.

"Why'd you ask about a boat?" I asked as we crossed the street.

"Figured that if that's how he tried to get rid of Long, he'd do the same with Cal."

"A guess, then?"

"A big one," said Charles. "What else do we have?"

Before we got to the car, Charles asked for my cell phone and punched in a number.

"Yeah ... five minutes," was all I heard before he handed the phone back to me.

"Folly View Marina," he said and slammed the door shut. "Mel's taking us for a ride."

I need to remember to ask Charles why he had memorized Mel's phone number.

Mad Mel had untied his Magical Marsh Machine from the dock as I slid to a stop in the gravel lot. A cloud of dust billowed up behind us. He must have been on the boat when Charles called.

"Let's see if I have my mission correct," said Mel as he threw the last rope into the boat. "All I have to do is find one damned bar owner in a small boat sticking something in the back of one frickin' country-music-singing cowboy floating around somewhere in seventeen gazillion square miles of ocean, river, or marsh. That about it?"

Charles had already climbed in Mel's machine and offered me a hand over the gunwale. He threw his cane on the bench seat and looked at Mel. "Couldn't have said it better myself."

Mel rolled his eyes.

"Here's my thought," I said. "If Gregory forced Cal to go with him, it wasn't to give him lessons on how to be part-owner in the bar. He's in big trouble. If they're in a boat, he plans to kill Cal—if he hasn't already."

"Well, a big duh to that," said Charles.

"So, where do we go?" asked Mel.

"As I was trying to say before I was so rudely interrupted," I said and stared at Charles, "Gregory didn't do a very good job dumping Long, so I'm guessing he doesn't know the marsh and its waterways that well."

Charles grabbed his cane and pointed it in the general direction of Secessionville. "He did know his way to where he dumped Long."

"Got it," said Mel. He pointed for Charles and me to sit. "If he's even in a boat," he mumbled.

That was the last I heard except for the roar of Mad Mel's Magical Marsh Machine's macho engine. Mel didn't let off the throttle until we were across the river and approached a boat pulling two teenagers on a huge truck inner tube. I took advantage of the relative quiet and dialed

Karen Lawson. Mel's machine eased past the other boat, and he looked over at me. I raised one finger to ask him to hold down the noise until I was off the phone.

Karen answered on the third ring. I gave her an abbreviated version of the events of the last hour. She said she knew where we were headed and said she would contact the Folly Beach police, the sheriff's office, and the Coast Guard. I told her I could be wrong and that Cal and Greg could be out for a pleasant boat ride. She said we'd deal with that if we had to, but until then, to stay away from Brile.

If we find him, I thought.

Charles and Mel closed in on me as soon as I shut the phone.

"Who was that, and what now?" asked Charles. Mel nodded at Charles's question.

"Karen Lawson, county sheriff's office," I said for Mel's benefit. "She said she'd contact law enforcement and for us to stay away from Brile."

Charles turned to Mel. "Did you hear that?" he asked. "We've got to find Brile—can't stay away from him if we don't know where he is."

Mel reached for the throttle lever. "Gotcha. If Brile's going to wipe out your country-crooning buddy, he could have it done and be back home eating pecans before the cops get there." He rammed the throttle with his palm; the sudden lurch of the boat nearly threw me overboard. I should have followed my advice to stay seated.

Chapter 51

A couple of hundred yards from Tony Long's next-to-final resting place, Mel pulled back on the throttle. This time, Charles lost his footing and grabbed the railing.

Charles glared at Mel. "Do you treat all your passengers this rough?" asked Charles as he regained his balance.

"Nope, you're special," said Mel. The boat was almost at a complete stop.

"Thanks," said Charles.

"Other passengers pay," responded Mel. He turned the boat to the right shore and pointed to the curve in the channel a hundred yards in front of us. "Didn't bring my damned machine gun; don't want to go barreling around that corner and run smack-dab into the killer barman." Mel pointed to the front of the boat. "Get a life jacket."

Charles reached under the front deck and grabbed two orange jackets and threw one to me. The idling engine masked the natural sounds of the marsh; we didn't hear any man-made noises. Mel inched the boat to the curve, where I could see the bow of a small fishing boat bob slightly with the gently rolling current.

Mel growled, "Attack!"

Greg leaned over the prone body of Cal. The Magical Marsh Machine leapt forward. Charles and I grabbed the railing so we wouldn't need to test the life jackets.

Mel turned us toward the small boat. Greg looked up from Cal, and for an instant, his face registered confusion, and then fear, and then anger. Greg grabbed Cal's right leg and lifted it over the side of his craft.

We were fifty feet from him. I was surprised—and pleased—to see Cal shake his head and then reach up and grab Greg's left arm.

"Incoming. Down!" screamed Mel.

Greg swung his right arm in our direction. A pistol was pointed at us. He fired two rounds before I knew what happened. The spent shells flew harmlessly into the marsh. Mel yanked the wheel to the left.

My knees were on the boat's fiberglass bottom. My right hand had a death grip on the side rail.

Cal held Greg's arm for dear life. Greg tried again to push Cal overboard, but the singer wasn't having any of it. Greg fired, but Cal had him so off-balance he had a better chance of hitting a pelican than us. Three misses, but how long could our luck hold?

Greg realized that he would have to do something with the human octopus clamped around his arm before he could deal the intruders. He lowered the automatic weapon and aimed it at Cal's leg.

Charles pointed his cane over Greg's head and screamed, "Greg, duck!"

It worked. Greg looked around to see what Charles was pointing at. Cal tightened his grip. And Mel had our boat speeding directly at the center of Greg's. We closed fast on the fishing boat.

I saw what Mel's plan was a split-second before we rammed the small boat. I grabbed the railing tighter and yelled for Charles to get down.

Our engine was loud, but it was nothing compared to the terrifying sound of metal on metal, fiberglass on fiberglass, and fiberglass on flesh.

Greg's boat, less than half the size and weight of Mel's Magical Marsh Machine, was lifted out of the water by the bow of Mel's with as much ease as someone snatching a leaf from the stream. The smaller craft twisted in the air.

Cal grabbed for the rail but missed. He looked like a rag doll as he was hurled through the air. He landed on his back in the creek, barely missing the bank and the razor-sharp oyster shells. Greg managed to hang onto the side and landed flat in the bottom when the disabled boat splashed back into the water. His head slowly appeared above the gunwale, and his right hand still held the deadly weapon. How he managed to hold onto the gun?

Mel yanked his machine in reverse and pulled away from Greg's wounded boat. Cal had pulled himself out of the water and collapsed in the marsh grasses. His left arm and leg sank beneath the soft, pluff mud. His right arm scraped against a row of oyster shells. He let out a yelp and then a string of profanities.

The roar of a boat engine was coming from behind us. I never thought I'd be happy to see Acting Chief King. I was so wrong. He was hunched down behind the wheel of a cream-and-ocean-green Bayliner Capri speedboat. I knew the city didn't have any watercraft larger than a jet ski, so it must have been his boat.

Greg had regained his balance, and without the burden of Cal yanking on his arm, he aimed the handgun at the rapidly-approaching chief. I screamed to warn King, but he either didn't hear me yell or chose to ignore me. He was no more than thirty feet from Greg when the killer fired.

The chief twisted, let go of the wheel, and grabbed his chest with his right hand. The boat abruptly turned to the right, and King flew out the left side like he had been jerked by a rope. The unmanned craft rammed the land and slid harmlessly on shore.

I grabbed a vest from storage and stepped off the side of the boat into the warm water. The chief bobbed face-down in the wake of his boat. He hadn't moved but drifted farther from me. Could I get to him before he went under for good? I had never been a strong swimmer. If it weren't for the life jacket, I would have gone down with the chief.

I gasped for breath and reached for his head. He had been under far too long, and I could see blood from the chest wound mix with the salt water. We were in the middle of the channel, and his head dipped beneath the surface each time I tried to pull him up enough to get the vest around him. I was losing the battle and was afraid that he had already lost his. Where was a mermaid when I needed one? I'd settle for Flipper.

It wasn't a mermaid or a dolphin, but something even better splashed in the water and grabbed my arm. Karen Lawson treaded water and put her arm under King's torso and grabbed the life jacket from me. I managed to lift his face above the surface. An oar tapped me on the arm. I twisted my head around and saw Brian Newman in a shiny, red speedboat inching up to me. He held the oar out for me to grab. Karen and I pulled and pushed the lifeless body against the side of the boat, and Brian reached over and gripped King's duty belt. Brian pulled, and Karen and I pushed the unresponsive body close enough for Brian to pull him in.

Brian carefully lowered King to the bottom of the boat. I looked over at Karen; her usually neat hairdo curled in all directions, and water dripped down her face. Her crisp, white blouse was nearly transparent and clung to her body. Mascara streaked down her cheeks. She had never looked better.

She turned to her dad and back to me as I floated on my back. She smiled. "Fancy meeting you here," she said.

I grinned and then heard Mel yell, "Enough of this crap! Damn the torpedoes!"

Mel pushed his hand against the throttle. His engine coughed and then roared. Water spewed in the air behind his magical craft. Greg had an old, wooden oar and was paddling his dented, twisted, powerless boat toward shore. He was only a few feet from one of the long private piers behind a large, old farmhouse in Secessionville. I didn't know if he could escape, but Mel wasn't going to let him find out.

For the second time in fifteen minutes, the Magical Mystery Machine rammed the killer's hapless craft. Greg lost his footing and reached for something solid. His luck had run out. He was thrown from the wadded-up boat—he flew left, while his gun catapulted right.

"Gotcha!" yelled Mel. He turned off the engine, threw both arms in the air like a referee signaling touchdown, and dove into the water. He surfaced behind Greg and wrapped his powerful arms around him. He would have made a python proud.

The next thing I heard was the thump-thump sound of the props on a Coast Guard helicopter swooping down on us from the east. From the opposite direction, I saw a Jet Ranger helicopter from the City of Charleston police department. When Karen said she would take care of the police, she meant it. I wouldn't have been surprised to see the Royal Canadian Mounted Police and a Boy Scout troop march through the marsh coming to our aid.

Brian waved at the Coast Guard's distinct orange chopper, and a rescue swimmer appeared on a rope being lowered from the air-sea rescue helicopter. The chopper was directly over us, and the turbulence from the rotor pushed me away from the boat. The life vest had earned its pay, and I was in no hurry to swim anywhere. I lay back in the water and watched the show.

Charles had Greg by the neck and roughly jerked him aboard with the help of Mel, who treaded water and pushed the bar owner. Brian helped the corpsman secure King in the basket to lift him to the chopper and medical care—if it wasn't too late. Karen maneuvered the boat to keep it stable. And Cal stood knee-deep in the marsh mud and applauded. Blood dripped from his oyster-shell-sliced arm, but he didn't seem too notice. His smile was as wide as his face would allow without cosmetic surgery.

Chapter 52

"Fellas," said Cal. He had a huge a smile of relief on his face. "Here's what happened."

Cal, Charles, Heather, Mel, Dude, Harley, Sean, and I were gathered in my living room. Space was tight, but as Charles had pointed out when he organized the let's-celebrate-being-alive party, my place was larger than the residences of the other invitees, with the exception of Sean's condo, but the lawyer wasn't terribly welcome at home. In fact, my humble abode was larger than Charles's, Heather's, and Harley's combined. Charles basked in his recent entry into the world of wealth and bought three large Woody's pizzas; Mel brought enough beer to host a homecoming frat party; and Cal brought his guitar to, as he put it, "liven the party if y'all start blabbering about that murder stuff." I chose not to mention that he would be the subject of the murder-stuff blabber.

Cal started to reach for his guitar at his feet but hesitated. "I was considering going into business with Greg. My good friend here, Chris—my good friend who almost got me killed—said I should find out as much about the business as I could before giving Greg an answer." He glared at me and then winked. "Said I needed to learn important stuff like if GB's could afford me or if he wanted to use me to sing free and then screw me, and other stuff I already forgot." He paused again and looked around to be sure he had our attention.

Dude's mouth was stuffed with pizza as he read the side of the Budweiser can, but everyone else stared at Cal. We were anxious to hear his story.

Cal nodded satisfaction with the almost-undivided attention and continued, "I'd learned from my detective friend, Charles, that the best way to detect was to be nosy—nosy and meddle in stuff that wasn't quite any of my business."

"Not exactly right," said Charles. "Close," he conceded.

"Not exactly legal either," added the only attorney present.

"Whatever," said Cal. "Well, the other day, Greg had gone to the post office to mail a box to Arkansas; so, I took the *opportunity* to commence detecting."

Mel belched and interrupted Cal's flow. Cal gave him a scornful look and continued. "The office door was open, and this old army surplus file cabinet was just sitting there behind the makeshift desk. Heck, it almost asked me to open the drawers."

"Makes sense," said Charles.

"Well, anyway, there were four or five folders in the top drawer, right in front." He smiled. "A bottle of Jim Beam was behind the files."

"Sip any?" asked Dude.

Cal didn't look at the surf shop owner. "I pulled the files out, put them on the desk, and started going through them. I didn't see anything but old invoices in the first three, but there was a red file folder with *TL* scribbled on the tab. I figured they were initials but I didn't think I knew anyone whose name they could be until I opened it and saw a note on letterhead with Aker and Long on the top. 'Course, I didn't really know Tony Long but heard of him. The note said something that I translated as 'I want out, and out now!' After that, there was some legal mumbo-jumbo; didn't mean a whit of spit to me."

"Wanted out of what?" asked Mel.

Cal rubbed his heavily bandaged and overly disinfected arm. "Well, Mr. United States Marine and saver of a country singer, under the note was a piece of paper that said something about Long footing the bill to keep the bar from going broke but if Mr. Brile ever screwed over the shyster, he would give the cops proof that Gregory was in deep porcupine poop with the law. He's wanted in Lincoln, Nebraska, for fraud and suspicion of murder."

"You be hanging with bad buds," added Dude. He was in stiff competition with Charles for being the master of the obvious.

Cal shrugged and then turned to Heather. He turned on his often-used stage smile. "Miss Heather, about the time I was thinking that I should possibly reconsider my business relationship with Greg, he bopped through the door and saw the folders on the desk. Since I use a bunch of fake smiles myself, I recognized his grin being more *sin* than *sin*cere."

Harley hadn't said anything and fidgeted with his pizza slice. He wanted to get in the action. "What happened?"

Cal focused on the biker. "Well, Harley, I started fumbling with words—not a good thing for a singer-songwriter, I concede. Anyway, I made up something about looking for information about beer and food purchases to learn more about the business. I told him I wanted it so I could be a better partner. Heck, I wasn't believing it myself and knew Brile wouldn't." He held out his arms and looked around the room. "I didn't know what to do. My detective training hadn't covered how to get out of that kind of mess. I slid the folders together and muttered that I was late for a meeting and asked him if he wanted me to put the folders back."

"Did he see you with the red one?" asked Sean.

"Don't think so; when I slipped them together, the lawyer folder was on the bottom."

"It wouldn't take him long to figure it out," added Mel.

"Nope," said Cal. "Didn't have much time to think about it; I got out of there as fast as these lanky legs could carry me." He raised his right leg in the air like we wouldn't have known which were his lanky legs. "I hoped he would forget about it."

"Aikona!" said Dude.

All heads turned his direction.

"What the hell does that mean, you damned commie-hippy-draft-dodger?" said Mel.

"Means no way, ain't going to happen," said Charles before Dude responded to Mel's polite question.

I grinned, and everyone else took the wise route and didn't ask Charles how he had known.

"He sure didn't forget," added Cal. He jumped out of the chair and started pacing the room on his lanky legs. "I thought you were the killer, Harley."

"Hmm," snarled Harley.

Cal stopped in front of Harley and looked down on the surprised biker. "It hadn't drifted by my mind that it could have been Greg. Even after I read the file, I wasn't sure. Flat out didn't know who to tell." He started pacing again. "Two knocks on my door yesterday nearly became the beginning of the end for me. Took away any doubt. You all know the rest, right?"

We each nodded as Cal moved his gaze around the room to each of us and then returned to his seat.

"I apologize, Harley, for thinking it was you."

Harley's gruff look softened. "No problem, Cal," he said, "I've been out of sorts a bit lately."

"Amen to that," interrupted Heather.

Harley looked at her and shrugged. "I miss Colleen. Sorry, guess there's a lot on my mind." He looked my way, but for only a second.

"Speaking of Colleen," said Heather, "why'd he kill her?"

Cal grinned, this time a real one. "Well, I have an answer for that one too," he said.

Harley gave him his undivided attention.

Cal made sure everyone was looking his way before he continued. "When Greg was taking me on our pleasant tour of the marsh, he kept mumbling about 'that biker bitch.' I figured he meant Colleen." He hesitated and looked at Harley. "Sorry Har, but that's what he called her."

Harley nodded but didn't say anything.

"You should have heard what he called me," said Cal. "Said he had committed the perfect murder when he shot Long and wasn't going to let me screw it up."

"Not perfect," interjected Dude.

"Anyway, I knew why he killed Long but had to ask him about Colleen. Didn't figure I had much to lose. He said that the biker bit— Colleen came to him the night of the fire and said that she had heard Greg arguing with Long a couple of weeks earlier. She didn't know what it was about. She was outside GB's taking a smoke the night of the fire and saw Greg slinking back across the street from the direction of the law office."

"Smoking be deadly," interjected Dude.

Harley gave him a dirty look, and Cal barely broke stride. He knew how to work a crowd.

"Greg said ... said Colleen cornered him and said that her mind would go blank if her bank account jumped by five grand."

Harley held his head down with a hand over each ear. "Shit," he whispered. "Why, Colleen, why?"

Cal stopped, took a swig of beer, and looked around the room.

"Umm, then what?" asked Charles, who, I'm sure spoke for everyone in the room except Cal.

Cal looked at Harley, blinked twice, and then lowered his head. "All he said was, 'That damned stupid bitch.' Sorry Harley."

"That's all?" said Charles.

"He repeated it," said Cal. "Then we got to the spot where you found us."

I looked around the room. Harley glared at Cal. Charles was about to ask something else and stir up no telling what. Tension was as thick as the humidity outside.

"My guess is that Greg told Colleen that he would pay her the five thousand dollars," I said. "He had already torched the law office and any evidence that Long may have had there. He would've told Colleen he was bringing the money to her apartment, so she would have been glad to let him in. Then ... then he killed her and tried to make it look like an accidental overdose."

Harley leaned forward, put his head between his hands, and looked at the floor. The room was silent; not even Charles spoke.

Harley finally looked up and around the room. "She never said anything," he said. "Not a word. I would have told her how big a mistake she was making. It wasn't worth it."

He looked at me when he finished. I gave a slight nod to let him know I understood.

I turned to Sean. "I own you an apology. I'm afraid I thought you did it." Charles nodded his head in agreement.

I continued, "Why'd you lie to us about being in your office until five the day of the fire?"

"Sorry," said Sean. "My wife and I had a counseling session. I left early for that." He looked around the room. "It's a little embarrassing, so I sort of left it out."

The room was silent. Then Cal stood and walked to the front window and looked out toward the street, and then turned back to the group. "I've been so bent out of shape about myself, I forgot to ask—any word on the police chief?"

"Acting Chief," clarified Charles.

"Karen Lawson called before you all got here," I said. "She said he was expected to make a full recovery."

"I hear he would have drowned if it wasn't for you," said Heather.

"Yeah," said Charles, "Chris screwed up again."

I ignored Charles and continued. "She also said that Acting Chief King told the mayor that he didn't want the job back; he had enough of the nuts over here and was retiring for good."

"Newman be back?" asked Dude.

"Starting next week," I said and smiled. I knew that breaking the news before Charles knew about it would drive him crazy—if he could go any further in that direction. "I propose a toast to peace, and a peace officer, being restored to Folly Beach."

We each took a sip—or two.

Mel set his beer on the table and looked at me. "What's the deal with you and that lady detective?" he asked.

"Whoa, good ques!" said Dude.

I had rapidly become the unwanted center of attention in the room.

Good ques, indeed, I thought.

Charles pointed his cane at me. "Chris, as President Coolidge once said, 'I have noticed that nothing I never said ever did me any harm.'"

Finally, a presidential quote that made sense.

Printed in the United States
By Bookmasters